大學生必懂的
英語學習

馬予華 / 主編

崧燁文化

前 言

《大學英語綜合教程》的編寫思路,既注意打好語言基礎,又側重培養應用能力,特別是實際使用英語進行涉外交際的能力。在培養閱讀能力的同時,加強聽、說、寫、譯等語言技能的綜合訓練,尤其注重口頭和書面實用表達能力的訓練與培養,以適應以後對外交往的需要。

在編寫過程中,我們力求突出以下一些特色:

1. 立足國情,博採眾長,充分吸收長期累積的學習英語的有效方法,認真借鑑國外的教學理論和經驗;全面落實《大學英語課程教學要求》提出的相關要求。

2. 堅持人本主義教育觀,重視開發學習者的「自我潛能」,注重「情感」和「態度」在學習活動中的作用,鼓勵學生開展課堂內外的自主學習活動,幫助學生成為「自我實現者」。

3. 英語綜合運用能力的培養應該建立在語言技能、語言知識、情感態度、學習策略和跨文化交際意識等諸方面的整體發展基礎上;交際能力的習得應該與學習者的人格發展有機地結合起來,通過全身心的體驗,輕鬆而快樂地學習和掌握英語。

4. 在課堂教學活動和課後學習活動的設計和安排等方面,力求為教師和學生提供較為開闊的自主空間,讓教師和學生都能根據各自的情況和已有的教學條件選擇適合自己需要的教學模式和學習風格。

本書共有 8 單元,每單元都由 Warming-ups、In-class Activities、Reading Passages、Skills Development and Practice、Practical Translation 和 Focused Writing 6 個部分組成,重點訓練學生的說、讀、寫、譯能力,提高學生實際使用英語進行涉外交際的能力,較好地體現了大學英語教學要突出全面培養並提高學

生的英語綜合應用能力的大方向。

　　由於編者的水準和經驗有限,教材中的不足之處在所難免,懇切希望廣大師生和讀者不吝賜教,以便我們進一步修訂和完善。

編者

目 錄

Unit 1 Education ……………………………………（ 1 ）
Unit 2 Man and Nature ……………………………（ 22 ）
Unit 3 Travel Around the World …………………（ 45 ）
Unit 4 Sports ………………………………………（ 79 ）
Unit 5 Health ………………………………………（ 103 ）
Unit 6 Lifestyle ……………………………………（ 129 ）
Unit 7 Man and Technology ………………………（ 152 ）
Unit 8 Job Interview ………………………………（ 170 ）

Unit 1　Education

Warming-ups

Task 1　Questions for Thought

Think about the following questions, then discuss with your partner.

1. What do you specialize in?
2. What is your favorite subject?
3. What are your goals for education in the future?
4. How do you do in college?

Task 2　Vocabulary Preview

Complete the following table by writing the English or Chinese equivalents of the words given. Then, check your answers with your partner.

課程		diploma	
必修課		graduate field work	
選修課		credit system	
基礎課		academic record	
專業課		attendance record	
退課		get a good/high grade (score, mark)	

In-class Activities

Task 1　Pair Work

Classify the following sentences as good or bad openers with which you'd like to start a conversation with someone on campus. Check your answers with your partner.

Start Your Conversation	Yes	No
1. I'd like to practice my English. Can I talk with you?		

表(續)

Start Your Conversation	Yes	No
2. Excuse me. Are you a student here?		
3. Excuse me. I'm new here. I don't know the way around. Is there anywhere people get together?		
4. Hello. My name's Chen. I'm looking for new friends.		
5. Can I ask you a few questions?		
6. It's getting a bit warmer now, isn't it? Are you planning to go to the yoga classes?		
7. What's your impression of the course so far?		
8. I'd like to help you with your Chinese. Can you help me with my English?		
9. Hello. Do you want somebody to practice Chinese with?		
10. Er, could you help me? I didn't understand what he meant by… did you?		

Task2 Group Work

A: Write down your information first according to the items given in the table.

B: Go around your group to interview each member for their information.

	You	Student 1	Student 2	Student 3	…
Name	LiNa				
Age to College	18				
Number of Years Learning English	6				
Major	Secretary				
Reasons for choosing the major	fond of office work				
Favorite Course	public relations				
Reasons for Enjoying the Course	a more practical course				

Task3 Discussion/Presentation

Some freshmen are taking a second-thought about their choice of major. As a sophomore, what suggestion will you give to them?

A: Discuss in groups about your opinions.

Statement1: My current major is not what I wanted.

Your opinion:

Statement 2: It's a hard road to my career success.

Your opinion:

B: After discussing, summarize all the opinions and make an oral speech entitled:

What If I Don't Like My Major?

The following might be useful and helpful in the speech:

Words and Expressions:

change major; second major; electives; study part-time

Reference Modal:

What do you do if you realize that you aren't interested in the career that you choose to major in? Should you stay in that area? What if you have no idea what career you want to pursue? And what will happen if you have changed your mind? Let's look into this issue. First,...

Task 4 Before reading Passage A, try to tell what you feel is the best part of your college life, and what is not so good as you used to expect.

1. Lecture
2. Class
3. Cafeteria
4. Library
5. Degree
6. Reading

Reading Passages

Passage A

<p align="center">Bachelor's Degress:
Has It Lost Its Edge and Its Value?
by <i>Lee Lawrence</i></p>

Once the hallmark of an educated and readily employable adult, the bachelor's degree is losing its edge. Quicker, cheaper programs offer attractive career route alternatives while the more prestigious master's is trumping it, making it a mere steppingstone.

Studies show that people with four-year college degrees earn more money than those without over their lifetime, that they are more likely to find jobs and, once employed, are almost twice as likely to be selected for on-the-job training.

This has prompted a stampede through college and university gates.

But studies are like photographs: They record the past. They say nothing about the clear and present danger that the bachelor's degree is losing value.

「As more and more people get a bachelor's degree, it becomes more commonplace,」says Linda Serra Hagedorn, immediate past president of the Association for the Study of Higher Education and associate dean and professor at Iowa State University in Ames, Iowa.

And, she adds, 「not all bachelor's are equal.」In many communities around the country, the bachelor's is not enough to make you stand out. 「「A bachelor's in what?」That's the question,」Professor Hagedorn says.

「A bachelor's is what a high school diploma used to be,」suggests Caryn McTighe Musil of the American Association of colleges and Universities.

After World War II and through decades of postwar economicgrowth, college attendance morphed from an exception into the desired norm. In 1950, some 34 percent of adults had completed high school; today, more than 30 percent have completed a bachelor's. In 2009, colleges and universities handed out more than 1.6 million bachelor's degrees, a number the National Center for Education Statistics (NCES) expects will grow to almost 2 million by 2020.

Spiraling degree inflation is what Richard Vedder, professor of economics at Ohio University and adjunct scholar at the American Enterprise Institute, calls it. The danger he sees is that growing numbers of Americans will be unnecessarily saddled with hefty student loans.

「The fact is that it is not a sure shot you're going to get the high-paying job,」Professor Vedder says, and the notion that the earnings differential 「is continuing to grow and expand is somewhat suspect.」

Bachelor's degree-holders may well earn 66 percent more than high school graduates and 35 percent more than people with two-year degrees, he says. But for every bachelor's degree-holder earning more than $54,000 a year, he notes, there is a mail carrier, taxi driver, bartender, parking attendant or other worker with a bachelor's earning less. Indeed, almost 16 percent of the country's bartenders and almost 14 percent of its parking lot attendants have a bachelor's or higher.

Vedder predicts more and more college-educated people will be in jobs that do not require a four-year degree.

Michael Hughes and Amanda Kusler met in just such a job, working as servers in a restaurant in Ann Arbor, Mich. It was 2007, and both had graduated from high school three years earlier.

Soon after they started dating, Kusler encouraged Hughes to re-enroll and pursue a degree. 「Especially nowadays,」 she believes, 「it's a norm to get your BA—doesn't matter what it's in.」

That was certainly the case for decades, says Anthony Carnevale, director of the Georgetown University Center on Education and the Workforce, but not anymore.

「It used to be that just getting the bachelor's made you employable,」 Mr. Carnevale says. But the research increasingly shows 「that the BA in and of itself is not what's valuable. Now, it more and more depends on what the degree is in.」

Kusler's aim was to work with children as a physical therapist, and there was no way to do that without a graduate degree.

But even in occupations that do not formally require postgraduate education, some employers have begun using graduate degrees as a filter.

「There's been some slight shifting to hiring more advanced degrees, particularly the master's,」 says Edwin Koc, director of strategic and foundation research at the National Association of Colleges and Employers. He notes that a number of his organization's members are now hiring people with a master's in engineering for jobs he'd assumed require only a bachelor's.

There is, however, also the undeniable fact that the supply of Americans with master's degrees is exploding. There are 50 percent more people in the job market today with a master's than there were in 2000. And the rate of growth is accelerating: When the economy is in turmoil and jobs are scarce, graduate enrollments typically rise.

This, in turn, fuels the feeling that Green, the accelerated master's student at Emory University, has: 「The master's seems like what you have to get where you want to go.」

With few good jobs immediately available and cuts in such postgrad havens as the Peace Corps, many are postponing these experiences to get their masters sooner rather than later.

Ironically, the push for master's degrees underscores the increasing need for the bachelor's while highlighting its weaknesses.

In theory, four years of undergraduate study nurtures critical thinking and the ability to adapt to a rapidly changing workplace.

But US college education has come under heavy criticism of late, and a bachelor's degree no longer guarantees that someone has actually acquired these crucial skills.

「There is this credential race going on,」 says Richard Arum, coauthor of 「Academically Adrift.」」「where there is less attention to the substance of the education and more to the credentials that are useful as signals in the labor market.」

Even though more than half of this year's college graduates have received no job offers, and even though the class of 2010 faced record unemployment, college graduates are still faring much better than those without a bachelor's.

「If nothing else,」 says Mr. McKendry, the California recruiter, 「a bachelor's shows that somebody has the mental capability and the initiative to complete something」 that less than 30 percent of the US population has achieved. But McKendry and his counterpart in a Snellings Staffing Services in New Jersey, Koleen Singerline, have independently lost their faith in the bachelor's as a predictor, in and of itself, of workplace success.

They point primarily to what they judge as a lack of workethic and an attitude of entitlement in the new generation. Still, they are forced by employers to use college degrees as a benchmark.

「There are really good people with a wonderful track record.」 says Ms. Singerline. 「but I often cannot get a client to consider them because the company policy is that to become a manager you must have a degree.」

This is where cultural factors come to bear. 「People would feel that it's unfair to report to somebody who has a lesser degree of education than they have.」 Hagedorn explains, 「That usually leads to an uncomfortable situation in the company.」

The crux is that 「education is still respected,」 as Hagedorn points out, and there will probably always exist an economic and social divide between those who have it and those who don't.

But workplace and educational institutions are evolving, and attitudes toward the bachelor's are also showing signs of change. Some employers are more interested in experience, skills, and attitude than they are in degrees; others require higher levels of education from the start.

Then, as Jack Hollister, president of the Employers' Association serving Northwest Ohio and Southeast Michigan, reports, there are employers who only 「look at bachelor's from certain schools and certain areas of study and require a minimum GPA.」

In other words, they no longer take a bachelor's at face value.

Words and Expressions

1. bachelor *n.* 學士
2. hallmark *n.* 檢驗印記；特點，標誌；質量證明
3. prestigious *adj.* 受尊敬的，有聲望的
4. stampede *n.* 驚逃；人群的蜂擁

5. commonplace *adj.* 平凡的，陳腐的；平庸的，普通的

6. morph *vt.* 改變

7. norm *n.* 規範；標準；準則；定額（勞動）

8. hang out 掛出，晾曬

9. inflation *n.* 通貨膨脹；膨脹；誇張；自命不凡

10. adjunct *adj.* 附屬的

11. exception *n.* 例外，除外；反對，批評；［法律］異議，反對

12. pursue *vt.* 追求

13. therapist *n.* 治療專家，特定療法技師

14. filter *n.* 濾波器；濾光器；濾色鏡

15. undeniable *adj.* 無可爭辯的；不可否認的，無法抵賴的；確實優秀的；無可疵議的

16. accelerate *vi.* 加快，加速

17. turmoil *n.* 混亂；焦慮

18. postgrad *n.* 研究所人數；官方網站

19. nurture *vt.* 培育；養育

20. credential *n.* 文憑；憑證

21. recruiter *n.* 招聘人員

22. initiative *n.* 主動性；主動權；主動精神

23. counterpart *n.* 合作者

24. independently *adv.* 獨立地，自立地，無關地

25. entitlement *n.* 授權；應得權益；命名、被定名

26. benchmark *n.* 基準，參照

27. crux *n.* 癥結；關鍵；中心

Content Awareness

1. Skim the text and then answer the following questions.

（1）What is the title of the article?

（2）What are the challenges for a bachelor's degree?
A. Cheaper programs.　　B. Master's degrees.　　C. Both A and B.

（3）Which of the following is not created by the「spiraling degree inflation」?
A. More and more Americans will be burdened with heavy student loans.
B. The earnings differential will continue to grow and expand.
C. More and more college-educated people will be in jobs that do not require a bachelor's degree.

(4) College graduates tend to do better in the job market than those without a bachelor's degree because _____.

A. they have mastered critical thinking skills

B. they have the mental capability and the initiative to complete something

C. they have the potential to obtain a master's degree

(5) People's attitudes toward a bachelor's degree _____.

A. are ambiguous   B. are changing   C. are not clear

(6) The main idea of this article is that _____.

A. a bachelor's degree has lost its value

B. a bachelor's degree will regain its value

C. a bachelor's degree is no longer taken at face value

2. According to the text, decide whether each of the following statements is True (T) or False (F).

(1) People with bachelor's degrees always earn more than those without.

(2) Not all bachelor's degrees are equal.

(3) More and more college-educated people may be employed in jobs that do not require a four-year degree.

(4) A master's degree highlights the weaknesses of a bachelor's degree and decreases the need for it.

(5) Employers are more interested in a master's degree than in anything else.

(6) People's attitude toward a bachelor's degree indicates that education is no longer respected.

Language Focus

1. Fill in the blanks with the correct forms of the given words.

Employ   economy   attend   graduate   pursue

Engineer   enrollment   criticize   academically   evolution

(1) He enrolled with an _____ agency for a teaching position.

(2) In recent years our country has placed great importance on _____ development.

(3) _____ at Professor Smith's lecture fell off sharply that evening.

(4) This university aims to more than double their _____ student population in five years.

(5) Life, liberty, and the _____ of happiness have been called the inalienable rights of man.

(6) Their inventions have contributed to the development of electrical _____.

8

(7) I must _____ the children for piano lessons before next week.

(8) All of our cultural heritage which is useful should be inherited, but in a _____ way.

(9) Many scholars were annoyed by his injection of politics into _____ discussion.

(10) He argued that organisms _____ gradually by accumulating small hereditary changes.

2. Fill in the blanks with words that are often confused.

attitude aptitude

(1) Does she show any _____ for music?

(2) He shows a very positive _____ to his work.

require acquire

(3) To remove any ambiguity we have to _____ more accurate information.

(4) If you _____ further information, you should consult the registrar.

search research

(5) The new law empowered the police to _____ private houses.

(6) Recent _____ has cast new light on the causes of the disease.

3. Fill in each blank with one suitable word.

Education is not an end, but a means to an end. In _____ words, we do not educate children _____ for the purpose of educating them; our purpose is to fit them for life.

In many modern countries it _____ for some time been fashionable to think that, by free education for all, one can solve all the problems of society and build a perfect nation. But we can already see that free education for all is not enough: we find in _____ countries a far larger number of people with university degrees _____ there are jobs for them to fill. Because of their degrees, they _____ to do what they think 「low」 work; and, in fact, work with the hands is thought to be dirty and shameful in such countries.

But we have only to think a moment to that the _____ that the work of a completely uneducated farmer is far more important than _____ of a professor: we can live _____ education, but we die if we have no food. _____ no one cleaned our streets and took the rubbish away from our houses, we should get terrible diseases in our towns.

In fact, when we say that all of us must be educated to fit us for life, it means that we must be _____ to do whatever job is suited to our brain and ability, and to realize that all jobs are necessary to society, that it is very _____ to be ashamed of one's work, or to scorn someone else's. Only such a type of education can be called valuable to society.

Passage B

Methods of Education: East and West

A teacher from Canada recently visited an elementary school in Japan. In one class, she watched 60 young children as they learned to draw a cat. The class teacher drew a big circle on the blackboard, and the 60 children copied it on their papers. The teacher drew a smaller circle on top of the first and then put two triangles on top of it; the children continued their cats in exactly the same way. The lesson continued until there were 61 identical cats in the classroom.

The Canadian teacher was startled by the lesson. The teaching methods—and their effects—were very different from those in her own country. An art lesson in a Canadian school would lead to a room full of unique pictures, not a series of identical cats. Why? What causes this difference in educational methods?

In any classroom in any country, the instructor teaches more than just art or history or language. Part of what's going on—consciously or not—is the teaching of culture: the attitudes, values and beliefs of the society. Every education system is inevitably a mirror that reflects the culture of the society it is a part of.

In many Western societies, such as the United States or Canada, which are made up of many different nationalities, religious groups and cultural orientations, individualism and independent thinking are highly valued. And these values are reflected by the education systems in these countries. Teachers emphasize the qualities that make each student special. Students are seldom expected to memorize information; instead, they are encouraged to think for themselves, find answers on their own and come up with individual solutions. At an early age, students learn to form their own ideas and opinions, and to express their ideas in class discussion.

In Japan, by contrast, the vast majority of people share the same language, history, and culture. Perhaps for this reason, the education system there reflects a belief in group goals and traditions rather than individualism. Japanese schoolchildren often work together and help one another on assignments. In the classroom, the teacher is the main source of knowledge: He or she lectures, and the students listen. There is not much discussion; instead, the students recite rules or information that they have memorized.

The advantage of the education system in Japan is that students there learn the social skill of cooperation. Another advantage is that they learn much more math and science than most American students. They also study more hours each day and more days each year than their North American counterparts do. The system is demanding, but it prepares children for a society that values discipline and self-control. There are, however, disadvantages. For one thing, many students say that after an exam, they forget much of the information they memorized. For another, the extremely demanding system puts enormous psychological pressure on students, and is considered a primary factor in the high suicide rate among Japanese school-age children.

The advantage of the education system in North America, on the other hand, is that students learn to think for themselves. They learn to take the initiative—to make decisions and take action without someone telling them what to do. The system prepares them for a society that values creative ideas and individual responsibility. There are drawbacks, however. Among other things, American high school graduates haven't studied as many basic rules and facts as students in other countries have. And many social critics attribute the high crime rate in the US at least partially to a lack of discipline in the schools.

New Words
1. triangle *n.* 三角形；三角形物體
2. inevitably *adv.* 不可避免地；必然地
3. reflect *vt.* 顯示；表明
4. initiative *n.* 主動的行動
5. partially *adv.* 部分地，不完全地

Content Awareness
Decide whether each of the following statements is true (T) or false (F).
(1) The method of teaching startled the Canadian teacher in the class she visited.
(2) By the statement「In any classroom in any country, the instructor teaches more than just art or history or language.」the author means instructors everywhere teach many different subjects.
(3) According to the author, the variety of nationalities, religious groups and cultural orientations there contributes to the high value placed on individualism in North America.
(4) The advantage of the Japanese system of education is that Japanese people share the same language, culture and history.
(5) According to the author, the most serious problem with the Japanese system is

that it prepares children for a society that values discipline and self-control.

(6) The author considers it appropriate for North American society to ⌈learn to take the initiative⌋.

(7) According to the author, the most serious problem with the North American system is that the lack of discipline may contribute to the high crime rate.

(8) According to the author, the Japanese system of education is better.

Language Focus

1. Complete the sentences by using the proper words above in the Word Match. Change their forms if necessary.

(1) The smooth surface of the lake _____ the light of the house.

(2) Our monitor used to take the _____ in organizing the New Year's party every year.

(3) The professor _____ the importance of keeping ourselves informed of the latest development in science and technology.

(4) There should be better _____ in schools.

(5) A teacher can't give _____ attention to each pupil if the classes are too large.

(6) Everyone was surprised when the mayor _____ a long poem to the visiting queen.

(7) Native speakers don't make _____ use of the formal rules of grammar.

(8) This is a very good car; its only _____ is that it uses a lot of petrol.

(9) The police are investigating a murder that happened on the campus last week, which was made to look like a _____.

(10) The coach said his team would _____ lose the match after the three best players were injured.

2. Word Match

Match the following words with their definitions within each group of five words.

reflect	repeat aloud from memory
initiative	not general or complete
emphasize	commencing move
recite	stress, single out as important
partial	show or express
discipline	shock
individual	the quality of having an inferior or less favorable position
startle	knowing and perceiving
disadvantage	being or characteristic of a single thing or person
conscious	a system of roles of conduct or methods of practice

表(續)

drawback	highly
suicide	the quality of being a disadvantage
inevitably	the act of killing oneself
cooperation	joint operation or action
extremely	unavoidably

Skills Development and Practice

Reading Skills

Reading for the Main Idea (1)
Topic Sentences

EXAMPLE:

There is a big difference between growing older and growing up. If you are nineteen years old and lie in bed for one full year and don't do one productive thing, you will turn twenty years old. If I am eighty-seven years old and stay in bed for a year and never do anything, I will turn eighty-eight. Anybody can grow older. That doesn't take any talent or ability. The idea is to grow up by always finding the opportunity in change.

QUESTIONS:

1. Where is the topic sentence of the paragraph?

_____

2. What is the main idea of the paragraph?

_____

Now reread the text and complete the following.
1. The topic sentence of Para. 2 is _____.
2. The topic sentence of Para. 3 is _____.
3. The topic sentence of Para. 4 is _____.

Practice 1: Read each of the paragraphs. Underline the topic sentences.

1. One way to improve your vocabulary in English is to read novels and stories in English. They often contain new words. It is not difficult to understand these new words because you can usually guess their meanings. The other words in the sentences will help you, and the story will also help you. An interesting story will help you guess the new words because the meanings of the new words are part of the meaning of the story.

2. In today's world, most graduate students don't regret spending time with their studies. They are finding that things are changing very fast. New developments are occurring in all fields. For many, graduate study has become a necessity.

3. Different language learners have different purposes of learning a new language. Some people learn a second language in order to learn about the culture of the people

who speak that language. They may be interested in the history and customs of these people, for example, or they may want to study the literature of the language. Other language learners want to travel to other countries. They need to know the languages of those countries so that they can talk to people and understand what they say. They want to make friends with the people they meet.

Translation Practice

Translation Skills

選擇詞義：根據詞在句中的搭配關係和上下文，正確地選擇詞義。

Practice 2：Translate the phrases into Chinese, pay attention to the meaning of the word「regular」.

1. regular reading _____
2. regular flights _____
3. regular job _____
4. regular visitor _____
5. regular speed _____
6. regular gasoline _____
7. regular verb _____
8. regular army _____

Translate the sentences into Chinese, and pay attention to the meaning of the word「study」.

1. Study reading is different from regular reading.
_____

2. You will find him in his study.
_____

3. He has made great progress in his studies.
_____

4. He is continuing his studies abroad.
_____

5. Scientists are studying the photographs of Mars (火星) for signs of life.
_____

6. My brother is studying at Peking University.
_____

7. He has been studying law these years.
_____

8. The prisoner studied ways to escape.
_____

Practice 3：Translate the sentences into Chinese.

1. Being on my own, talking with friendly people, and having Fridays off—these are just some things I like about college.

2. Finally—to add to my likes of college—I love having Fridays off; I wouldn't be able to cope with five days of classes in a row.

3. The first day of school our teacher introduced himself to our math class and challenged us to know someone we didn't already know.

4. We elderly people usually don't have regrets for what we did, but rather for things we didn't do.

5. We'll never forget this wonderful woman who taught by example that it's never too late to be all you can possibly be.

Practice 4: Translate the sentences into English with the words or expressions given.

1. 在我進大學的第二周裡，我得出去找一家書店，在那裡買幾本英語辭典。（where）

2. 那些參加會議的人都是我的同學。（who）

3. 她昨天早上起得遲，沒有趕上火車。（sleep in）

4. 我很快就適應了大學生活。（adjust to）

5. 他們已查清了這個人是誰。（find out）

6. 船應該在什麼時候開？（be supposed to）

Practical Translation

詞彙的翻譯

翻譯詞彙時最忌諱的可以說是一個詞對應一個詞地「死譯」，如此翻譯的結果往往令人啼笑皆非。比如：bring down the house 不能按字面意思翻譯為「推倒房子」，而應該譯為「全場喝彩」；at the right angle 說的不是「恰巧呈角度」，而是「呈直角」；know you to a hair 不是「我瞭解你的頭髮」，而是「對你了如指

掌」。諸如此類的誤譯都有一個共同點，即不考慮詞的深層含義以及詞在短語中的含義，而是生搬硬套地逐詞翻譯，從而曲解了原文。

翻譯一個詞，必須先從它在上下文中所處的位置及與其他詞的搭配關係去理解，去進行貼切的翻譯。總的來說，翻譯詞彙應注意如下三方面的問題：

1. 一詞多義

有時單詞在不同的上下文中含義不同，應注意利用上下文加以區別。例如本課出現的 rest, negotiate, odds 等詞在不同的上下文中有不同的含義，以它們中最為常見的詞 rest 為例：

（1）It was an experience I will treasure for the rest of my life.

譯文：在有生之年我都將珍惜這次經歷。

解析：這裡 rest 是「剩餘」的意思，是名詞。

（2）He's tired and exhausted, and has been advised to rest for two weeks.

譯文：他很疲憊，別人都建議他休息兩週。

解析：這裡 rest 是「休息」的意思，是動詞。

（3）The car accelerates rapidly from rest.

譯文：這輛車從靜止到加速用時很短。

解析：這裡 rest 是「靜止」的意思，是名詞。

2. 短語的含義

在一些固定搭配的短語裡，詞義也會相應地發生變化，應注意累積這一類短語。例如：

all but：幾乎，差不多；as yet：迄今，至今；as anything：非常地；anything but：根本不；apart from：除了；but for：要不是；by no means：絕對不行；by any means：無論如何；far from：決非；for one：至少……；not so much... as：與其……不如；let alone：更不用說；no less than：簡直是。

在將英語習慣用語翻譯成漢語時，千萬不能望文生義。例如：pull one's leg 不是「拖後腿」的意思，而是「愚弄某人，開某人的玩笑」；break a leg 不是「摔斷一條腿」，而是「祝好運」的意思。

還有些英語習慣用語，其細微的差別就可能造成意義的迴異。例如：be black and white 指「是非分明」，與之近似的 be in black and white 意思卻是「白紙黑字」；out of the question 指「不可能的」，out of question 表達的卻是「沒問題」。

3. 兩種語言的文化背景差異

在翻譯一些具有鮮明民族色彩的詞語時，如成語、典故，由於兩種語言的社會文化背景不同，直譯往往不能使讀者明白意思。有學者主張加註釋，可這樣做又容易使譯文太囉嗦。在這種情況下，譯者可以在理解詞彙引申含義的基礎上，結合上下文將其譯為符合譯入語文化的句子。例如：

(1) as rich as Croesus

譯文：十分富有，富可敵國

解析：Croesus（克羅伊斯）是公元 6 世紀小亞細亞呂底亞國王，十分富有。如果直譯為「像克羅伊斯一樣富有」，而讀者又不知「克羅伊斯」為何許人，這句話就變得令人十分費解。

(2) The room had a Spartan look.

譯文：房間看起來很簡樸。

解析：古希臘斯巴達人以生活簡樸而著稱。對待這一典故，直接把詞的引申意義翻譯過來更容易理解。

Translation Practice

Translate the following paragraphs into Chinese.

Paragraph One

Sometimes, psychographic profiles can be quite detailed. Take the Accord. Honda Motor reports that their car's owners like to vacuum their garages. You can't say they're not clean.

Paragraph Two

We also found that sometimes messages sent out by seemingly similar cars can be quite different. Consider two premier British luxury sedans: Bentley's Arnage and Rolls' Phantom. Both are stately and fast, but each attracts a different kind of customer.

Paragraph Three

The Bentley buyer wants an understated heirloom that he or she can pass down through the generations; over 80% of all Bentleys ever made are still on the road today. The Phantom buyer, on the other hand, is looking for instant recognition. The Car has a presence that really demands attention wherever it goes.

Focused Writing

Formal Letters

Professional communication is different from personal communication, so the style of a formal letter is distinct from that of a personal letter. Formal letters are usually also business letters such as letters sent with a job application, cover letters, letters to institutions such as government ministries or educational establishments and letters to the service industries as well as all the usual day-to-day letters involved in businesses.

Formal letters differ from personal letters in two facets. Firstly, the format of a formal letter is somewhat different from that of a personal letter. Secondly, the language of a formal letter, as the name indicates, is more formal than that of a personal letter. It follows that the intimate and conversational style appropriate for a personal letter is out of place in a formal letter.

The format is, in general, similar in both types of letters in terms of the address of the sender, the date and the main body. However there are some additional points to note as follows.

The addressee's address. In a formal letter, the addressee's address, that is, the address of the recipient which you will also write on the outside of the envelope, is placed on the left, one or two lines below the line of the date (which is still on the right) and above the salutation. In a personal letter, this address is omitted.

The salutation. This usually takes the form 「Dear Mr...」 or 「Dear Ms...」 if you know the surname of the recipient. Note that only the surname appears after Mr. / Mrs. /Miss. /Ms. It is not correct to address a letter 「Dear Mr. Tom Black」. It should be Dear Tom (informal) or Dear Mr. Black (formal). If you don't know the name of the recipient or you don't know who is supposed to receive the letter, simply write 「Dear Sirs」 or 「Dear Sir or Madam」.

The complimentary close. 「Yours sincerely」 or 「Yours faithfully」 are two most commonly used forms, but their usage should never be confused. 「Yours sincerely」 is used when you know the name of the recipient and have started the letter with their name; whereas, 「Yours faithfully」 should be used if you don't and have therefore started Dear Sirs or Dear Madam.

The signature. A formal letter requires your full signature, and usually your full name and title will be printed below your signature. This is because signatures are often unclear.

Headed notepaper. If you are writing on behalf of a business, then it is likely that you will use notepaper that has been preprinted with the name and logo and often the address of the company. If you are writing a business letter on your own behalf, then it is important to ensure that your address is clearly written at the top right of the page so that any reply can be sent.

Two samples of formal letters are given below to help you see how a formal letter should be laid out and the tone of the formal writing.

Sample 1: A Letter of Enquiry

Living Science Weekly
45-49 Rush Road
Nottingham
NO2, 2ST
England

June 23rd, 2010

The General Manager
Ryder Wholesale Medical Supplies Ltd.
90-100 Rue de la Pompe
Paris 75004
France

Dear Sir,

  The magazine Living Science Weekly of which I am Chief Feature Writer will shortly be running a series of articles on scientists who are prominent in different fields of science. We understand that your Senior Research Scientist, Dr J. L. Bonfils, is engaged in research on a new type of anesthetic and we would therefore be very interested in his views for one of our articles.

  I am writing to you first in case you feel it inappropriate for Dr. Bonfils to talk to us and to assure you that the subject matter of the interview will not in any way breach the confidentiality associated with his current research.

  I would be most grateful if Dr. Bonfils could spare me a little of his very valuable time, during the next two weeks I can be available at any time to suit Dr. Bonfils except for on the 19th and 24th and would be happy to meet anywhere convenient for him.

  I look forward to hearing from you.

Yours faithfully,
Edward Sawyer

  Note: This is a letter requesting whether a senior member of Ryder Medical Supplies could be available for an interview by a feature writer of a magazine. The writer first briefly introduces himself and then says why he is writing (i.e. asking for an interview). He also indicates why he has not approached Dr. Bonfils directly. Then he mentions that the interview will have to be in the next two weeks (no doubt he has deadlines to meet but it is not necessary for him to go into detail about that) but makes it as easy as possible for Dr. Bonfils to accommodate him since he is asking for a favor.

  The ending ⌈I look forward to hearing from you⌋ is the best and most commonly used way to indicate that you hope for an early response.

  It is important for all business letters to be written as concisely and as clearly as possible so that they are easy to read and understand.

  A cover letter is a letter that is included with a document or object to explain why it is being sent to the recipient. For example, a cover letter would be necessary if something was being returned after purchase in order to explain what is wrong and what you expect the seller to do about it. A cover letter should be sent with a CV or resume when applying for a job highlighting the main reason why you think you are suitable for the job and expressing your hope for the opportunity to meet (i.e. to get an interview). In this circumstance the letter should be short, do not be tempted to repeat everything that is in your CV. There are many situations in which a cover letter will be necessary. See the sample below.

Sample 2: A Cover Letter for Manuscript Submission

<pre>
                                                    The Dept of Education
                                                    University of Birmingham
                                                    Edgbaston
                                                    Birmingham
                                                    B15, 2TT

                                                    June 6th, 2008
</pre>

The Editor in Chief
ELT Journal
Markham Road
London
SW18, 9LT
Dear Mr. Drummond,

  I am enclosing a manuscript entitled ⌈Improving Scores on the IELTS Speaking Test⌋ to be considered for publication in the ELT Journal.

  The paper presents three strategies for teaching students who are taking the IELTS speaking test. The first strategy is aimed at improving confidence and uses a variety of self-help materials from the field of popular psychology. The second strategy encourages students to think critically and invokes a range of academic perspectives. The third strategy invites a close inspection and utilization of the marking criteria published in the IELTS handbook. These strategies were applied to a group of students who sat the test in September 2005 and their scores are presented and analyzed. There is evidence that the strategies were effective in raising scores on the speaking component by as much as 12%.

  I confirm that this manuscript has not been published elsewhere and is not under consideration by another journal. The study was supported by a grant from the Wellcome Trust, U.K. The author has no conflicts of interest to declare.

  Please address correspondence to:
  Dr. Steve Issitt
  Deputy Director of EAP Summer Courses
  University of Birmingham
  I look forward to hearing from you at your earliest convenience.

Yours sincerely,
Steve Issitt
Dr. S. Issitt
S. Issitt@bham.ac.uk
Tel: 0121, 41, 45702

Note: A cover letter for a manuscript submission is your opportunity to directly address the editor of your target journal in order to persuade him or her to consider your paper. The following principals apply in this situation:

· Some journals have different editors for the different areas of research that the journal covers so you should choose the most appropriate editor based on area and occasionally also editor profiles. Always try to address your letter personally to the appropriate editor, e.g., 「Dear Dr. Smith」. It is easy to telephone to ask. If one cannot be identified, address your letter to the Editor-in-Chief.

· Begin by providing the title of your manuscript, the section/publication type in which you would like to see it published, and the name of the journal you are submitting it to.

· You then need to provide a very brief background and rationale for your study, explaining why you did what you did. This can be followed by a brief description of the results.

· The following paragraph is very important. You will need to explain the significance of your findings to the research community, and specifically to the readers of your target journal. If you find it difficult to explain why the readers of that journal would be interested in your findings, then you may need to select a more appropriate journal. Editors will only send papers to review that they think will be of interest to their readers. Studying the 「aims and scope」 of your chosen journal might help with this.

· The last paragraph of the letter should contain any statements or declarations required by the target journal. These usually include declarations of any conflicts of interest, grant support or other sources of funding, a statement that all authors have read and approved the manuscript and a statement that the same manuscript has not been submitted elsewhere. Confirmation of each author's qualification for authorship may also be required.

· Finally, add your contact details and your name printed after your signature.

Writing Assignment

Write a formal letter to a tourist office asking for information about a place you intend to visit. Be sure to be specific about what information you would like to know.

Unit 2　Man and Nature

Warming-ups

Task 1　Questions for Thought

Think about the following questions, then discuss with your partner.

1. What environmental problems are existing in today's world?
2. Who do you think is more responsible for pollution, individuals or the government?
3. What is low-carbon life? What is the significance of low-carbon life?
4. What can you do to reduce pollution and protect our environment?

Task 2　Vocabulary Preview

Complete the following table by writing the English or Chinese equivalents of the words given. Then, check your answers with your partner.

地震		environment-friendly	
噪聲		garbage	
沙塵暴		recycle	
臺風		over exploitation	
災難		landslide	
溫室效應		desertification	

In-class Activities

Task 1　Individual Work

A: Which of these problems do you think will cause the most damage to the world? Why? Rank them from 1 (the most serious) to 6 (the least serious).

… More and more people are living in cities.

… Rivers, lakes, and oceans are becoming more polluted.

… The air in our cities is becoming more polluted.

... The greenhouse effect is causing the earth's temperature to rise.

... The population of the world is growing too quickly.

... Holes are developing in the earth's ozone layer, the part of the atmosphere that protects the earth from dangerous radiation.

B: How 「green」 are you? Give each item in the quiz a number from 1 to 5. 1=always, 2=often, 3=sometimes, 4=hardly ever, 5=never

How Green You are

	1. turn off the lights when you leave home
	2. avoid using more water than you need
	3. use low-energy light bulbs
	4. avoid using plastic shopping bag
	5. recycle paper, glass, and cans
	6. avoid throw things away if they can be reused, repaired or recycled
	7. do not leave litter
	8. do not smoke
	9. walk or use a bike when traveling short distances
	10. minimize the use of the electric appliances (micro-wave oven, hairdryer)
	11. avoid using air-conditioning in the summer
	12. avoid using disposable wooden chopsticks

C: Add up your number from the quiz above, and then calculate your score referring to the interpretation below. Now, do you know how green you are?

Score	
12-23	You are so green, it's unbelievable! Are there more things do to protect the environment?
24-35	You are very environmentally aware. You care about and respect the world around you.
36-47	You do something to protect the environment, but there's always room for improvement.
48-60	You're not green at all. Be aware of the things you can do and try. Everything you do will help.

Task 2 Pair Work

Suppose you and your partner are from different country or place. Try to start a conversation with him/her on environment. An example is given to you.

A: Is the environment a big issue in your country? It is in mine.

B: It is in mine, too. The biggest issue is water. The climate is dry and so water conservation is very important.

A: What methods do you use to conserve water?

B: Water is rationed. We can only use a certain amount each month. It means that we cannot use some modern household items, like washing machines. They use too much water.

A: I see. I think the biggest environment problem in my country is air pollution.

B: Yes, I agree. The air here is much more polluted than in my country. Of course, my country is more agricultural and has much less industry.

A: We have reduced emission of air pollution in recent years, but cars are still a major source of them. Factories have become cleaner as stricter environment pollution laws have been introduced.

B: The problem is now on a truly global scale. I don't believe that any single country can do anything about it.

A: I think you're right. There needs to be an international response to this problem.

Task 3 Role-play

Read the following dialogue first, and then act it out with your partner. Each of you should assume a role, and then switch the role.

(Situation: You and your friend are worried about the environment problems, and talking about some solutions.)

A: There are so many environment problems in the world today. Do you think we can really solve them all or will destroy the world?

B: I hope that world leaders can get together and agree on a plan for action, but I doubt it'll happen before it's too late.

A: We need to solve the problem of air pollution before we destroy the atmosphere. There is lots of clean, modern technology, but companies in developed countries say it is expensive. Developing countries put more emphasis on economic development than on environment protection.

B: Everyone is looking at the issue in the short term, rather than the long term. It's the same with the destruction of the rainforests. Countries and companies just want the wood. They're not thinking about the long-term damage to the forests. We should also remember that the forests are an important natural habitat for thousands of species of animal and plant life.

A: In other parts of the world, especially in Africa, there is a problem with desertification. Climate change and over-farming are causing farmland to turn into desert. It means that people cannot grow enough food.

B: It also means that people sometimes fight over the farmland that remains. Damaging the environment actually leads to conflict between people.

A: Have you ever thought about joining an organization committed to protecting the environment? You could get involved with projects to improve the environment.

B: I think I'd like to do that. I could take the things I learn here back to my country when I have finished my studies.

Task 4   Debate/Discussion

Which is more important, increasing standard of people living, or protecting the environment? Why?

A: Work in groups and make discussion with your peers.

Argument 1: Increasing standard of people living is more important.

Your opinion:

Argument 2: Protecting the environment is more important.

Your opinion:

B: After discussing, summarize all the opinions and make an oral speech about:

Developing Economy and Protecting Environment

The following might be useful and helpful in the speech:

Words and Expressions:

backward, sustainable development strategy, to strike a balance between…, rational exploitation and utilization of natural resources, long-term development, low-carbon economy

Reference Modal:

Some people think that we should develop our economy first, because third world countries must improve their economies if they want to raise their citizen's standard of living. People need jobs and that means we need industry. Some hold that protecting the important since we are facing many serious environmental issues. We have only one globe. In my opinion…

Reading Passages

Passage A

Mission Zero

Ray C. Anderson (July 28, 1934–August 8, 2011) was founder and chairman of Interface, Inc., one of the world's largest manufacturers of modular carpet for commercial and residential applications. He was 「known in environmental circles for his advanced and progressive stance on industrial ecology and sustainability.

「If it exists, it must be possible」, asserts Amory Lovins, co-founder and chief scientist of the Rocky Mountain Institute think tank. He is talking about my company. Fellow industrialists, I dare say, thought my ambition impossible to realize when fourteen years ago I described my aspirations for Interface Inc. to turn into what it actually is becoming today. Indeed, around then, the CEO of a major competitor looked at me in the eye, and said, 「Ray, you are a dreamer.」 Yet, as Amory says, 「If it exists...」

The 「impossible」 that exists today is a petroleum-intensive carpet manufacturer (for both energy and raw material) that has reduced net greenhouse gas (GHG) emissions by 88 percent, in absolute tons, and its water usage by 79 percent since 1996, even as sales have grown by two-thirds and earnings have doubled. In 1994 Interface set out on a mission 「to be the first industrial company that, by its deeds, shows the entire industrial world what sustainability is, in all its dimensions: people, process, product, profit, and place.」 Our definition of sustainability is to operate our petro-intensive company so as to take from the Earth only that which is naturally and rapidly renewable, and to do no harm to the biosphere.

Cumulatively, we have avoided $ 372 million in costs by eliminating waste, in a quest that is half way to achieving waste-free perfection by 2020. We define waste as any cost that does not add value for our customers. This translates ambitiously into doing everything right the first time, every time. We even define energy that still comes from fossil fuels as waste, something to be eliminated. Indeed, while offsets have a critical role to play in helping Interface (and, indeed, all of us) to reach our sustainability goals, we will not achieve them until we begin to redefine fossil fuel energy in this way. Sounds incredible? Remember, 「If it exists...」

Indeed our belching smokestacks, our gushing effluent pipes, our mountains of waste—all completely legal—provided tangible proof that business was good. They meant jobs, orders coming in, products going out, and money in the bank.

That all changed with a question that came from our customers: 「What is Interface doing for the environment?」 We had not heard that question before, and had no good answers. For a 「customer-intimate」 company, this was untenable. Looking for an answer—and a determination to respond with credible, demonstrable, and measurable results and transparent accountability—set us on this course.

Can taking a profitable business apart at the height of its success make business sense? The waste elimination initiative alone—and the avoided costs of $ 372 million over 13 years—have more than offset all the investments and expenses incurred in pursuit of our goal which we now call 「Mission Zero」: zero environmental impacts by the year 2020. This has allowed the business case for sustainability to develop and become crystal clear. Costs are down, not up—dispelling a myth and exposing the false choice between the environment and the economy.

Amazingly, this initiative has produced a better business model, a better way to bigger and more legitimate profits. It out-competes its competitors in the rough and tumble of the marketplace, but not at the expense of the Earth or future generations. Instead it includes Earth and generations not yet born in win-win-win relationships. As validation of this, the Interface Share price has moved from $ 2 to $ 20 in four years, as we have dug out of the deepest, longest recession in our industry's history, a recession we might not have survived without the enormous boost of sustainability.

But, what about the big picture? What does the Interface journey have to teach us? A sustainable society into the indefinite future depends totally and absolutely on a vast, ethically driven redesign of the industrial system, triggered by an equally vast mind-shift—one mind at a time, one organization at a time, one technology at a time, one building, one company, one university curriculum, one community, one region, one industry at a time—until the entire system has been transformed into a sustainable one existing ethically in balance with Earth's natural systems, upon which every living thing, even civilization itself, utterly depends.

One person, you, can make the difference in your organization. The key is: Do something, then do something else.

Notes

1. Amory Lovins: an American environmental scientist and writer, Chairman and Chief Scientist of the Rocky Mountain Institute. Having worked in the field of energy policy and related areas for four decades, he was named by *Time* magazine one of the world's 100 most influential people in 2009.

2. The Rocky Mountain Institute (RMI): an organization in the United States dedicated to research, publication, consulting, and lecturing in the general field of sustainability, with a special focus on profitable innovations for energy and resource efficiency. For more information, please check: http://www.rmi.org.

Content Awareness

Choose the best answer to each question with the information from the passage.

(1) What was the attitude of other industrialists when the author announced what he wanted to achieve 14 years ago?

A. Supportive.

B. Opposed.

C. Approving.

D. Suspicious.

(2) The author believes that to achieve sustainability, his company must _____.

A. try by all means to avoid any harm to the biosphere

B. be more profitable to afford the rising cost of petroleum

C. focus more on the people, process, product, profit and place

D. take only that is natural as its energy and material

(3) According to the definition of the author, which of the following is regarded as waste?

A. Anything that increases production cost.

B. Anything from fossil fuels used as energy.

C. Anything that added value for customers.

D. Anything that offsets the rising costs.

(4) For Interface, the goal of 「Mission Zero」 is to _____.

A. be completely legal in its waste disposal

B. turn itself to a customer-intimate company

C. draw a line between the environment and the economy

D. achieve waste-free perfection while remaining profitable

(5) Which of the following statements about Interface is true?

A. Interface has increased its costs to achieve the goal of 「Mission Zero」.

B. The success of Interface is grounded on its emphasis on sustainability.

C. To protect the Earth, Interface has given up competition in the market.

D. The Interface share price has sharply risen because of the recession.

Language Focus

1. Decide on the meaning of the suffix or prefix (in italics) of each compound word, and make a sentence with each of the given compound words.

Word	Meaning in the context
(1) petroleum-*intensive*	☐ giving extreme and constant care or attention
	☐ involving a lot of effort, energy, or attention
	☐ indicating the use of a lot of a particular thing
labor-intensive	
knowledge-intensive	
(2) waste-*free*	☐ without a particular thing
	☐ without cost or payment
	☐ not limited or controlled
alcohol-free	
duty-free	
(3) customer-*intimate*	☐ having thorough knowledge something
	☐ relating to very private or personal matters
	☐ having a very close and friendly relationship
client-intimate	
user-intimate	
(4) *co*-founder	☐ partner or associate in an activity or job
	☐ to the same extent or degree
	☐ in a less important or assistant position
co-sponsor	
co-author	
(5) *out*-compete	☐ away from the central part or area
	☐ in a better, faster or further way
	☐ showing the result of an action

Unit 2 Man and Nature

29

表(續)

Word	Meaning in the context
out-sell	
out-rank	

2. Choose the word or expression that is closest in meaning to the underlined part in each sentence below.

(1) Apple turned into a profitable business with a few very popular products.

A. built up　　　　　　　　　　B. set up
C. moved　　　　　　　　　　　D. became

(2) After many years of doing nothing about banning smoking in public, the government set out on it.

A. set down　　　　　　　　　　B. set aside
C. set off　　　　　　　　　　　D. set up

(3) An uproar came from the audience as the most promising racing athlete stopped half way.

A. midway　　　　　　　　　　　B. right away
C. on the wrong track　　　　　　D. off the track

(4) Replacing the battery is an easy job; you don't have to take your watch apart.

A. take... away　　　　　　　　　B. take... to pieces
C. pull... down　　　　　　　　　D. pull... away

(5) It's almost impossible to catch a taxi at the height of the rush hour anywhere in this city.

A. at the peak of　　　　　　　　B. at the point of
C. at the moment of　　　　　　　D. at the beginning of

(6) It doesn't make sense to spend so much on this phone when you can buy a much cheaper one with similar functions.

A. seem responsible　　　　　　　B. make it possible
C. tell anything　　　　　　　　　D. have a good reason

(7) All the team members display high levels of energy and motivation in pursuit of the objectives.

A. to achieve　　　　　　　　　　B. to follow
C. to work out　　　　　　　　　D. to move toward

(8) The whole world is following closely how the country will dig out of its financial trouble.

A. deal with　　　　　　　　　　B. control

30

C. settle   D. work out

3. Translate the following paragraphs into English.

(1) 十年前，當公司還處在生產的鼎盛時期時，我們就決定投資新技術，將公司轉型為技術密集型企業。由於擁有先進技術，我們在激烈動盪的市場競爭中脫穎而出。現在我們的成本下降了百分之三十，銷售業績卻上漲了三分之二，利潤翻了一番。

(2) 我們將可持續性定義為保持企業盈利，但不以環境為代價。從商業的角度看，這合理嗎？事實上，在追求可持續發展目標的過程中，我們的收益已經超過了所有的投資和開支。可持續發展的推進起到了如此重要的作用，幫助我們撐過了史上最深重的經濟衰退。

Passage B

What Is Animal Welfare?

Introduction

Human understanding of animals—especially their sentience, needs and natures—is developing all the time. The physical states of poor welfare are more readily accessible and understandable (particularly for veterinarians, who undertook much of the early work on welfare). But new research leads naturally to greater understanding of mental states and needs and natures. This is particularly true of ethological research, including 「preference testing」 where animals' preferences are measured and assessed. This may be why earlier definitions of welfare centered on physical states, whereas the latest definitions have reflected the complex, multi-faceted nature of animal welfare.

Welfare and Rights

In brief, the difference between animal welfare and animal rights can be explained as below:

Animal welfare denotes the desire to prevent unnecessary animal suffering (that is, whilst not categorically opposed to the use of animals, want to ensure a good quality of life and humane death).

Animal rights denote the philosophical belief that animals should have rights, including the right to live their lives free of human intervention (and ultimate death at the hands of humans). Animal rightists are philosophically opposed to the use of animals by humans (although some accept 「symbiotic」 relationships, such as companion animal ownership).

Welfare and Conservation

The key difference between conservation and animal welfare is that conservation cares about species (and extinction) whereas animal welfare cares about the individual animal (and its suffering). Animal welfarists believe that each individual animal has an intrinsic value and should be respected and protected. They recognize that animals have biologically determined instincts, interests and natures, and can experience pain and suffer, and believe that they should therefore be permitted to live their lives free from avoidable suffering at the hands of humans. It is not difficult to see why the conservation movement has attracted support more readily than the animal welfare movement. Animal welfare requires greater altruism and empathy than conservation. Care for conservation can be generated by human-centered objectives, such as not wanting species to become extinct because of the loss for future generations (of humans). Although many people now recognize that animals feel pain and suffer, this comes lower down on their list of priorities for action—and may indeed challenge their own lifestyle and habits.

Welfare Defined

Welfare is not just absence of cruelty or 「unnecessary suffering」. It is much more complex. It includes the following different states:

Physical State: Traditional definitions center on the physical state of animals. However, it is a simplistic view that welfare is only poor when survival or reproduction is impaired by a physical problem.

Mental State: Mental states play an important role in welfare. These states are becoming increasingly understood and explored, including by scientists.

Naturalness: The third state-naturalness-refers to the ability of the animal to fulfill its natural needs and desires. The frustration of these harms its welfare. This third dimension has been recently recognized and added.

The definition of animal welfare is often debated. However, these three states, which are given in the definition by WSPA in its 「Concepts of Animal Welfare」 veterinary training resource, provide the most comprehensive to date.

Five Freedoms

The 「five freedoms」, which were originally developed by the UK's Farm Animal

Welfare Council (FAWC), provide valuable guidance on animal welfare. They are now internationally recognized, and have been adapted slightly since their formulation. The current form is:

· Freedom from hunger and thirst—ready access to water and a diet to maintain health and vigor

· Freedom from discomfort—by providing an appropriate environment including shelter and a comfortable resting area

· Freedom from pain, injury and disease—by prevention or rapid diagnosis and treatment

· Freedom to express normal behavior—by providing sufficient space, proper facilities and company of the animal's own kind

· Freedom from fear and distress—by ensuring conditions and treatment which avoid mental suffering

They cover all three of the states identified by WSPA above.

They are ideal states, and it is recognized that some freedoms may conflict in a situation where animals are cared for by man, e.g. the conflict between treatment (such as veterinary treatment) to cure illness/disease and freedom from fear and distress (that may be caused by the handling and procedure)

Needs

The term 「needs」 is often used in discussions on welfare, as needs are the things that should be provided to ensure an animal's welfare.

A need is:「A requirement, fundamental in the biology of the animal, to obtain a particular resource or respond to a particular environmental or bodily stimulus.」Needs may include a range of provisions such as food, water, comfort, avoidance of infectious disease and environmental enrichment. For animals under our care it is a human ethical responsibility to provide for their needs.

Different needs have different levels of importance to animals. Observing effects after withdrawal of needs provides an indication of their relative importance.

Sentience

There is now widespread recognition of the 「sentience」 of animals, which reinforces the need to protect welfare. The European Union has officially recognized animals to be 「Sentient Beings」 (1997). Sentience implies that animals:

· are aware of their own surroundings

· have an emotional dimension

· are aware of what is happening to them

· have the ability to learn from experience

- are aware of bodily sensations—pain, hunger, heat, cold, etc.
- are aware of their relationships with other animals
- have the ability to choose between different animals, objects and situations

Welfare Assessment

Animal welfare has developed into a science in its own right and as a result there is a growing amount of research into this subject. This research is funded by governments, corporations and industry bodies, welfare groups and other agencies. It is often used as the basis for the reform of animal welfare legislation. It is also used to improve conditions for animals reared for food, used in research, kept in captivity or as companion animals.

Three components are important for a welfare assessment:
- use the Five Freedoms as the framework
- assess welfare inputs and outputs
- quantify problems using severity, duration and number of animals affected

Inputs are the factors that affect welfare. Outputs are the actual impact of these factors on welfare.

Examples of three types of welfare inputs are:
- stockman—Empathy, knowledge, observation skills
- environment—Housing, bedding, feed quality, water provision
- animal—Suitable breed, age, and sex for the system

Physiological measures of welfare include:
- heart rate
- respiratory rate
- adrenal habituation
- blood pressure
- catecholamines (adrenaline and noradrenaline)
- enzymes and metabolites

However, measures of welfare should be applied with caution. WSPA's 「Concepts of Animal Welfare」 refers to different 「components」 of welfare, of which welfare science is one.
- Welfare science
- Animal ethics
- Welfare law

It is arguable that law is simply the practical application of the current state of science and ethics in a society, as accepted by consumers and (ultimately) politicians. However, the important point here is that science is not the only criteria for judging welfare, as other less tangible factors are also involved. It is, therefore, important that the 「precautionary principle」is applied, and where there are any cases of doubt, then the action taken should favor the animals (just in case the alternative course would impair welfare).

Welfare and Death

Welfare concerns the「quality」of animal life, whereas death affects the「quantity」of animal life. However, both may be the subjects of ethical concern by humans. The manner of death is relevant to an animal's welfare, e.g. the method of slaughter is important. Also, high death rates can indicate poor welfare conditions—poor husbandry conditions can cause disease and death and production pressures and overwork can also cause early death.

Content Awareness

Skim the text and answer the questions below.

(1) What is the title of this article?

(2) The first paragraph tells us that _____.

A. animal welfare should have our attention

B. animal welfare has a complex and multi-faceted nature

C. animal welfare needs new definitions

(3) Which of the following statements is true?

A. Both animal welfarists and animal rightists are against the use of animals

B. Animal welfarists are not against the use of animals.

C. Animal rightists are not against the use of animals.

(4) Conservation cares about _____.

A. the whole species

B. the individual animal

C. the human objectives

(5) The dimension to animal welfare that has been recently recognized is _____.

A. physical state   B. mental state

C. naturalness

(6) There are now _____ internationally recognized animal freedoms.

A. three   B. five

C. six

(7) In the discussions on animal welfare,「needs」are _____.

A. provided by human beings for animals

B. fundamental in obtaining provisions

C. important to animals on different levels

(8) Sentience implies that animals _____.
A. have the ability to respond sensibly to what is happening to them
B. have the ability to understand their own surroundings
C. have the awareness of bodily sensations
(9) Assessment of animal welfare _____.
A. relies on science alone
B. applies the 「precautionary principle」
C. involves more intangible factors than science
(10) Which of the following statements is true?
A. Animal death is not an ethical concern for humans.
B. The method of slaughter is not relevant to animal welfare.
C. High death rates indicate poor welfare conditions.

Language Focus
1. Fill in the blanks with the correct forms of the given words.
preference   suffer   humane   fulfill
extinction   originally   loss   arguable
(1) All theories _____ from practice and in turn serve practice.
(2) The _____ of my dream is apparently as far off as ever.
(3) All this gracious living isn't for me; I _____ the simple life.
(4) It is _____ to treat animals cruelly.
(5) The small _____ boiled over into a serious quarrel.
(6) I took a wrong turn and we got _____ in the mountains.
(7) Dinosaurs have been _____ for millions of years.
(8) A doctor's task is to work for the relief of patients' _____.
2. Fill in the blanks with words that are often confused.
humane   human
(1) We're all mortals, with our _____ faults and weaknesses.
(2) Is it _____ to kill animals for food?
source   resource
(1) There's a great shortage of _____ materials in many schools.
(2) An overcrowded workplace can be a major _____ of stress.
(3) Immeasurable quantity of natural _____ was lost forever through misuse.

access assess

(1) They _____ his house at 1,500,000 dollars.
(2) Supervisors have many opportunities to _____ the ability of candidates.
(3) The only _____ to the town is across the bridge.

3. Fill in each blank with one suitable word.

How do the birds find their way on their enormously long journeys? The young birds are not taught the road by their _____, because often the parents fly off first. We have no _____ how the birds find their way, particularly as many of them fly _____ night, when landmarks could hardly be _____. And other birds migrate over the sea, where there are no _____ at all. A certain kind of plover, for _____ nests in Canada. At the end of the summer these birds _____ from Canada to South America; they fly 2,500 miles, non-stop, over the ocean. Not only is this very long flight an extraordinary feat of endurance, but there are no landmarks on the ocean to _____ the birds.

It has been suggested that birds can sense the magnetic lines of force stretching from the north to south magnetic _____ of the earth, and so direct themselves. But all experiments hitherto made to see whether magnetism has any _____ whatsoever on animals have given negative results. Still, where there is such a biological mystery as migration, even improbable experiments are worth trying. _____ was being done in Poland, before the invasion of that country, on the possible influence of magnetism on path-finding. Magnets were attached to the birds' heads to see _____ their direction-sense was confused thereby. These unfinished _____ had, of course, to be stopped.

Skills Development and Practice

Reading Skills

Reading for the Main Idea (2)
Topic Sentences

Practice 1: Read the paragraphs and underline the topic sentence(s) of each paragraph.

1. I have always been told that it is best to buy American-made products, especially, American cars. However, I have come to the conclusion that foreign cars are a better investment than American cars. For one thing, the foreign cars get better gas mileage. The price of gas and oil is getting higher and higher. So any car owner must be con-

cerned about how far his car will take him on a gallon of gas. In this category the foreign cars leave the American cars far behind. Another important advantage of the foreign cars is their dependability. While parts and labor for foreign car repairs are expensive, the facts show that foreign cars do not require repair nearly as often as American cars.

2. When prices are high, producers can get more money for their goods. When prices are low, consumers can get more goods for their money. These changes in the prices of goods can cause changes in production and consumption. As the prices of goods go up, producers will make more goods in order to make more money. As the prices go down, consumers will buy more goods because of the low prices.

3. The key to good driving is to move your eyes every two seconds. Keep checking near, then far, and to both sides. Don't focus on the objects ahead. And remember to check your mirrors, too. Keep your eyes moving while driving.

Practice 2: Read the paragraphs and choose the statements that best express the main ideas of them.

1. Everybody knows that tomatoes are grown for food, yet there was a time when they were grown only to be admired in a garden. They had many colours—yellow, pink and red. They looked bright and so pretty that they were known as 「love apples」.

　　A. Tomatoes are grown mainly for food.

　　B. Tomatoes were grown in the garden for people to admire.

　　C. Tomatoes have many colours.

　　D. Tomatoes are known as 「love apples」.

2. English is spoken by pilots and airport control operators on all the air-ways of the world. Over 70 percent of the world's mail is written in English. More than 60 percent of the world's radio programs are in English. Clearly English is an international language.

　　A. English is very important for pilots.

　　B. English is spoken by airport control operators.

　　C. English is used more often in the world's mail than in radio programs.

　　D. English is used everywhere in the world.

3. Language, too, is the product of labour. In farming and hunting and in war, people had to work in groups. They had to say something to one another. This led to the use of speech organs. The organs of the mouth learned to produce different speech sounds, and gradually man learned to speak.

　　A. Man learned to speak a long time ago.

　　B. People used to work in groups.

　　C. Language comes out from labour.

D. Man could only say something very easy at the beginning.

Translation Practice

Translation Skills

引申詞義：根據上下文和邏輯關係將詞義加以引申。

Practice 3：Translate the sentences into Chinese.

1. Victory always goes to the strong.

___

2. The key won't go in the lock.

___

3. In two years, he was a national phenomenon.

___

4. The wisest thing to do is to skim over the chapter to be read.

___

5. I am busy packing my things for the long journey.

___

6. An idea formed in my mind.

___

7. Do you want regular or king size?

___

8. It is difficult to say exactly how the music we call「rock」or「rock and roll」began. Its roots go back to many different countries and many different kinds of music and musicians.

___

9. No one thinks of early rock and roll without thinking of Elvis Presley, the「King of Rock and Roll.」

___

10. He continued to record, but his music rarely had the life of his early songs.

___

11. Music is a part of the history of America. It expresses the problems and feelings of its people. As the years pass, the music grows and changes.

___

___

12. Even when people cannot understand the same language, they can share the

same music. Many people learn and practice English by singing songs. Understanding American music can help you understand American people, their history and culture.

Practice 4: Translate the sentences into English.
1. 他的觀點和我的差不多。

2. 這位教師對學生有很大的影響。

3. 她沒鎖門就出去了。

4. 這些照片使我回想起了我的學生時代。

5. 到 2050 年我們將把中國建成世界上中等發達（medium-developed）國家之一。

6. 瞭解中國的歷史和文化有助於瞭解中國人民。

Practical Translation

複合詞的翻譯

　　現代英語中，詞的複合形式多樣，比較靈活。複合詞的詞性轉換也經常發生，同一個詞在一些語境中充當名詞，而在另一些語境中則充當動詞或形容詞。因此，在英漢翻譯中，不必拘泥於詞性或詞的形式，而是要結合複合詞的構成和漢語的語言習慣進行調整，在不失其含義的前提下，給出恰當的譯文。

　　1. 最常見的複合結構之一是用名詞的複合結構充當名詞或形容詞修飾語，其在漢語中的作用與「的」字結構相似，一般直譯。例如：

　　（1）The best thing local officials can do to promote affordable housing is to get out of the way—stop requiring one-acre lots and two-car garages, and stop blocking low-income and high-density projects.

　　譯文：為促進廉價房的發展，當地政府最好不要橫加阻攔——不要再要求房產項目必須占地一英畝（1 英畝＝4,046.856,422,4 平方米）、具有雙車位的車庫；不要再阻止面向低收入人群的高容積率項目。

　　（2）Eventually, politicians may rediscover housing not as an urban poverty issue, but as a middleclass quality-of-life issue, like gas prices or health care.

譯文：總會有那麼一天，從政者會發現住房問題像油價問題或醫療問題一樣，不只是城市貧民的問題，還是中產階級的生活質量問題。

（3）This creates all kinds of lousy outcomes children who don't get to see their parents, workers who can't make ends meet when gas prices soar, exurban sprawl, roads clogged with long-distance commuters emitting greenhouse gases.

譯文：這產生了各種弊端：油價飛漲、城市向郊外延伸、路上堵滿了長途往返的通勤者、不停地釋放著溫室氣體，使得孩子們見不到父母，工人們入不敷出。

（4）The new phone system uses state-of-the-art technology.

譯文：新的電話系統採用了最先進的技術。

2.「形容詞+名詞+-ed」和「形容詞+動詞+-ed」結構是兩種常見的形容詞構成方式。例如：

Seventy years after President Franklin D. Roosevelt declared that the Depression had left one-third of the American people "ill-housed, ill-clothed and ill-nourished," Americans are well-clothed and increasingly over nourished.

譯文：富蘭克林·羅斯福總統曾經說經濟大蕭條造成三分之一的美國人住房簡陋、衣衫襤褸、營養不良，70年後的今天，美因人卻是穿著考究、營養日益過剩。

解析：句中分別使用了「形容詞+名詞+-ed」結構的複合詞 ill-housed, ill-clothed, well-clothed 以及「形容詞+動詞+-ed 分詞」結構的複合詞 ill-nourished，對仗工整，排比效果明顯。在翻譯時，根據漢語的習慣可把它們譯為主謂結構的名詞短語「住房簡陋、衣衫襤褸、穿著考究、營養不良」。

Translation Practice

Translate the following paragraph into Chinese.

Opened in 1980, the House of the Future was designed to be a showcase for state-of-the-art electronic innovations. The structure itself is a 3,100 square foot, copper-trimmed prism rising out of the Arizona desert. Computer-controlled solar collectors on the south face of the house provide 75% of the heating and 95% of the domestic hot water needs. Inside, the house is as startling as it is outside. For the moment, the only permanent resident of the House of the Future is the computer. That monotone voice which greets visitors belongs to a unique, Motorola-designed five-unit computer network which serves as the nerve center of the building.

Focused Writing

Letters of Application

The role of a letter of application

A letter of application will almost certainly be required when applying for any position, be it a job, an internship or a place on a graduate/professional program. The role of the application letter is to draw a clear link between the position you are seeking and your qualifications as listed in your resume. It must not merely repeat the contents of your resume but should highlight the most relevant information emphasizing why you are right for the position.

The format of a letter of application

An application letter customarily laid out as follows:

The sender's address;

The date;

The addressee's address;

The salutation;

The body of the letter, which is usually comprised of:

—an introductory paragraph, stating the purpose of the letter. When applying for a job, people usually indicate the source of their information about the job, say, a newspaper advertisement or a personal contact. If applying for a graduate program, people usually mention by name their sponsor, mentor or a senior tutor who has recommended that they apply;

—main body paragraphs, highlighting the main qualifications and presenting evidence closely tied to the job or the graduate program;

—a closing paragraph, indicating your hope to be able to meet to explore further how you may be of help to the company;

The complimentary close;

The signature.

Differences between academic and business letters of application

Though academic and business letters of application are very similar in terms of function and layout, the content differs significantly in quantity and kind. When you are applying for a graduate program or a faculty position with a college or university, the application letter needs to leave a strong impression as a promising researcher or teacher. Thus, an academic application letter should be long enough to highlight in some detail your accomplishments during your academic years. However, the application letter for other job vacancies is relatively brief and concise because it is usually accompanied by a copy of your CV.

Sample 1: An Academic Application Letter

Tel: 008810, 4509, 876 Email: limin@ hotmail. com	The School of Management Shanghai Jiaotong University 535, Fahuazhen Road Shanghai, P. R. China, 200052

July 5th, 2009

The American Graduate School
of International Management
15429 N. 59th Ave.
Glendale
Arizona 85306-6003

Dear Siror Madam, 　　With the enclosed application and supporting documentation, I am expressing my sincere interest in being accepted into the Master of International Management Graduate Program at The American Graduate School of International Management.	The introductory paragraph: Li Min states his interest in being admitted.
I feel confident that I am well equipped for graduate studies in international business, and I feel certain I could one day become a distinguished alumnus of your fine institution. As you will see from my resume. I already hold a B. Sc. degree in Business and Marketing and I read, write, and speak English fluently. My English language skills were refined and improved while working as an interpreter at the 2008/2009 Canton Fair (China) and as a tour guide for foreign delegations.	Main body paragraphs: supporting evidence of his eligibility for the graduate program①.
In addition to my experience as an interpreter and tour guide, I have extensive work experience which I believe will help to make me a valuable member of the MIM program. While working in summer and part-time jobs to finance my college education, I gained experience in a wide range of positions working in retail: sales and marketing and in the construction, hospitality, and transportation industries.	Supporting evidence of his eligibility for the graduate program②.
As you will see when you read my essay, my goal is to become the chief executive officer of a company doing business in Asia, and I feel my background thus far, combined with the program of graduate studies offered by the American Graduate School of International Business, will help me achieve that aim. I feel I would be a credit to the business community because of my strong conviction of the economic necessity that making a profit must be balanced by regard for customers and respect for employees.	Supporting evidence of his eligibility for the graduate program③.
I can assure you in advance that I would be an asset to the next entering class and as a graduate. If I can provide any further information please do not hesitate to contact me. Thank you for your consideration of my application. 　　I look forward to hearing from you. Yours sincerely, Li Min Enclosures: Application Form, Essay, Resume, Letter of Reference	The closing paragraph, re-emphasizing his confidence and offering more information if required.

Sample 2: A Business Application Letter

> 34 Second Street
> Troy
> New York 12180
>
> May 4th, 2009
>
> MS. Gail Roberts
> Recruiting Coordinator
> Department DRR 1201
> Data base Corporation
> Princeton, New Jersey 05876
>
> Dear MS. Roberts,
> Your advertisement for software engineers in the January issue of the IEEE Spectrum caught my attention. I was drawn to the ad by my strong interest in both software design and Database.
> I have worked with a CALMA systemin developing VLSI circuits, and I also have substantial experience in the design of interactive CAD software. Because of this experience, I can make a direct and immediate contribution to your department I have enclosed a copy of my resume, which details my qualifications and suggests how I might be of service to Database.
> I would like very much to meet with you to discuss your open positions for software engineers. If you would like to arrange an interview, please contact me at the above address or by telephone at (518) 271-9999 or email: jsmith@yahoo.com
> Thank you for your time and consideration.
>
> Yours sincerely,
> Joseph Smith
> Encl: Resume

Introduction: the source of information about the job vacancy.

Main body: supporting evidence of his qualifications for position.

Closing: requesting an interview and facilitating that request.

Writing Assignment

1. Write a letter of application for an internship at an international company.

2. Write a letter of application for a position on a doctoral program at Cornell University in America.

Unit 3   Travel Around the World

Warming-ups

Task 1   Questions for Thought

Think about the following questions, then discuss with your partner.
1. If you want to know somebody's plans, what would you say?
2. What places would you recommend a foreigner to visit in China?
3. What are the main tourist attractions in Beijing?

Task 2   Vocabulary Preview

Complete the following table by writing the English or Chinese equivalents of the words given. Then, check your answers with your partner.

地陪		cultural heritage site	
全陪		package tour	
觀光遊		thestatue of liberty	
鐘樓		the temple of heaven	
五星酒店		Chinese garden architecture	
招待所		handicraft	

In-class Activities

Task 1   Individual/Pair Work

A: Planning your holiday? Whether you're going to Yunnan or USA? It's important to make sure you're well-prepared. Decide what you will take into consideration before you leave. Check (√) and compare your answers with your partner.

What to consider before traveling	How to get information	Preparations made for traveling abroad
☐ Weather	☐ Surf the Internet	☐ Visit the travel agency
☐ Politics	☐ Go to the railway station	☐ Buy the ticket the day before you leave
☐ Destination	☐ Go to a local travel agency	☐ Have a budget in mind
☐ Budget	☐ Talk to a passersby	☐ Learn about political information for the countries you plan to visit
☐ Religion	☐ Talk to their sales representatives	☐ Book your hotel in advance
☐ Transportation	☐ Read a travel brochure	☐ Pack your passport in your backpack
☐ Language lessons	☐ Ask your hotel for local information	☐ Keep a separate purse of money for emergencies
☐ Accommodation	☐ Watch TV news	☐ Make 2 copies of your passport identification page

Task 2 Pair work

1. Suppose you're talking about your plan to a tourist attraction with your friend. Try to start a conversation with him/her. An example is given to you.

A: Is there anywhere you'd like to go this summer vacation?

B: No where in particular. Do you have anything in mind?

A: Well, some of us are thinking about going to Tai Mountain in Shandong. Would you like to join us?

B: OK. I'd love to. I like climbing mountains.

A: Me too. You'll lose yourself in the beautiful scenery there.

B: Really? I can't help feeling excited already. By the way, what should I wear?

A: Just bring warm clothes. It's said it is cold in the mountain, especially in the evening.

2. Suppose you're a tourist guide. You're now introducing some scenic spots in Zhangjiajie to a group of tourists. An example is given to you.

A: Here we are, ladies and gentlemen. This is Zhangjiajie. We can take some time to go around. Please be back to the bus at 4 pm.

B: Wow, what a beautiful scenery!

A: Yes. It's really a nice place. The mountains have gradually eroded to form a spectacular landscape of peaks and huge rock columns rising out the forest. There are waterfalls, caves, streams everywhere.

B: This place is unique. Oh, look at the people there! They're dressed differently.

A: Yes, they're people of minority group Tujia. This area is home for three minority groups of Tujia, Miao and Bai.

B: Ah, I see.

A: On the way up, it is Jumping Fish Pool.

B: So beautiful!

A: Did you enjoy yourself?

B: Yes, I had a great day!

A: It's nearly 4 now. Shall we go back to the bus?

B: All right, let's go.

3. Suppose you're planning a trip to Hawaii. You're calling a travel agency for some information about the trip. An example is given to you.

A: Blue Skies Travel Agency. Can I help you?

B: I'm planning a trip to Hawaii. I wonder if you could give me some information about the trip.

A: Certainly. What would you like to know?

B: Well, first of all, we want to know the air fare to Hawaii. And what will the weather like?

A: I see. When do you want to go?

B: May, or maybe June. And I'd like to know about the inclusive holidays and good hotels and...

A: (interrupts) Certainly. Just give me your name and address. I'll send you all the information you want.

B: That's a good idea. By the way, can you give us a brochure, please?

A: Of course. Here you are.

B: Thanks.

Task 3 Pair Work

A: Form groups as travel agencies, and each has to work out an itinerary (a travel plan) for a group of foreign tourists who are coming to visit China. Discuss in your group and fill in the following travel plan.

Destination	_____ in _____
Cost per person (check)	RMB 120; RMB 880; RMB 1,200
Duration	_____ days _____ nights
Times to go	_____ (season)
Styles of travel	an individual tour in a group with a travel agency

表(續)

Destination	_____ in _____
Transportation	First, take _____ to _____ Then, go to _____ by _____ Finally, travel around
Sights	
Accommodation	

B: Now give an oral promotion of the tourist attraction you decide to recommend. Information you may include:

· Location

· Famous scenic spots

· Tourist features

Task 4　Role-play

(Situation: You are thinking of having a holiday in Wuxi and go to the travel agency for further details about the town. Your partner works in the agency.)

Ask your partner as many questions as you can to get as much information as possible with the help of the following two cards.

Card A
You want to know: —climate —accommodation —time to go —transportation —sights —duration —styles

Card B
Climate: mild and rainy in spring; sunny in summer; low rainfall in autumn and winter Accommodation: hotels, guest houses, holiday inns, motels Time to go: Spring, summer, autumn Transportation: Bus, train, plane, car, ship Sights: Yuantouzhu (the Turtle-head Park), The Taihu Lake, Lingshan Budda, Jichang Garden, Li Garden... Duration: One-day tour, two-day tour Styles: An individual tour, a group tour, a guided tour

The following may be helpful in your conversation:

I'm thinking of having a holiday in Wuxi this summer. I wonder if you could tell me something about the city.

· Climate:

What's the weather like in Wuxi?

· Accommodation:

Where do most tourists stay in Wuxi?

Which hotel is the best one in Wuxi?

· Time to Go:

What time is better for traveling in Wuxi in a year?

· Transportation:

What is the best way to go to Wuxi?

How long will it take me to get to Wuxi by train from...?

How about going there by bicycle?

· Sights:

Are there any interesting places for tourist to visit?

What places in Wuxi should a tourist visit?

Could you describe them to me?

· Duration:

How long will you stay in Wuxi?

· Styles:

What would you like, an individual tour or a group one?

Task 5　Discussion/Debate

Nowadays, an increasing number of people are looking for ways of eco-friendly tour. Recently your class is planning a bicycle trip to a place half an hour's drive from your college.

A: Work in groups and make discussion on 「the Advantages and Disadvantages of Travel by Bicycle.」

The following might be useful and helpful in the speech:

Positive Side
—save lots of money —protect the environment —exercise and strengthen our bodies —a way to enjoy the beautiful scenery —be closer to nature —stop wherever you like to...

Negative Side
—much slower than other transportation —tiring over long distance —at the mercy of weather —at the risk of people in automobiles —hard to carry much in the say of needed supplies...

B: For a long time, Peking University has been a hot spot for millions of pupils and their parents. But suddenly the University Authority says 「Peking University is no longer open to group tours of primary school students and adults」.

What's your opinion about this decision? Work in groups and carry out a debate on:

Should Peking University Refuse Tourists?

The following might be useful and helpful in the debate:

Words and Expressions:

taxpayer's money; the whole country; public; experience its academic atmosphere; ignore the university's regulations; a place for students to gain knowledge the right to deal with its own affairs; disturb student's daily study and life

Reference Modal:

Positive Side:

Peking University is not only for the current students, but also a university for the whole country.

Negative Side:

The university is a place for students to gain knowledge and not a profit-making tool.

Reading Passages

Passage A

OSLO

I remember on my first trip to Europe going alone to a movie in Copenhagen. In Denmark you are given a ticket for an assigned seat. I went into the cinema and discovered that my ticket directed me to sit beside the only other people in the place, a young couple locked in the sort of passionate embrace associated with dockside reunions at the end of long wars. I could no more have sat beside them than I could have asked to join in—it would have come to much the same thing—so I took a place a few discreet seats away.

People came into the cinema, consulted their tickets and filled the seats around us. By the time: the film started there were about 30 of us sitting together in a tight pack in the middle of a vast and otherwise empty auditorium. Two minutes into the movie, a woman laden with shopping made her way with difficulty down my row, stopped beside my seat and told me in a stem voice, full of glottal stops and indignation, that I was in her place. This caused much play of flashlights among the usherettes and fretful re-examining of tickets by everyone in the vicinity until word got around that I was an American tourist and therefore unable to follow simple seating instructions and I was escorted in some shame back to my assigned place.

So we sat together and watched the movie, 30 of us crowded together like refugees in an overloaded lifeboat, rubbing shoulders and sharing small noises, and it occurred to me then that there are certain things that some nations do better than everyone else and certain things that they do far worse and I began to wonder why that should be.

Sometimes a nation's little contrivances are so singular and clever that we associate them with that country alone—double-decker buses in Britain, windmills in Holland (what an inspired addition to a flat landscape: think how they would transform Nebraska), sidewalk cafes in Paris. And yet there are some things that most countries do without difficulty that others cannot get a grasp of at all.

The French, for instance, cannot get the hang of queuing. They try and try, but it is beyond them. Wherever you go in Paris, you see orderly lines waiting at bus stops, but as soon as the bus pulls up the line instantly disintegrates into something like a fire drill at a lunatic asylum as everyone scrambles to be the first aboard, quite unaware that this defeats the whole purpose of queuing.

The British, on me other hand, do not understand certain of the fundamentals of eating, as evidenced by their instinct to consume hamburgers with a knife and fork. To my continuing amazement, many of them also turn their fork upside-down and balance the food on the back of it. I've lived in England for a decade and a half and I still have to quell an impulse to go up to strangers in pubs and restaurants and say, ⌈Excuse me, can I give you a tip that'll help stop those peas bouncing all over the table?⌋

Germans are flummoxed by humor, the Swiss have no concept of fun, the Spanish think there is nothing at all ridiculous about eating dinner at midnight, and the Italian should never, ever have been let in on the invention of the motor car.

One Of the small marvels of my first trip to Europe was the discovery that the world could be so full of variety, that there were so many different ways of doing essentially identical things, like eating and drinking and buying cinema tickets. It fascinated me that Europeans could at once be so alike—that they could be so universally bookish and cerebral, and drive small cars, and live in little houses in ancient towns, and love soccer, and be relatively unmaterialistic and law-abiding, and have chilly hotel rooms and cosy and inviting places to eat and drink—and yet be so endlessly, unpredictably different from each other as well. I loved the idea that you could never be sure of anything in Europe.

I still enjoy that sense of never knowing quite what's going on. In my hotel in Oslo, where I spent four days after returning from Hammerfest, the chambermaid each morning left me a packet of something called Bio Tex Blå, a ⌈minipakke for ferie, hybel og weekend⌋, according to the instructions. I spent many happy hours sniffing it and experimenting with it, uncertain whether it was for washing out clothes or gargling or cleaning the toilet bowl. In the end I decided it was for washing out clothes—it worked a treat—but for all I know for the rest of the week everywhere I went in Oslo people were saying to each other, ⌈You know, that man smelled like toilet-bowl cleaner.⌋

When I told my friends in London that I was going to travel around Europe and write a book about it, they said, ⌈Oh, you must speak a lot of languages.⌋

⌈Why, no.⌋ I would reply with a certain pride, ⌈only English,⌋ and they would look at me as if I were crazy. But that's the glory of foreign travel, as far as I am concerned. I don't want to know what people are talking about. I can't think of anything that excites a greater sense of childlike wonder than to be in a country where you are ignorant of almost everything. Suddenly you are five years old again. You can't read anything, you have only the most rudimentary sense of how things work, you can't even reliably cross a street without endangering your life. Your whole existence becomes a series of interesting guesses.

I get great pleasure from watching foreign TV and trying to imagine what on earth is going on. On my first evening in Oslo, I watched a science program in which two men in a studio stood at a lab table discussing a variety of sleek, rodent-like animals that were crawling over the surface and occasionally up the host's jacket. ⌈And you have sex with all these creatures, do you?⌋ the host was saying.

⌈Certainly,⌋ replied the guest, ⌈You have to be careful with the porcupines, of course, and the lemmings can get very neurotic and hurl themselves off cliffs if they feel you don't love them as you once did, but basically these animals make very affectionate companions, and the sex is simply out of this world.⌋

⌈Well, I think that's wonderful. Next week we'll be looking at how you can make hallucinogenic drugs with simple household chemicals from your own medicine cabinet, but now it's time for the screen to go blank for a minute and then for the lights to come up suddenly on the host of the day looking as if he was just about to pick his nose. See you next week.⌋

After Hammerfest, Oslo was simply wonderful. It was still cold and dusted with greyish snow, but it seemed positively tropical after Hammerfest, and I abandoned all thought of buying a furry hat. I went to the museums and for a day-long way out around the Bygdøy peninsula, where the city's finest houses stand on the wooded hillsides, with fetching views across the icy water of the harbour to the downtown. But mostly I hung around the city center, wandering back and forth between the railway station and the royal palace, peering in the store windows along Karl Johans Gate, the long and handsome main pedestrian street, cheered by the bright lights, mingling with the happy, healthy, relentlessly youthful Norwegians, very pleased to be alive and out of Hammerfest and in a world of daylight. When I grew cold, I sat in cafes and bars and eavesdropped on conversations that I could not understand or brought out my *Thomas Cook European Timetable* and studied it with a kind of humble reverence, planning the rest of my trip.

Thomas Cook European Timetable is possibly the finest book ever produced. It is impossible to leaf through its 500 pages of densely printed timetables without wanting to dump a double armload of clothes into an old Gladstone and just take off. Every page whispers romance：「Montreux—Zweisimmen—Spiez—Interlaken」.「Beograd—Trieste—Venezia—Verona—Milano」,「Göteborg—Laxå（Hallsberg）—Stockholm」,「Ventimiglia—Marseille—Lyon—Paris」. Who could recite these names without experiencing a tug of excitement, without seeing in his mind's eye a steamy platform full of expectant travelers and piles of luggage standing beside a sleek, quarter-mile-long train with a list of exotic locations slotted into every carriage? Who could read the names「Moskva—Warszawa—Berlin—Basel—Geneve」and not feel a melancholy envy for all those lucky people who get to make a grand journey across a storied continent? Who could glance at such an itinerary and not want to climb aboard? Well, Sunny von Bulow for a start. But as for me, I could spend hours just poring over the tables, each one a magical thicket of times, numbers, distances, mysterious little pictograms showing crossed knives and forks, wine glasses, daggers, miner's pickaxes (whatever could they be for?), ferry boats and buses, and bewilderingly abstruse footnotes.

Words and Expressions

1. abstruse *adj.* 深奧的, 高深的

2. asylum *n.* 精神病院

3. auditorium *n.* 聽眾席, 觀眾席

4. bookish *adj.* 嗜書的；好讀書的；喜歡學習的

5. cerebral *adj.* 要運用智力的；訴諸理性的

6. chambermaid *n.*（尤指旅館裡的）打掃臥室的女服務員

7. contrivance *n.* 發明物, 新裝置

8. dagger *n.* 匕首, 短劍

9. disintegrate *v.*（使）粉碎；崩裂；分崩離析

10. double-decker *n.* 雙層公共汽車

11. eavesdrop *v.* 偷聽

12. fetching *adj.*（尤指因著裝得體而）動人的, 迷人的, 吸引人的

13. flummox *v.* 使（某人）徹底不知所措（困惑不解）

14. fretful *adj.*（尤指為無足輕重的小事）煩躁的；發牢騷的

15. gargle *v.* 漱口（喉）

16. glottal stop *n.* 喉塞音, 聲門塞音

17. hallucinogenic *adj.* 引起幻覺的, 致幻的

18. itinerary *n.* 旅行計劃；預訂行程

19. laden *adj.* 裝滿的, 滿載的

20. law-abiding *adj.* 守法的；安分守己的

21. lemming *n.* 旅鼠
22. lunatic asylum *n.* 精神病院，瘋人院
23. materialistic *adj.* 實利主義的，物質主義的
24. unmaterialistic *adj.* 非實利主義的
25. passionate *adj.* 情欲強烈的，多情的
26. pickax *n.* 鎬，鶴嘴鋤
27. pictogram *n.* 象形文字
28. porcupine *n.* 豪豬，箭豬
29. pore *v.* （長時間）仔細閱讀；凝視，註視
30. quell *v.* 減輕，消除（疑慮）
31. relentless *adj.* 嚴厲的；無情的；堅決的
32. relentlessly *adv.* 無情地；殘酷地
33. reverence *n.* 尊敬，崇敬
34. rodent *n.* 嚙齒動物（如老鼠、兔子等）
35. rudimentary *adj.* （有關某學科的知識或理解）基本的，初步的，粗淺的
36. sleek *adj.* （頭髮，皮毛）平直光滑的，有健康光澤的
37. thicket *n.* 灌木叢，小樹叢
38. usherette *n.* （影院的）女引座員，女服務員
39. windmill *n.* 風車；風力磨坊
40. get the hang of sth. 得知……的竅門；熟悉某物的用法
41. let sb. in on sth. 允許（某人）知道（秘密），同意分享
42. out of this world 出色的；了不起的
43. pore over 專心閱讀，鑽研
44. work a treat 非常好

Proper Names
1. Basel 巴塞爾（瑞士西北部城市，在萊茵河畔）
2. Beograd 貝爾格萊德（塞爾維亞首都）
3. Copenhagen 哥本哈根（丹麥首都）
4. Hammerfest 哈默菲斯特（挪威北部港市）
5. Lyon 里昂（法國東南部城市）
6. Marseilles 馬賽（法國東南部港市）
7. Oslo 奧斯陸（挪威首都）
8. Stockholm 斯德哥爾摩（瑞典首都）
9. Trieste 的里雅斯特（義大利東北部港市）
10. Verona 維羅納（義大利北部城市）

Notes

1. Bygdøy is a peninsula on the western side of Oslo, Norway.

2. Karl Johans Gate (Karl Johan Street), named after King Karl Johan, is the main street of the city of Oslo. The street includes many of Oslo's tourist attractions: Royal Palace, Oslo Cathedral, Central Station and Stortinget, the National Theater, the old University Buildings, the Palace Park and the pond「Spikersuppa」(「the nail soup」), which is a skating rink in winter.

3. Thomas Cook is a British travel agent, born in Melbourne, England. He became a missionary in 1828 and later was an active temperance worker. In 1841 he chartered a special train to carry passengers from Leicester to Loughborough for a temperance meeting. The success of the guided excursion led to the formation of a travel agency bearing his name. Cook organized personally conducted tours throughout Europe and procured traveling and hotel accommodations for tourists making independent trips. He also provided travel services for the British government on several occasions.

4. Gladstone is the same as Gladstone bag, a small suitcase or portmanteau consisting of a rigid flame on which two compartments of the same size are hinged together.

5. Montreux (蒙特勒) is the French name for a resort town in Southwest Switzerland, on the northeast shore of Lake Geneva. Zweisimmen (茨韋西門) is a municipality in the district of Obersimmental in the canton of Berne in Switzerland. Spiez (施皮茨) is a city in the district of Niedersimmental in the canton of Bem in Switzerland. Interlaken (因特拉肯) is the German for the chief town of the Bernese Alps in Central Switzerland. Venezia is the Italian name for Venice (威尼斯). Milano is Italian name for Milan (米蘭). Göteborg is Swedish name for Gothenburg (哥德堡). Laxå Municipality (Laxå kommun) is a municipality in Örebro County in central Sweden. Hallsberg (哈爾斯貝里) is a bimunicipal locality and the seat of Hallsberg Municipality, Örebro County, Sweden. Ventimiglia (文蒂米利亞) is a town in northern Italy.

6. Moskva is the Russian name for Moscow. Warszawa is the Polish name for Warsaw. Genève is the French name for Geneva.

7. A storied continent refers to a continent being the subject of many stories, namely, quite famous.

8. Martha Sharp Crawford von Bülow (1932—2008), known as Sunny von Bülow, was an American heiress, socialite, and philanthropist. Her husband, Claus von Bülow, was convicted of attempting her murder by insulin overdose, but the conviction was overturned on appeal. A second trial found him not guilty, after experts opined that there was no insulin injection and that her symptoms were attributable to over-use of prescription drugs. The story was dramatized in the book and movie, *Reversal of Fortune*. Sunny

von Bülow lived almost 28 years in a persistent vegetative state until her death in a New York nursing home on December 6th, 2008.

Content Awareness

1. Work in pairs to complete the outline of the text.

The author's experience in the cinema	A. His experience in the cinema: A small group of people _____ B. His feelings: Some countries _____
Some interesting things about different nations in Europe	A. Some inventions are associated with a particular country. a. The British: b. The Dutch: _____ c. The French: _____ B. Some strange things done by people from a particular nation. a. The French: _____ b. The British: _____ c. The German: _____ d. The Swiss: _____ e. The Spanish: _____ f. The Italian: _____
Benefits of traveling to Europe	A. One can never be sure of anything in Europe since they alike in certain ways but different in others. a. Similarities: bookish and cerebral, and drive _____, and live in _____, and love soccer, and be relatively _____, and have chilly hotel rooms and _____. b. Differences: even eating and drinking and buying cinema tickets can be different. Example: a packet of something called _____. B. One can only know the basic things in life which results in a series of interesting guesses. Example: _____ C. _____. Example: the author's activities in Oslo.
Attractions of *Thomas Cook European Timetable*	One would feel excited and couldn't wait to take the trip.

2. Read the following statements and decide whether they are true or false according to the text. Put 「T」 before a true statement and 「F」 before a false one.

(1) The author didn't sit beside the young couple because he didn't like the discreet atmosphere.

(2) All the other audience thought the author didn't follow the seat instruction simply because he was a foreigner.

(3) In the author's opinion, the windmills in Holland help add variety to the landscape.

(4) The author found it ridiculous to tell the British not to eat hamburgers with a fork and knife.

(5) One can never be sure of what's going on in Europe since Europeans are from different nations.

(6) The packet of something called Bio Tex Blå is mainly used for washing the toilet bowl.

(7) The author's friends in Britain assume that one has to speak a lot of languages in order to travel around Europe.

(8) Being in a different and unfamiliar country can bring a lot of problems, which displeases the author.

(9) The author's experience in watching foreign TV programs shows that one can still understand the idea without knowing the language.

(10) The author wandered in the main street of Oslo in order to learn more about the history and culture of the city.

(11) It is impossible to look through Thomas Cook European Timetable since it has 500 pages.

(12) The author would spend time reading *Thomas Cook European Timetable* to plan his trip.

Language Focus

1. Choose the answer that is closest in meaning to the underlined word in the sentence.

(1) After the first visit, I came home laden with flats and pots and cardboard boxes.

A. filled   B. loaded
C. charged   D. left

(2) The boy appeared fretful and disappointed that he couldn't join the others on their excursions.

A. annoyed   B. restless
C. relentless   D. anxious

(3) The project disintegrated owing to lack of financial backing.

A. broke up   B. turned up
C. used up   D. torn up

(4) This latest setback will have done nothing to quell the growing doubts about the future of the club.

A. cast   B. express
C. reduce   D. avoid

(5) The tools that the ancient Egyptians used to build their temples were extremely rudimentary.

A. simple   B. imperative
C. obscure   D. periodic

(6) In most cases, it is difficult to detect that someone is eavesdropping.

A. peeping   B. overhearing
C. cheating   D. whispering

(7) Most patients derive enjoyment from leafing through old picture albums.

A. turning   B. coming
C. skimming   D. seeing

(8) Kids these days are very materialistic. They only seem to be interested in expensive toys and computer games.

A. concerned with money   B. interested in materials
C. enthusiastic about substance   D. keen on information

(9) We dumped our bags at the nearby Grand Hotel and hurried towards the market.

A. threw away   B. put down
C. took back   D. packed up

(10) The only sounds were the distant, melancholy cries of the sheep.

A. dissatisfied   B. painful
C. unhappy   D. sharp

2. Fill in each of the blanks with an appropriate word from each group. Change the form if necessary.

discreet   discretion   discrete

(1) These small companies now have their own _____ identity.
(2) We were all pretty open with each other but very _____ outside.
(3) You can trust her to keep your secret—she's the soul of _____.

audit   auditor   auditory   auditorium

(1) The external _____ come in once a year.
(2) We gathered in an _____ and watched a videotape.
(3) The yearly _____ takes place each December.
(4) It's an artificial device which stimulates the _____ areas of the brain.
(5) The fund is _____ annually by an accountant.

conceive   contrive   conception   contrivance

(1) The _____ of the book took five minutes, but writing it took a year.

(2) This was a steam-driven _____ used in the 19th century clothing factories.

(3) Miraculously, he managed to _____ a supper out of what was left in the cupboard.

(4) He was immensely ambitious but unable to _____ of winning power for himself.

gargle   giggle   gasp   gossip

(1) Once one child starts _____ it starts the whole class off.

(2) The circus audience _____ with amazement as she put her head in the lion's mouth.

(3) The advertisement promises that _____ mouthwash will freshen your breath and kill germs.

(4) There has been much _____ about the possible reasons for his absence.

passion   passionate   affection   affectionate

(1) She gave her daughter a (n) _____ kiss and put her to bed.

(2) He spoke with considerable _____ about the importance of art and literature.

(3) Their father never showed them much _____.

(4) I remember many _____ arguments taking place around this table.

relevant   relentless   reluctant

(1) Many parents feel _____ to talk openly with their children.

(2) Ridge's success is due to a _____ pursuit of perfection.

(3) For further information, please refer to the _____ leaflet.

revere   reverence   reverent

(1) I stood there, gazing down, and feeling a _____ for these spectacles of the natural world.

(2) The Bishop's sermon was received in _____ silence.

(3) Most of us _____ Hamlet, but few of us read it regularly.

pore   peer   peep   perceive

(1) I saw her _____ through the curtains into the room.

(2) She _____ through the mist, trying to find the right path.

(3) A key task is to get pupils to _____ for themselves the relationship between success and effort.

(4) Aunt Bella sat at the table, _____ over catalogs, surveying the ac-

counts, calculating.

3. Fill in each of the blanks with an appropriate word from the box. Change the form if necessary.

adventure	challenging	discover	diverse	enlighten
enrich	gain	joyful	memory	opportunity
outweigh	perspective	similarity	span	specific

Traveling provides tremendous opportunities for fun, adventure and discovery. When we visit places in other countries, we _____ a better understanding of the people living there. We learn their cultures, history and background. We discover the _____ they have with us, as well as their differences from us. It is interesting to learn from people with _____ backgrounds. Traveling helps to _____ our lives. It increases our knowledge and widens our _____. When we visit interesting places, we discover and learn many things. We _____ new people, surroundings, plants and animals. If we want to make our travels more exciting and _____, we can choose to plan our own tour and select the _____ places we want to visit. Traveling not only provides us fun and _____, it also provides us marvelous insights and _____ our minds. Traveling provides _____ for us to share our happiness with our friends and family. When we travel with our friends and family, we create _____ that would last a lifetime. It is indeed a (n) _____ thing to share the experience of a special trip with those we love. Giving them a wonderful traveling experience far _____ the benefit of buying presents for them. Goods have a limited life _____, whereas memories last forever.

Passage B

Going on a Journey

By *William Hazlitt*

One of the pleasantest things in the world is going a journey; but I like to go by myself. I can enjoy society in a room; but out of doors, nature is company enough for me. I am then never less alone than when alone.

「The fields his study, nature was his book.」

I cannot see the wit of walking and talking at the same time. When I am in the country I wish to vegetate like the country. I am not for criticizing hedge-rows and black cattle. I go out of town in order to forget the town and all that is in it. There are those who for this purpose go to watering-places, and carry the metropolis with them. I like more elbow-room and fewer incumbrances. I like solitude, when I give myself up to it, for the sake of solitude; nor do I ask for

⌈A friend in my retreat,

Whom I may whisper solitude is sweet.⌋

The soul of a journey is liberty, perfect liberty, to think, feel, do, just as one pleases. We go a journey chiefly to be free of all impediments and of all inconveniences; to leave ourselves behind much more to get rid of others. It is because I want a little breathing-space to muse on indifferent matters, where contemplation

⌈May plume her feathers and let grow her wings,

That in the various bustle of resort

Were all too ruffled, and sometimes impaired⌋.

that I absent myself from the town for a while, without feeling at a loss the moment I am left by myself. Instead of a friend in a post-chaise or in a Tilbury, to exchange good things with, and vary the same stale topics over again, for once let me have a truce with impertinence. Give me the clear blue sky over my head, and the green turf beneath my feet, a winding road before me, and a three hours' march to dinner—and then to thinking! It is hard if I cannot start some game on these lone heaths. I laugh, I run, I leap, I sing for joy. From the point of yonder rolling cloud I plunge into my past being, and revel there as the sun-burnt Indian plunges headlong into the wave that wafts him to his native shore. Then long-forgotten things like ⌈sunken wrack and sunless treasuries⌋ burst upon my eager sight, and I begin to feel, think, and be myself again. Instead of an awkward silence, broken by attempts at wit or dull common-places, mine is mat undisturbed silence of the heart which alone is perfect eloquence. No one likes puns, alliterations, antitheses, argument, and analysis better than I do; but I sometimes had rather be without them. ⌈Leave, oh, leave me to my repose!⌋ I have just now other business in hand, which would seem idle to you, but is with me ⌈very stuff of the conscience.⌋ Is not this wild rose sweet without a comment? Does not this daisy leap to my heart set in its coat of emerald? Yet if I were to explain to you the circumstance that had so endeared it to me, you would only smile. Had I not better then keep it to myself, and let it serve me to brood over, from here to yonder craggy point and from thence onward to the far-distant horizon? I should be but bad company all that way, and therefore prefer being alone. I have heard it said that you may, when the moody fit comes on, walk or ride on by yourself, and indulge your reveries. But this looks like a breach of manners, a neglect of others, and you are thinking all the time that you ought to rejoin your party. ⌈Out upon such half-faced fellowship,⌋ say I. I like to be either entirely to myself, or entirely at the disposal of others; to talk or be silent, to walk or sit still, to be sociable or solitary. I was pleased with an observation of Mr. Cobbett's, that he thought ⌈it a bad French custom to drink our wine with our meals, and that an Englishman ought to do only one thing at a time.⌋ I cannot talk and think, or indulge in melancholy musing and lively conversation by fits and starts.

⌈Let me have a companion of my way,⌋ says Sterne, ⌈were it but to remark how the shadows lengthen as the sun declines.⌋ It is beautifully said; but, in my opinion, this continual comparing of notes interferes with the involuntary impression of things upon the mind, and hurts the sentiment. If you only hint what you feel in a kind of dumb show, it is insipid; if you have to explain it, it is making a toil of a pleasure. You cannot read the book of nature without being perpetually put to the trouble of translating it for the benefit of others. I am for this synthetical method on a journey in preference to the analytical. I am content to lay in a stock of ideas then, and to examine and anatomise them afterwards. I want to see my vague notions float like the down of the thistle before the breeze, and not to have them entangled in the briars and thorns of controversy. For once, I like to have it all my own way; and this is impossible unless you are alone, or in such company as I do not covet. I have no objection to arguing a point with anyone for twenty miles of measured road, but not for pleasure. If you remark the scent of a bean-field crossing the road, perhaps your fellow-traveller has no smell. If you point to a distant object, perhaps he is short-sighted and has to take out his glass to look at it. There is a feeling in the air, a tone in the colour of a cloud, which hits your fancy, but the effect of which you are unable to account for. There is then no sympathy, but an uneasy craving after it, and a dissatisfaction which pursues you on the way, and in the end probably produces ill-humour. Now I never quarrel with myself, and take all my own conclusions for granted till I find it necessary to defend them against objections.

It is not merely that you may not be of accord on the objects and circumstances that present themselves before you—these may recall a number of objects, and lead to associations too delicate and refined to be possibly communicated to others. Yet these I love to cherish, and sometimes still fondly clutch them, when I can escape from the throng to do so. To give way to our feelings before company seems extravagance or affectation; and, on the other hand, to have to unravel this mystery of our being at every turn, and to make others take an equal interest in it (otherwise the end is not answered), is a task to which few are competent. We must ⌈give it an understanding, but no tongue.⌋ My old friend Coleridge, however, could do both. He could go on in the most delightful explanatory way over hill and dale a summer's day, and convert a landscape into a didactic poem or a Pindaric ode. ⌈He talked far above singing.⌋ If I could so clothe my ideas in sounding and flowing words, I might perhaps wish to have some one with me to admire the swelling theme; or I could be more content, were it possible for me still to hear his echoing voice in the woods of All-Fox-den. They had ⌈ that fine madness in them which our first poets had ⌋; and if they could have been caught by some rare instrument, would have breathed such strains as the following:

⌈ Here be woods as green

As any, air likewise as fresh and sweet

As when smooth Zephyrus plays on the fleet

Face of the cuffed streams, with flowers as many

As the young spring gives, and as choice as any;

Here be all new delights, cool streams and wells,

Arbour's overgrown with woodbines, caves and dells,

Choose where thou wilt, whilst I sit by and sing,

Or gather rushes to make many a ring

For thy long fingers; tell thee tales of love,

How the pale Phoebe, hunting in a grove,

First saw the boy Endymion, from whose eyes

She took eternal fire that never dies

How she convey'd him softly in a sleep,

His temples bound with poppy, to the steep

Head of old Latmos, where she stoops each night,

Gilding the mountain with her brother's light,

To kiss her sweetest. ⌋

...

I have no objection to going to see ruins, aqueducts, pictures, in company with a friend or a party, but rather the contrary, for the former reason reversed. They are intelligible matters, and will bear talking about. A person would almost feel stifled to find himself in the deserts of Arabia without friends and countrymen; there must be allowed to be something in the view of Athens or old Rome that claims the utterance of speech; and I own that the Pyramids are too mighty for any single contemplation. In such situations, so opposite to all one's ordinary train of ideas, one seems a species by one's self, a limb torn off from society, unless one can meet with instant fellowship and support. There is undoubtedly a sensation in travelling into foreign parts that is to be had nowhere else; but it is more pleasing at the time than lasting. It is too remote from our habitual associations to be a common topic of discourse or reference, and, like a dream or another state of existence does not piece into our daily modes of life. It is an animated but a momentary hallucination. It demands an effort to exchange our actual for our ideal identity; and to feel the pulse of our old transports revive very keenly, we must「jump」all our present comforts and connections. Our romantic and itinerant character is not to be domesticated. Dr. Johnson remarked how little foreign travel added to the facilities of conversation in those who had been abroad. In fact, the time we have spent there is both delightful and, in one sense, instructive; but it appears to be cut out of our substantial, downright existence; and never to join kindly on to it. We are not the same, but another, and perhaps more enviable individual, all the time we are out of our own country. We are lost to ourselves, as well as our friends. So the poet somewhat quaintly sings:「Out of my country and myself I go.」Those who wish to forget painful thoughts do well to absent themselves for a while from the ties and objects that recall them; but we can be said only to fulfill our destiny in the place that gave us birth. I should on this account like well enough to spend the whole of my life in travelling abroad, if I could anywhere borrow another life to spend afterwards at home!

Words and Expressions

1. vegetate *v.* 植物
2. hedge *n.* 樹籬；用樹籬圍起；樹籬下的，樹籬旁的
3. metropolis *n.* 都市
4. incumbrance *n.* 阻礙物，累贅
5. impediment *n.* 妨礙，阻止；障礙物
6. plume *n.* 羽毛；羽毛飾；羽毛狀物
7. resort *n.* 度假村
8. ruffle *v.* 弄皺；激怒；連續地輕敲；擾亂
9. impair *v.* 損害
10. truce *n.* 休戰；停戰（協定）
11. yonder *det.* 在那邊，在遠處
12. headlong *adv.* 頭向前地；急速地；輕率地
13. waft *v.* 飄蕩
14. pun *n.* 雙關語
15. alliteration *n.* 頭韻
16. repose *n.* 安息
17. conscience *n.* 良心；愧疚
18. emerald *n.* 翡翠，翠綠色，綠寶石
19. craggy *adj.* 崎嶇的
20. moody *adj.* 喜怒無常的；（無緣無故）不高興的

21. indulge *v.* 放縱

22. reverie *n.* 遐想

23. melancholy *n.* 憂鬱；悲哀；愁思

24. insipid *adj.* 平淡的

25. perpetually *adv.* 永恆地；終身地；不斷地

26. synthetical *adj.* 綜合的

27. anatomise *v.* 解剖

28. thistle *n.* 薊

29. entangle *v.* 糾纏

30. briar *n.* 荊棘

31. controversy *n.* 爭議

32. covet *v.* 妄想

33. throng *n.* 人群

34. extravagance *n.* 奢侈，揮霍；奢侈品；過分（的事情）；放縱的言行

35. affectation *n.* 假裝；裝模作樣

36. unravel *v.* 解開

37. poppy *n.* ［植］罌粟（花）；罌粟屬植物；深紅色

38. aqueduct *n.* 溝渠；引水渠；導水管

39. stifle *v.* 扼殺

40. utterance *n.* 說話方式；表達；說話

41. discourse *n.* 話語

42. hallucination *n.* 幻覺，幻想；錯覺

43. itinerant *adj.* 巡迴的

44. substantial *adj.* 實質性的

45. for the sake of 為了……起見

46. at a loss 困惑，不知所措

47. in hand （工作等）在進行中，待辦理；在控制中

48. at the disposal of 在處置

49. fits and starts 時斷時續

50. in preference to 優先於

51. on this account 為了這個緣故

Notes

1. Hazlitt's「On Going a Journey」is to be found in *Table Talk*, *Essays on Men and Manners*（1822）.

2. The woods of All-Fox-den refer to Wordsworth's house in Somerset, where Haz-

litt visited Coleridge and Wordsworth in April 1798.

Content Awareness

1. Answer the following questions according to the passage.

(1) What's one of the pleasantest things in the world and what does the author like?

(2) What's the soul of a journey?

(3) What may make the author happier compared with exchanging good things with a friend?

(4) What silence does the author prefer?

(5) In what sense does the author agree with Mr. Cobbett?

(6) Does the author prefer having a company in travelling? Why?

(7) Does the author object to going to see ruins in company with a friend or a party? Why?

(8) What is the author's view concerning travelling abroad?

2. Write a summary of the text.

_____
_____
_____
_____

Language Focus

1. Find the words from the text that are almost the same in meaning to the words in bold type in the following sentences.

(1) He said, and broke away to enjoy his grief and anger in **loneliness**. (　)

(2) The main **obstacle** to growth is a lack of capital. (　)

(3) Each morning the priest spent an hour in quiet **thoughtfulness**. (　)

(4) This place has become a famous summer **scenic spot**. (　)

(5) The peace negotiations should not **damage** the country's independence and integrity. (　)

(6) The owl hunts while you **sleep** in bed. (　)

(7) Ben dislikes waste and **luxury**. (　)

(8) He is indulging in **imaginations** about the future. (　)

(9) Aunt Polly had drooped into a settled **depression**, and her gray hair had grown almost white. (　)

(10) She said she was a good cook, but the food she cooked is **flavorless**. (　)

(11) The mayor will try to accord the **arguments** over the housing scheme. (　)

(12) He made a **pretense** of indifference. (　)

(13) My imprudent **remarks** incurred her displeasure. (　)

(14) I told him that such a proposal could be of no signification, but to **trap** us both in great difficulties. (　)

(15) Brain drains may represent a **great** reduction in some labor force skills and specialties. (　)

2. Choose a proper word from the list to fill in each blank in the following passage. Change the form if necessary.

 direction whoever negative difference alike movement magnetic
 loseman change childlike goal set alternative on

Wherever you are, and _____ you may be, there is one thing in which you and I are just _____ at this moment, and in all the moments of our existence. We are not at rest; we are _____ a journey, our life is a _____, a tendency, a steady, ceaseless progress towards an unseen _____. We are gaining something, or _____ something, every day. Even when our position and our character seem to remain precisely the same, they are _____. For the mere advance of time is a change. It is not the same thing to have a bare field in January and in July, the season makes the _____. The limitations that are _____ in the child are childish in the _____.

Everything that we do is a step in one _____ or another, even the failure to do something is in itself a deed. It _____ us forward or backward. The action of the _____ pole of a _____ needle is just as real as the action of the positive pole. To decline is to accept—the other _____.

3. Translation

A. Put the following paragraph into Chinese.

Instead of a friend in a post-chaise or in a Tilbury, to exchange good things with, and vary the same stale topics over again, for once let me have a truce with impertinence. Give me the clear blue sky over my head, and the green turf beneath my feet, a winding road before me, and a three hours' march to dinner—and then to thinking! It is hard if I cannot start some game on these lone heaths. I laugh, I run, I leap, I sing for joy. From the point of yonder rolling cloud I plunge into my past being, and revel there as the sun-burnt Indian plunges headlong into the wave that wafts him to his native shore. Then long-forgotten things like ⌈sunken wrack and sunless treasuries⌋ burst upon my eager sight, and I begin to feel, think, and be myself again. Instead of an awkward silence, broken by attempts at wit or dull common-places, mine is that undisturbed silence of the heart which alone is perfect eloquence. No one likes puns, alliterations, antitheses, argument, and analysis better than I do; but I sometimes had rather be without them.「Leave, oh, leave me to my repose!」

B. Put the following paragraphs into English.

今天，仰望藍天，聆聽小草在腳下生長，呼吸春天的氣息，細細品嘗大地的果實，然後放開雙手擁抱你的所愛。讓上帝喚醒你那神聖的知覺。

這真是一個奇跡！無論冬天多麼漫長，無論霜雪多麼嚴寒，自然總能獲勝。沒有哪個季節像春天那麼讓人翹首企盼……每年春花的爛漫總讓我驚訝不已：野生報春花和紫羅蘭的嬌嫩，公園裡藏紅花的多彩，還有高大的鬱金香和傲然的水仙花。

每個春天都是想像這樣一幅圖景：溫暖的春風彌漫著泥土的氣息，陽光照射著每一寸土壤，土壤把陽光染成深紅色，空氣中滲透著泥土的清香，腳下的小草與頭上的藍天遙相呼應。

獨一無二的，是自然界永恆的奇跡。

4. Answer the following questions in writing or through oral discussion.

(1) Why do we travel?

(2) Which one do you prefer, travelling with company or travelling alone?

Skills Development and Practice

Reading Skills

Guessing Unknown Words (1)
Understanding Word Formation

Practice 1: Being aware of how words are formed will help you discover the meaning of a great number of unfamiliar words in your reading. A good knowledge of word formation is also a fast way of increasing your vocabulary. Look at the examples.

EXAMPLES:

1. My homework is *incomplete* because I did not have time to finish it.

2. People often *misspell* my name.

3. Is this cushion cover *washable*?

QUESTIONS:

1. Are the italicized words new to you?

2. After you have read the following help box, can you guess the meaning of each one? Write down the meaning of the words in the given space.

a. incomplete _____

b. misspell _____

c. washable _____

HELP
in- = not *mis-* = wrong or wrongly *-able* = that can be V-ed
Common Prefixes (前綴) and Suffixes (後綴)

Prefix	Meaning	Example
in-	not	*in*+active: not active
en-	cause to be	*en*+large: cause to become large
dis-	not	*dis*+like: not like
re-	again or back	*re*+write: write again
mis-	bad (ly) or wrong (ly)	*mis*+understand: understand wrongly
un-	not	*un*+happy: not happy

Suffix	Meaning	Example
-ence	act, state, quality	differ+*ence*: the state of being different
-ion	act or process	comprehend+*ion*: act or process of understanding
-ity	quality or state	equal+*ity*: the state of being equal
-ness	state or condition	neat+*ness*: the state of being clean and orderly
-ize	cause to be more	modern+*ize*: make… more modern
-en	cause to be or have	sharp+*en*: cause to be more pointed
-able	capable of	break+*able*: capable of being broken
-less	without	friend+*less*: having no friend
-ful	full of	color+*ful*: full of colors
-ive	having the tendency or quality of	protect+*ive*: having the quality to protect

Practice 2: Use your knowledge of word formation to guess the meaning of the underlined word in each of the sentences.

1. We were <u>saddened</u> to hear of the death of your mother.

   A. mad   B. worried

   C. surprised   D. sad

2. Many children complained that <u>readable</u> books were rare those days.

   A. cheap   B. interesting

   C. easy   D. serious

3. Man's achievement on earth is great; however, he has been <u>endangered</u> by

breaking the balance of nature.

    A. in danger   B. in trouble

    C. defeated   D. creating danger

4. They promised to create more jobs for <u>unemployed</u> young people.

    A. not being used   B. being out of work

    C. poor   D. useful

5. Even though very expensive, this kind of engine is highly efficient and needs servicing <u>infrequently</u>.

    A. rarely   B. instantly

    C. constantly   D. suddenly

6. I'm sorry, I thought those letters had already been sent. It seems that I was <u>misinformed</u>.

    A. not informed   B. incompletely ordered

    C. wrongly told   D. given little information

7. The woman had been dead for about 3 days and her face was not <u>recognizable</u>.

    A. that can be seen   B. that can be recovered

    C. that can be recognized   D. that can be covered

8. The old house is <u>enclosed</u> with trees.

    A. protected   B. prevented

    C. covered   D. surrounded

9. It proved to be a <u>fruitful</u> meeting.

    A. crowded   B. lively

    C. popular   D. productive

10. There is a great <u>selection</u> of books on that topic.

    A. difference   B. choice

    C. need   D. lack

Translation Practice

Translation Skills

轉譯詞類：英語名詞可轉譯成漢語的動詞、形容詞等。

Practice 3: Translate the sentences into Chinese, paying attention to the italicized words.

1. International trade is the *exchange* of goods and services produced in one country for goods and services produced in another.

2. His music was an exciting *mixture* of white country music and black blues.

3. We know that the *mastery* of a foreign language is not easy.

4. A *change* of state from a solid to a liquid form requires heat energy.

5. Keep this dictionary on your desk for easy *reference*.

6. Have you any *idea* where he lives?

7. The experiment was a *success*.

8. Don't make the *mistake* of using the title「Mr」with the first name.

Practice 4: Translate the sentences into Chinese.

1. We have always been told that honesty is the best policy. However, when it comes to the Internet, this saying flies out of the window.

2. We should not take everything we read or see at face value. This is especially true if we visit chat rooms.

3. If you give out your personal information online, you have no way of knowing how the information can be used against you.

4. The idea behind this is that at no time should you be left along with an unknown person.

5. Most of the big sites and some of the little sites allow you to choose a user name and password so that you can enter the site and get access to your account.

6. Just as you would for「real world」shopping, know the return and refund policies for the sites on the Internet that you shop at.

Practice 5: Translate the sentences into English with the words or expressions given.

1. 我直到昨天才知道你已决定自己要去面见网友的消息。（not... until, in

person)

2. 說到互聯網，你不應該公開自己的個人信息。（when it comes to, keep... private）

3. 在任何時候你都不應該把他的手機號碼公布在網上。（at no time, give out）

4. 在網上與別人交易前，你得確保你能夠退掉自己不喜歡的商品或者受損的商品。（make sure）

5. 你用自己的用戶名和密碼就能登錄這個網站，進入你自己的帳戶。（get access to）

6. 有些人很善於在網上偽裝自己的身分。（be good at）

Practical Translation

語篇層次的翻譯——連貫

一個完整的語篇應該銜接得當，連貫性好。在翻譯過程中，我們應該注意翻譯不是以單個詞或句為轉換單位，而是以語篇為單位進行轉換，而語篇要注重整體性和一致性，也就是語篇的連貫性，語篇的連貫性決定了語篇的整體質量。為了實現語篇的連貫，有效的詞彙和語法銜接手段必不可少，但銜接手段是實現語篇連貫的必要但不充分條件，除此之外，我們還應注重語篇邏輯順序的調整和視角的轉換。

1. 邏輯順序的調整

在邏輯關係的敘述上，英語常先總結後分析，先結果後原因，句子重心取前置式。而漢語句子則恰恰相反，先原因後結果，先條件後推論，先分析後總結，句子重心取後置式。因此在英譯漢過程中，為使漢語語篇連貫，有必要根據漢語的邏輯關係進行合理的調整。

例1：We should not be surprised that increasing numbers of people choose to live entirely indoors, leaving buildings only to ride in airplanes or cars, viewing the great outside, if they view it at all, through sealed windows, but more often gazing into screens, listening to human chatter, cut off from「the realities of earth and water and the growing seed.」（Scott Russel Sanders：「A Few Earthly Words」）

譯文：越來越多的人們選擇完全足不出戶的生活，離開樓群也只是為了開汽車或者乘飛機，透過密封的窗戶去看一看外面的大千世界，假設他們去看的話，也不過如此。但是，在更多的時候，他們凝視著屏幕，傾聽人們的閒聊，與「土地、水和正在生長的種子的現實世界」隔絕開來。這一切我們都不必大驚小怪。（範守義譯）

解析：原句是一個完整的「形合」英語長句，採用了各種語法手段，如賓語從句、獨立主格結構、狀語從句等來進行銜接，而且在邏輯關係上也體現了英語句子先下結論後分析說明的特點，句子重心取前置式。在翻譯過程中，為了符合漢語「意合」的表達習慣，原語中顯性的語法和詞彙手段被隱去，整個句子被切分成漢語中靠隱性的意義和邏輯關係銜接的三個單句。而且譯文充分考慮漢語先分析後下結論的特點，對句子的整體結構進行了大調整，原語中表示結論的句子 We should not be surprised 在目標語中被放到最後，形成了一個自然的結論，句子重心取後置式。譯文銜接順暢，邏輯性強，讀來非常連貫和通順。

例 2：It is a curious fact, of which I can think of no satisfactory explanation, that enthusiasm for country life and love of natural scenery are strongest and most widely diffused in those European countries which have the worst climate and where the search for the picturesque involves the greatest discomfort.

譯文：歐洲有些國家，天氣糟透，要找到景色如畫的所在，這裡的人們得辛苦一番。奇怪，他們就喜歡過鄉村生活，也最愛欣賞自然美景，而且這種情形在這裡是個普遍現象。這是實情，可我怎麼也想不出令人滿意的原因。

解析：原句是一個典型的英語「形合」的句子，採用了各種語法手段，如定語從句、同位語從句等，而在邏輯關係上也符合英語先下結論後分析說明的特點，先提出總說的句子：a curious fact, I can think of no satisfactory explanation，然後，如撥開雲霧般，一層層地進行分析和說明，讓讀者心中的疑惑一一解開。翻譯過程中，為了體現漢語句子「意合」的特徵，不僅要有顯性的銜接手段的調整，如去掉原句中的連接詞，將一個長句切分成三個語義銜接的句子等，而且要按照漢語習慣對句子的「隱性」邏輯順序進行調整，體現漢語句子先分析後總結的特點，這樣漢語句子不僅銜接恰當，而且語篇流暢。因此，漢語譯文先分說一些歐洲國家的天氣和尋找美景所需付出的代價，然後語義出現轉折，做進一步的分析和說明，最後高屋建瓴地進行總結：「這是實情，可我怎麼也想不出令人滿意的原因。」漢語句子重心在最後，前面的分析和說明是為最後結論的自然出現作鋪墊，而最後的結論起到了昇華主旨內容的作用。

2. 視角的轉換

從社會認知系統上講，東西方不同的哲學和認識論在社會歷史背景中建構了不同的心理學理論。西方人往往把注意力更多地放在客體和自身目標之上，在觀察事物時，視點更多聚焦於事物而不是觀察者本身；中國人在觀察事物時，更多

地是從自己的角度出發。體現在語言結構和邏輯的連貫性上就是英語句子常以物作主語，且一般不能省略，並由此產生謂語形式的被動化。而漢語句子多用人稱主語，當人稱不言而喻時，常常對其進行隱藏或省略，從而使漢語中出現大量的省略句和無主句。所以為使語篇連貫，有必要弄清楚兩種語言的思維差異，努力調整自己的思維模式，在翻譯過程中注意視角的轉換，翻譯出地道和連貫的語篇。

例 3：This is always a feast about where we are now. Thanksgiving reflects the complexion of the year we're in. Some years it feels buoyant, almost jubilant in nature. Other years it seems marked by a conspicuous humility uncommon in the calendar of American emotions. (November 25th, 2004, The New York Times)

譯文：感恩節這一餐總是關乎到我們的處境，反應出一年的年景。有些年的感恩節我們心情愉悅，幾乎是喜氣洋洋，但有些年頭我們卻把感恩節過得相當低調，不敢驕傲，這並不是美國人慣有的情緒。（葉子南譯）

解析：英語原文的第三、四句是以 it 作主語的句子，it 指代「感恩節」，有的年份它呈現給我們一派活力萬千、愉悅開心的氣氛，有的年份它又要求人低調。但在漢語中，感恩節不能和愉悅的心情、喜氣洋洋的氣氛連用，也不能和低調、驕傲等詞搭配，只有感恩節的參與者「我們」才能感受到這份節日的喜悅，體會到那份低調和不敢輕易驕傲的心情。因此為使譯文地道、連貫，譯者有意將原文中的物稱主語變成漢語中的人稱主語，這樣譯文讀起來才順暢、連貫。

例 4：Friday started with a morning visit to the modern campus of the 22,000-student University of Michigan in nearby Ann Arbor, where the Chinese table tennis team joined students in the cafeteria line for lunch and later played an exhibition match.

譯文：星期五那天，中國乒乓球隊一早就到安伯亞附近去參觀擁有 22,000 名學生的密歇根大學的現代化校園。他們和該校學生在校內自助餐廳排隊取午餐，然後進行了一場表演賽。

解析：英語原文是個典型的以物稱 Friday 作主語的句子，表述了那一天所發生的事情。英語中以某個年份、某個日子作主語的句子很多，都表示在某一年或某一天所發生的事情。在漢語譯文中，我們不能照搬原文的結構，不能將原文的物稱作主語，只能從漢語表達習慣和語篇連貫的角度出發，找到動作真正的發出者，調整句子結構，將原文中物稱主語轉換成漢語中的人稱主語，這樣，不僅原語和目標語在語義上是完全對等的，而且譯文在語篇連貫性方面也恰到好處。

Translation Practice

Translate the following sentences into Chinese.

1. Such is human nature in the West that a great many people are often willing to

sacrifice higher pay for the privilege of becoming white collar workers.

2. Cosmopolitan Shanghai was born to the world in 1842 when the British man-of-war Nemesis, slipping unnoticed into the mouth of the Yangtze River, reduced the Wusong Fort and took the city without a fight.

3. A study of the letter leaves us in no doubt as to the motives behind it.

4. The happiness—the superior advantages of the young women round about her, gave Rebecca inexpressible pangs of envy. (W. M. Thackeray: *Vanity Fair*)

5. Poor Joe's panic lasted for two or three days; during which he did not visit the house. (W. M. Thackeray: *Vanity Fair*)

Focused Writing

Precis or Summaries

A precis is a summary. Writing a precis is valuable training in composition. Since the writing requires you to be clear and concise, you must choose your words carefully and arrange them skillfully to get the maximum amount of meaning into the minimum space.

In addition to its value as a writing exercise, writing a precis is excellent reading practice. In order to summarize another's ideas in your own words, you must thoroughly understand the idea.

In order to avoid any chance of being accused of plagiarism, you MUST include a citation of the original whenever you summarise it. This must include, as a minimum, the author's name, the original title, date of publication, publisher and where published.

In writing a precis, bear in mind the following dos and don'ts:

(1) A precis is a short summary. It is not a paraphrase, which merely says in different and simpler words exactly what the passage being paraphrased has to say. A paraphrase may be as long as the passage itself.

(2) A precis gives only the 「heart」 of a passage. It omits any repetition and details such as examples, illustrations, and adjectives unless they are of particular importance to the understanding of the text.

(3) A precis is written entirely in the words of the person writing it, not in the words of the original selection. Avoid the temptation to lift long phrases and whole sentences from the original.

(4) A precis is NOT a personal interpretation of a work or an expression of your opinion; it is, rather, an exact replica in miniature of the work, often reduced to one-third to one-quarter of its size, in which you express the complete argument.

(5) As a writer, you decide what goes into your precis or summary based on what the summary needs to do for the reader. For example, if you write a summary to remind yourself about the content of an article you read as part of a large research project, you'll only include the information you need for your research. If you write a summary of a book or article as part of a literary review, the summary will be based on how much you believe your target readers need to know about the book before they read your review.

In writing a precis, you should proceed as follows:

(1) Skim and scan the text to identify the topic and to understand how the information has been organized.

(2) Read carefully, sentence by sentence. Make a note of the writer's main points in your own words. Spotting the topic sentences will help you to do this. Look up in the dictionary any words whose meaning is not absolutely clear and be sure you have the correct meaning based on the context.

(3) As you read, take brief notes in your own words about the main ideas.

(4) Do not use the wording of the original except for any key words which are indispensable. If you cannot put the ideas into your own words you do not understand them very well! Be especially careful not to just copy the topic sentences. If you do have to use any of the words from the original text, be sure to put them in quotation marks.

(5) Do not add any opinions or ideas of your own.

(6) Write in the third person—the passive voice.

(7) Revise your writing until you are sure that you have an accurate summary which flows logically and makes sense to anyone who has not read the original.

(8) Usually you will find your precis is too long, if it is more than one-third the length of the original, continue your revision until you have reduced the precis to about a quarter. In this careful revision lies the principal value of the precis as a composition exercise.

Below is a sample summary of the text 「Is Affordable Housing Becoming an Oxymoron?」by Hal R. Varian.

Sample

> In his article, 「Is Affordable Housing Becoming an Oxymoron?」(2005), Hal R. Varian suggests that house prices are rising in America due to low mortgage rates and lack of supply. High prices create demand as people invest in property to benefit from capital gains and government subsidies to help first time buyers also increase demand. High demand without increased supply forces prices up.
>
> Increasing property taxes could decrease prices but would not solve the problem. In California it has helped encourage people to extend their homes rather than move to a bigger house. However this means fewer houses on the market and therefore higher prices.
>
> Whilst raising interest rates has helped dampen demand in some places, an increase in supply would reduce prices. Varian concludes by pointing out that this requires that land be made available near places of employment, but crowding homes together in urban areas is unpopular among home owners as it devalues their home and standard of living.
>
> (159 words)
>
> Varian, Hal R.; 「Is Affordable Housing Becoming an Oxymoron?」; *New York Times*, October 21, 2005

In this summary, the author first identifies the main points that Varian thinks cause high property prices and groups them together in the first paragraph. Then the first possible solution to the problem (increasing property taxes) is mentioned but shown to also increase demand. Finally, the summary identifies that although higher interest rates does help, what is required is more housing. However this means more land and therefore increased crowding which is unpopular.

Note 1: Reference is made to Varian twice. In a longer summary, it may be necessary to refer to him more often. It is important for readers to know that you are still summarizing and have not moved on to your own or someone else's opinion.

Note 2: As in the text itself, the result, as indicated in the title, is inferred rather than clearly stated. i.e. that affordable housing may not be possible.

Note 3: Full bibliographic details should be available, especially the date when the original text was published.

Writing Assignment

Find an essay and write a precis. Remember to ensure that it is no longer than 1/4 of the original in length.

Unit 4 Sports

Warming-ups

Task 1 Questions for Thought

Think about the following questions, then discuss with your partner.
1. Do you think it's good to do regular exercises?
2. What sports do you prefer? Why?
3. Why are so many people crazy about sports?
4. Can you name a few sports that China is strong at? Which one do you like best?

Task 2 Vocabulary Preview

Complete the following table by writing the English or Chinese equivalents of the words given. Then, check your answers with your partner.

奧林匹克		champion	
運動員		table tennis	
極限運動		draw	
蹦極		gymnasium	
馬拉松		bodybuilding	
打破紀錄		jogging	

In-class Activities

Task 1 Presentation

Introduce your favorite pastime. Your presentation should include:
- the things you always do in your spare time
- your favorite pastime
- the benefits of the pastime

Task 2 Pair/Group Work

A: Suppose you are talking about what sports you like and what your family members like. Practice the following dialogue with your partner.

Jane: What would you like to do other than work?

Jerry: Well, sports might be my hobby.

Jane: What kinds of sports do you like?

Jerry: I used to like ice-skating, but I'm interested in badminton.

Jane: I like it woo.

Jerry: Whom do you usually play with, Jane?

Jane: Usually with my younger sister and elder brother.

Jerry: Where do you go to play? Gymnasium?

Jane: Yes.

Jerry: How come you like badminton?

Jane: My parents love it and they always say it's a great sport. Then gradually I found it was really interesting. So now, I like it.

Jerry: It seems that family influence is very important.

Jane: There you have it.

B: Suppose you are talking about which athlete you like best and why you like him or her. Practice the following dialogue with your partner.

Kate: He is only an amateur athlete, but he is the best one.

John: Whom are you talking about?

Kate: He is Spiriton Louis, the first marathon winner at the first Olympic Games in Athens in 1896.

John: Yes, he is great, but I don't think he is the best in modern games.

Kate: Who is your bravest hero?

John: Jesse Owen. I think he is the greatest. He was one of the first black American athletes to win gold. His 8.06-meter long jump record remained unbroken for 25 years.

Kate: We have our own favorite athletes. But they may not be the best, or we can say all of them are best.

John: I couldn't agree more.

Task 3 Pair/Group Work

What's your opinion on football? Exchange your ideals with your partner. The following words and patterns may help you express your opinion.

- I think...
- As far as I am concerned...
- In my opinion...
- From my point of view...

Words: mad, exciting, boring, proud, injury, dangerous, interesting, safe, black eyes, yellow card, red card, injury, friendship...

Task 4 Read the following dialogue first, then act it out with your partner and each of you should assume a role, and then switch the role

(Situation: Li Ming and Jane meet in the gymnasium. Jane is an exchange student who is now studying in China. They begin to talk about some benefits brought by sports.)

Li Ming: What sports do you like?

Jane: I'm fond of the shuttle cock, and playing basketball. How about you?

Li Ming: I like dancing, swimming and so on.

Jane: Which one do you like best?

Li Ming: I think there is nothing better than swimming for exercise.

Jane: Why?

Li Ming: Because it can boost our whole body capacity.

Jane: How many strokes are there usually?

Li Ming: There are freestyle, backstroke, butterfly, frog stroke and etc.

Jane: I heard exercise can also boost brain function.

Li Ming: Yes. Exercise can improve blood flow and spur cell growth, and exercise can lose weight.

Jane: A growing keep-fit fever is sweeping over China, isn't it?

Li Ming: In order to live a happy life, everyone wants to have a good health and a long life.

Jane: What do they play with usually?

Li Ming: For people around the retirement age, they do some Taijiquan, perform sword and practise the Chinese Wushu.

Jane: How about young people?

Li Ming: They are now flocking into gyms.

Task 5 Discussion/Presentation

A: Read the following viewpoints on fast food. Do you agree with the statements? Why or why not? Work in groups and make discussion with your peers.

Student 1: Sports can lead people to live a longer life.

Your opinion:

Student 2: The most important thing is to participate.

Your opinion:

Student 3: Sports help to train a person's character.

Your opinion:

B: After discussing, summarize all the opinions and make an oral presentation entitled.

Sports and Health

The following might be useful and helpful for your presentation:

Words and Expressions:

healthy body; healthy mind; energetic; stimulate the circulation of blood; activate our digestion; live longer

Reference Modal:

A healthy body is necessary for a healthy mind. As is known, to have a sound mind, we must first have a sound body. This is of vital importance. Only by keeping ourselves healthy and strong can we feel energetic and vigorous in studying and working and live a happy life...

Reading Passages

Passage A

Yoga in America
by Douglas Dupler

Yoga originated in ancient India and is one of the longest surviving philosophical systems in the world. Some scholars have estimated that yoga is as old as 5,000 years: artifacts detailing yoga postures have been found in India from over 3,000 B. C. Yogis claim that it is a highly developed science of healthy living that has been tested and perfected for all these years. Yoga was first brought to America in the late 1800s when Swami Vivekananda, an Indian teacher and yogi, presented a lecture on meditation in Chicago. Yoga slowly began gaining followers, and flourished during the 1960s when there was a surge of interest in Eastern philosophy. There has since been a vast exchange of yoga knowledge in America, with many students going to India to study and many Indian experts coming here to teach, resulting in the establishment of a side variety of schools. Today, yoga is thriving, and it has become easy to find teachers and practitioners throughout America. A recent Roper poll, commissioned by Yoga Journal, found that 11 million Americans do yoga at least occasionally and 6 million perform it regularly. Yoga stretches are used by physical therapists and professional sports teams, and the benefits of yoga are being touted by movie stars and *Fortune* 500 executives. Many prestigious school of medicine have studied and introduced yoga techniques as proven therapies for illness and stress. Some medical schools, like UCLA, even offer yoga classes as part of their physical training program.

There are several different schools of hatha yoga in America; the two most prevalent ones are Iyengar and Ashtanga yoga. Iyengar yoga was founded by B. K. S. Iyengar, who is widely considered as one of the great living innovators of yoga. Iyengar yoga puts strict emphasis on form and alignment, and uses traditional hatha yoga techniques in new manners and sequences. Iyengar yoga can be good for physical therapy because it allows the use of props like straps and blocks to make it easier for some people to get into the yoga postures. Ashtanga yoga can be a more vigorous routine, using a flowing and dance-like sequence of hatha postures to generate body heat, which purifies the body through sweating and deep breathing.

Yoga routines can take anywhere from 20 minutes to two or more hours, with one hour being a good time investment to perform a sequence of postures and a meditation. Some yoga routines, depending on the teacher and school, can be as strenuous as the most difficult workout, and some routines merely stretch and align the body while the breath and heart rate are kept slow and steady. Yoga achieves its best results when it is practiced as a daily discipline, and yoga can be a life-long exercise routine, offering deeper and more challenging positions as a practitioner becomes more adept. The basic positions can increase a person's strength, flexibility and sense of well-being almost immediately, but it can take years to perfect and deepen them, which is an appealing and stimulating aspect of yoga for many.

Yoga is usually best learned from a yoga teacher or physical therapist, but yoga is simple enough that one can learn the basics from good books on the subject, which are plentiful. Yoga classes are generally inexpensive, averaging around 10 dollars per class, and students can learn basic postures in just a few classes. Many YMCAs, colleges, and community health organizations offer beginning yoga classes as well, often for nominal fees. If yoga is part of a physical therapy program, it can be reimbursed by insurance.

Yoga can also provide the same benefits as any well-designed exercise program, increasing general health and stamina, reducing stress, and improving those conditions brought about by sedentary lifestyles. Yoga has the added advantage of being a low-impact activity that uses only gravity as resistance, which makes it an excellent physical therapy routine; certain yoga postures can be safely used to strengthen and balance all parts of the body.

Meditation has been much studied and approved for its benefits in reducing stress-related conditions. The landmark book, *The Relaxation Response*, by Harvard cardiologist Herbert Benson, showed that meditation and breathing techniques for relaxation could have the opposite effect of stress, reducing blood pressure and other indicators. Since then, much research has reiterated the benefits of meditation for stress reduction and general health. Currently, the American Medical Association recommends meditation techniques as a first step before medication for borderline hypertension cases.

Modem psychological studies have shown that even slight facial expressions can cause changes in the involuntary nervous system; yoga utilizes the mind/body connection. That is, yoga practice contains the central ideas that physical posture and alignment can influence a person's mood and self esteem and also mat me mind can be used to shape and heal the body. Yoga practitioners claim that the strengthening of mind/body awareness can bring eventual improvements in all facets of a person's life.

Yoga can be performed by those of any age and condition, although not all poses should be attempted by everyone. Yoga is also a very accessible form of exercise; all that is needed is a fiat floor surface large enough to stretch out on, a mat or towel, and enough overhead space to fully raise the alms. It is a good activity for those who can't go to gyms, who don't like other forms of exercise, or have very busy schedules. Yoga should be done on an empty stomach, and teachers recommend waiting three or more hours after meals. Loose and comfortable clothing should be worn.

Beginners should exercise care and concentration when performing yoga postures, and not try to stretch too much too quickly, as injury could result. Some advanced yoga postures, like the headstand and full lotus position, can be difficult and require strength, flexibility, and gradual preparation, so beginners should get the help of a teacher before attempting them.

Yoga is not a competitive sport; it does not matter how a person does in comparison with others, but how aware and disciplined one becomes with one's own body and limitations. Proper form and alignment should always be maintained during a stretch or posture, and the stretch or posture should be stopped when there is pain, dizziness, or fatigue. The mental component of yoga is just as important as the physical postures. Concentration and awareness of breath should not be neglected. Yoga should be done with an open, gentle, and non-critical mind; when one stretches into a yoga position, it can be thought of as accepting and working on one's limits. Impatience, self-criticism and comparing one self to others will not help in this process of self-knowledge. While performing the yoga of breathing (pranayama) and meditation (dyana), it is best to have an experienced teacher, as these powerful techniques can cause dizziness and discomfort when done improperly.

Although yoga originated in a culture very different from modern America, it has been accepted and its practice has spread relatively quickly. Many yogis are amazed at how rapidly yoga's popularity has spread in America, considering the legend that it was passed down secretly by handfuls of adherents for many centuries.

There can still be found some resistance to yoga, for active and busy Americans sometimes find it hard to believe that an exercise program that requires them to slow down, concentrate, and breathe deeply can be more effective than lifting weights or running. However, ongoing research in top medical schools is showing yoga's effectiveness for overall health and for specific problems, making it an increasingly acceptable health practice.

New Words

1. adept *adj.* 熟練的
2. adherent *n.* 信徒；擁護者；追隨者
3. align *v.* 使……排成一線
4. artifact *n.* 手工藝品
5. cardiologist *n.* 心臟病專家
6. disciplined *adj.* 受過訓練的，遵守紀律的
7. hypertension *n.* 高血壓
8. indicator *n.* 指示物
9. innovator *n.* 創新者
10. meditation *n.* 默念，默想；冥想，打坐
11. nominal *adj.* （金額）極小的，微不足道的，象徵性的
12. posture *n.* 姿勢，體態
13. practitioner *n.* （某種活動的）從事者，實踐者
14. prestigious *adj.* 有聲望的，有威信的
15. prevalent *adj.* 流行的，普遍的
16. prop *n.* 支柱；支撐物
17. reimburse *v.* 償還
18. reiterate *v.* 反覆地說，重申
19. sedentary *adj.* （工作等）坐著做的，案頭的
20. stamina *n.* 持久力，耐力，毅力

21. strenuous *adj.* 艱苦的，要花功夫的
22. tout *v.* 贊揚；吹捧
23. well-being *n.* 舒適；健康；幸福
24. yogi *n.* 瑜伽師；瑜伽教授者

Notes

1. Douglas Dupler is a writer for *Gale Encyclopedia of Alternative Medicine and Gale Encyclopedia of Nursing and Allied Health*, 2002, from which the text is extracted.

2. Eastern philosophy includes the various philosophies associated with the countries of Asia, including India, China, Iran, and Japan. The term can also sometimes include Persian philosophy and Islamic philosophy, though these may also be considered Western or Central Asian philosophies.

3. Founded in 1946, the Roper Center is a large archive of public opinion data containing thousands of polls conducted by leading survey organizations in 75 countries.

4. Yoga Journal is an American based media company that publishes a magazine, a website, DVDs, and holds conferences devoted to yoga, food and nutrition, fitness, well-being, and fashion and beauty.

5. UCLA is the abbreviated name for University of California, Los Angeles.

6. With 「ha」 meaning 「sun」 and 「tha」 meaning 「moon」, hatha yoga is commonly translated as the yoga that brings union 「of the pairs of opposites」.

7. The Iyengar method of Yoga is initially learnt through the in-depth study of asanas (posture) and pranayama (breath control).

Content Awareness

Read the following statements and decide whether they are true or false according to the text. Put T before a true statement and F before a false one.

_____ (1) Yoga became immediately popular in the US after it was introduced in the late 1800s.

_____ (2) Not only therapists but also movie stars encourage the practice of yoga.

_____ (3) Iyengar yoga emphasizes on a flowing and dance-like sequence of hatha postures.

_____ (4) One hour sessions of yoga practice is recommended.

_____ (5) Your insurance company may pay for your yoga class if your physical therapist prescribes it.

_____ (6) For people who sit a lot at work yoga is particularly beneficial.

_____ (7) Meditation can reduce blood pressure, so those with high blood pressure should use meditation instead of medication.

_____ (8) Yoga should always be practiced under the guide of an experienced teacher.

_____ (9) Yoga is a competitive sports, so yoga practitioners should always try their best.

_____ (10) Yoga may cause pain, dizziness or fatigue if not done correctly.

_____ (11) When practicing Yoga, one should keep an open, gentle, and non-critical mind.

_____ (12) Americans like yoga because it follows a fast and energetic pattern.

Language Focus

1. Choose the answer that is closest in meaning to the underlined word in the sentence.

(1) The speaker announced the establishment of a new college.
A. breakdown   B. setup
C. output   D. construction

(2) He has traveled extensively in China, recording every facet of life.
A. detail   B. comer
C. step   D. aspect

(3) This negative attitude is surprisingly prevalent among young boys.
A. liberal   B. previous
C. common   D. definite

(4) At that point, the public sector deficit was estimated to be around £45 billion.
A. forecasted   B. judged
C. determined   D. boasted

(5) It was claimed that some doctors were working 80 hours a week.
A. revealed   B. required
C. stated   D. pleaded

(6) Wildlife seems to flourish in the area.
A. grow well   B. pass out quickly
C. settle down easily D. make up conveniently

(7) He lives in Australia now, so we only see him very occasionally.
A. regularly   B. sometimes
C. scarcely   D. often

(8) She has been commissioned to write a new national anthem.

A. asked   B. required

C. ordered   D. contracted

(9) One of the most prestigious universities in the country is looking for a new president.

A. popular   B. prosperous

C. admired   D. accountable

(10) He wouldn't let me reimburse him for the cost of his journey.

A. pay   B. charge

C. switch   D. punish

(11) Gaining confidence is a major component when developing leadership skills.

A. reason   B. legend

C. part   D. necessity

(12) We need to be given greater flexibility in the use of resources.

A. capacity to sustain   B. ability to maximize

C. rise of productivity   D. ability to make changes

(13) He'll never get anywhere working for himself—he lacks self-discipline.

A. military training   B. self control

C. a vivid imagination   D. a sense of belonging

2. Fill in each of the blanks with an appropriate word or phrase from the box. Change the form if necessary.

medical	practice	write	describe	mental
state of being	exercise	include	picture	soul
individual	adapt	experience	control	fundamental

Yoga is an ancient system of relaxation, exercise, and healing with origins in Indian philosophy. Early descriptions of yoga are _____ in Sanskrit, the classical literary language of India. The first known work is *The Yoga Sutras*, written more than 2,000 years ago, although yoga may have been _____ up to 5,000 years ago. The initial concepts have been _____ over time through translation and scholarly interpretation, but the _____ principles describing the practice of yoga in the quest of the _____ remain largely intact. Yoga has been _____ as ⌈the union of mind, body and spirit⌋, which addresses physical, _____ intellectual, emotional and spiritual dimensions towards an overall harmonious _____. The philosophy of yoga is sometimes _____ as a tree with eight branches. These eight limbs are: pranayama (breathing exercises), asana (physical postures), yama (moral behavior), niyama (healthy habit), dharana (concentration), prathyahara (sense withdrawal), dhyana (contemplation), and samadhi (higher consciousness). There are several schools of yoga practice, such as hatha yoga, karma yoga, bhakti yoga, and raja yoga. These schools vary in the proportions of the _____ of the eight limbs. However, they are all similar in working towards the goal of self-realized and _____ of mental, physiological, and psychological parameters through yogic _____. In the United States and Europe, hatha yoga is commonly practiced, _____ pranayama and asanas. Yoga is often practiced by healthy _____ with the aim to achieve relaxation, fitness, and a healthy lifestyle. Yoga has also been recommended and used for variety of _____ a conditions. Yoga techniques can be learned in classes or through videotape instruction. Classes last from 30 to 90 minutes and are offered at various skill levels.

3. Translate the following sentences into Chinese.

(1) Then I discovered that somewhere inside the wonderful device lived an amazing whose name was 「Information Please」and there was nothing she did not know.

_____

_____

(2) The pain was terrible, but there didn't seem to be any reason to cry because there was no one home to give sympathy.

_____

_____

(3) Why is it that birds should sing so beautifully and bring joy to all families, only to end up as a heap of feathers on the bottom of a cage?

_____

_____

(4) 「Information Please」belonged to that old wooden box back home and I somehow never thought of trying the tall, shiny new phone that sat on the table in the hall.

_____

_____

(5) Often, in moments of doubt and confusion, I would recall the peaceful sense of security I had then. I appreciated now how patient, understanding, and kind she was to have spent her time on a little boy.

_____

_____

Passage B

Olympic Effort

No matter how much her legs screamed or back ached, she couldn't stop. Her son was dying, she had no insurance, so she couldn't stop. The medical bills were stacked to the sky, and she had no money.

Gymnastics once saved Oksana Chusovitina. Now, she needed it to save her boy.

「If I don't compete, then my son won't live,」Chusovitina said after her son was found to have cancer before his third birthday. 「It's as simple as that. I have no choice.」To get better medical care for her son Alisher, she moved to Germany in 2003.

The story deeply moved the gymnastics world. Maybe that's why Chusovitina, the first female gymnast to compete in five Olympics, heard a loud cry on every tumbling pass and back-flip from the thousands in the National Indoor Stadium at the team qualification this week.

Chusovitina, more than twice the age as many competitors, has pushed her 33-year-old body beyond where it was meant to go.

Her son is well now, but she won't stop.

「I feel perfect,」she said, 「I feel young.」

From a few feet away, she was with the young competitors she's trying to beat. She finished fourth in the vault during the qualification and will compete for a medal in that event this weekend.

Whether it's flawless technique, or simply a gift from the heavens, Chusovitina has turned into an inspiration to gymnasts all over the world.

「I don't know how she does it,」said U. S. gymnast Alicia Sacramone, one of the medal favorites in the vault. 「She's a role model to so many of us.」

「She was always doing very difficult routines. She was doing harder routines than the boys, that's what I remember. She was really amazing,」said Valeri Liukin, a member of the men's Unified Team at the 1992 Barcelona Olympics with Chusovitina.

Chusovitina was born and brought up in the former Soviet Union. She rocketed up the gymnastics ladder, winning the country's junior all-around title in 1988 when she was 13 years old.

She was elevated to the senior level the following year before most of this year's Olympic gymnasts were born.

Chusovitina helped the Unified Team win the team gold in Barcelona. She became one of the world's top vaulters, winning a record eight of her 10 world titles on the apparatus.

「She's quick,」said German national coach Ursula Koch.「You cannot teach that. She's a phenomenon.」

Her body sometimes hurts, but…

「She doesn't speak about pain,」Koch said.

The workouts are shorter. Chusovitina spends much more time sharing more than 25 years of knowledge with her teammates than sharpening her routines. She's more efficient.

「She's like an idol,」said a 17-year-old teammate,「She doesn't do routines 20 times in training. She does it once and well. She knows her body very well. She knows when something is wrong, she stops.」

Koch insisted Chusovitina could tumble, jump and flip forever. Hermann said「maybe one or two years more… or maybe to London (for the 2012 Olympics).」

Asked to explain how she's pulled it off and persevered through the years of pounding, Chusovitina broke into a wide smile and flashed the little English she knows：

「My secret.」

Words and Expressions

1. scream *v.* 發出尖銳刺耳聲，尖叫；（因受傷、受驚嚇或激動而）尖叫，驚呼
2. ache *v.* & *n.* 疼痛，酸痛
3. insurance *n.* 保險
4. medical *adj.* 醫療的，醫學的
5. bill *n.* 帳單；法案
6. stack *v.* 堆起，堆放

    n. (整齊的)（一）堆，（一）疊
7. gymnastics *n.* 體操，體操訓練
8. gymnast *n.* 體操運動員
9. tumbling *n.* 空翻，翻跟頭
10. backflip *n.* 直體後空翻
11. indoor *adj.* 室內的，屋內的
12. stadium *n.* (有看臺的) 體育場，運動場
13. competitor *n.* (體育比賽的) 參賽者；(商業) 競爭對手
14. vault *n.* 跳馬
15. event *n.* (比賽等的) 項目；發生的事情，事件
16. flawless *adj.* 完美無瑕的，無缺點的

17. technique *n.* 技巧，技術
18. gift *n.* 天賦，才能；禮物
19. heaven *n.* 上天，上帝；天，天空
20. inspiration *n.* 鼓舞人心的人（或物），啓發靈感的人（或物）
21. unified *adj.* 聯合的，統一的
22. former *adj.* 從前的，以前的，早先的
23. rocket *v.* 迅速上升，猛漲
    n. 火箭
24. ladder *n.* 階梯，途徑；梯子
25. junior *adj.* 青少年的；職位較低的，資歷較淺的
26. all *adj.* （體育方面）全能的，全面的
27. title *n.* （體育比賽）冠軍；標題，題目
28. elevate *v.* 提升，提高
29. senior *adj.* 較年長的；地位（或等級）較高的，年資較深的
30. vaulter *n.* 跳馬運動員
31. apparatus *n.* 器械，設備，裝置
32. coach *n.* 教練，輔導教師
33. workout *n.* 鍛煉，健身
34. knowledge *n.* 知識，學識，瞭解
35. efficient *adj.* 有效率的，高效能的
36. flip *v.* 翻，翻轉，空翻
37. forever *adv.* 永遠
38. persevere *v.* 堅持不懈，鍥而不舍
39. pounding *n.* 反覆的打擊
40. turn into 變成
41. bring up 養育
42. pull it off 取得成功
43. break into 突然呈現⋯⋯，突然發出（或冒出）⋯⋯

Content Awareness

Answer the questions according to the passage.

（1） What did Chusovitina say after her son was found to have cancer?

（2） Why did the audience cheer Chusovitina widely in the National Indoor Stadium?

（3） Where was Chusovitina born and brought up?

（4） Why do her teammates think she is more efficient?

（5） What can we learn from her answer「my secret」?

Language Focus

1. Fill in the blanks with the words or expressions given. Change the form if necessary.

effort   insurance   bill   event   technique

model   former   all-round   title   senior

knowledge   efficient   turn into   bring up   break into

(1) He mentioned in an article that parents should be the true role _____ for their children.

(2) What it comes down to is which method is smarter and more _____.

(3) When asked what had made him stay in competitive gymnastics for so many years, he said gymnastics had _____ way of life for him.

(4) Chusovitina won the USSR Junior Nationals in 1988 and began competing at the _____ international level in 1989.

(5) Chusovitina had no medical _____ to pay for Alisher's treatment.

(6) I think we can learn from each other by sharing _____ of how we have trained at home.

(7) Hundreds stand in line outside the U. S. Capitol to pay their last respects to _____ President Gerald Ford.

(8) She _____ tears repeatedly as she described the battle, saying she would have walked across the marathon finish line if necessary to finish the race.

(9) I was born and _____ in Beijing, and attended college in Shanghai.

(10) When asked about winning the national vault _____ at the 2002 Championships, Tricase said, 「It was the most amazing thing for me to win vault.」

(11) Other competitors might match her level of difficulty but her _____ is better.

(12) In 1988, at the age of 13, Chusovitina won the _____ title at the USSR National Championships in the junior division.

(13) Anyone interested in sport can make the _____ to improve and get proper training.

(14) They had to take out a loan to pay their last fuel _____.

(15) Chinese Kang Xin took the women's balance beam _____, beating Chusovitina into second place.

2. Fill in each of the following blanks with a preposition or an adverb.

(1) Dan was elevated _____ Senior Vice President in August of 2007.

(2) As their eyes met, his face broke _____ a huge smile.

(3) If I had more practice, I could have pulled it _____.

(4) Her parents died when she was a child and she was brought _____ by

her aunt.

(5) In one year he turned from a problem child _____ a model student.

(6) I just don't feel _____ doing anything tonight.

(7) I think we can solve this problem without resorting _____ legal action.

(8) In order to be a winner, you have to believe _____ yourself.

(9) What it came down _____ was whether our students could compete at a fair level.

(10) If you talk to your friends or family about your goals, they can really help keep you _____ track.

3. Combine each pair of sentences into one by using that. Pay attention to the difference in structure.

MODEL:

a. We are delighted at the news.

We are going to spend our summer vacation in Qingdao.

<u>We are delighted at the news that we are going to spend our summer vacation in Qingdao.</u>

b. We are delighted at the news.

You've told us the news.

<u>We are delighted at the news (that) you've told us.</u>

(1) Tony made a suggestion.

We should not stay up late every day.

_____

(2) Here comes the news.

Some American students will come to our university.

_____

(3) The suggestion is very good.

She put it forward at the meeting.

_____

(4) She was sad at the news.

Her husband had been killed in an accident.

_____

(5) I agreed with their decision.

They made it last night.

_____

Skills Development and Practice

Reading Skills

Guessing Unknown Words (2)
Using Contextual Clues
利用上下文

Practice 1: Another effective way to determine the meaning of a word is using contextual clues. The language before or after the word you may not know often gives you enough hint as to the meaning of the new word. Look at the examples.

EXAMPLES:

1. He works as a *dustman* and cleans the street every day.

2. He is a *resolute* man. Once he sets up a goal, he won't give it up halfway.

3. All the other members are of the same opinion. They are *unanimous*.

4. You may borrow from the library any *periodicals*: Nature, New Society, News Week, or The Listener.

5. We don't like that man. He is as *sly* as a fox.

6. Most of them agreed; however, John *dissented*.

QUESTIONS:

1. Are the italicized words above new to you?

2. Read each sentence above again and pay more attention to the context. Write down the possible meaning of each word in the space given below.

(1) dustman: _____   (2) resolute: _____

(3) unanimous: _____   (4) periodicals: _____

(5) sly: _____   (6) dissented: _____

Practice 2: Use contextual clues to guess the meaning of the italicized word in each of the sentences.

1. We decide to *persevere* rather than give up.

2. We will meet you in the *foyer*, the entrance hall of the theatre.

3. What he said was just *flattery*, for he praised me so much that I am sure he did not mean what he said.

4. Unlike his sister, who is a warm, interested person, John is *apathetic* to everyone and everything.

5. The social sciences have always been my *forte* but foreign languages remain my weakness.

6. The people really enjoy gathering in the *plaza*, which is much like a public square, to talk freely with each other.

7. How can you *extol*, or praise, such work?

8. Return the money of your own *volition* rather than be forced to hand it over.

Translation Practice

Translation Skills

轉譯詞類：英語形容詞可轉譯成漢語的動詞或名詞。

Practice 3: Translate the sentences into Chinese, paying attention to the italicized words.

1. Every time you meet someone in a social situation, give him your *undivided* attention for four minutes.

_____

2. In most cases, countries do not trade *the actual goods* and services.

_____

3. He didn't succeed in ringing her up, for he dialled the *wrong* number.

_____

4. The man is *difficult* to deal with.

_____

5. I'm *sure* the meeting will be a success.

_____

6. It will be *good* for you to eat more fruits and vegetables.

_____

Practice 4: Translate the sentences into Chinese.

1. We can become accustomed to any changes we choose to make in our personality.

_____

2. He keeps looking over the other person's shoulder, as if hoping to find some one more interesting in another part of the room.

_____

3. There is a time for everything, and a certain amount of paly-acting may be best for the first minutes of contact with strangers.

_____

4. The author declares that interpersonal relations should be taught as a required course in every school, along with reading, writing, and mathematics.

5. In Great Britain today, good manners at table include eating with the mouth closed; not letting any of the food fall off the plate; using the knife only for cutting; and not trying to take food across the table.

_____

6. I have nothing to say until I see my lawyer.

_____

Practice 5: Translate the sentences into English with the words or expressions given.

1. 安全行車的規則對每個人都適用。(apply to)

_____

2. 祖寧博士建議我們多交些新朋友。(suggest)

_____

3. 英國人習慣於靠左邊開車。(be accustomed)

_____

4. 她盯著那姑娘看，好像是第一次見到她似的。(as if)

_____

5. 這兩兄弟看上去一模一樣。(the same as)

_____

6. 那場雨使得我們不能去打網球了。(prevent)

_____

Practical Translation

語篇層次的翻譯——銜接

　　語篇（discourse）是在交際功能上相對完整和獨立的一個語言片斷。為了進行有效的交際活動，語篇應銜接（cohesion）得當，連貫性（coherence）好。銜接手段（cohesive device）是一種謀篇手段，是生成語篇的重要條件之一，也是譯者在翻譯過程中首先要考慮的問題，因為它直接關係到譯文的質量。銜接自然的譯文讀起來通順、流暢、連貫；缺乏銜接或銜接不當的譯文晦澀難懂，影響閱讀，也影響交際功能的實現。

　　英語和漢語分屬不同的體系：英語屬於印歐語系（Indo-European Family），漢語屬於漢藏語系（Sino-Tibetan Family）。它們在許多方面都有各自的規律和特點。從語篇層面上說，需要強調英漢兩種語言在形合（hypotaxis）和意合（parataxis）方面的差異。由於英漢兩種語言邏輯思維的不同，英語重「形合」，句子內部的連接或句子間的連接採用顯性的語言手段來實現，主要是通過各種語法手

段和詞彙手段,以表示其結構和邏輯關係。因此,英語中長句多。漢語重「意合」,句中各成分之間或句子之間的結合少用甚至不用形式銜接手段,主要靠句子內部的隱性邏輯聯繫,注重邏輯事理的順序以及意義和主旨上的銜接和連貫。因此,漢語中短句多,短句間的邏輯關係靠意義來表達,語法處於次要地位。在翻譯過程中,要牢記英漢兩種語言在形合和意合上的差別,注意形合和意合之間的轉換和調整。

例1: I had so worked upon my imagination as really to believe that about the whole mansion and domain there hung an atmosphere peculiar to themselves and their immediate vicinity—an atmosphere which had no affinity with the air of heaven, but which had reeked up from the decayed trees, and the grey wall, and the silent tam—a pestilent and mystic vapor, dull, sluggish, faintly discernible, and leaden-hued. (Edgar Allan Poe:「The Fall of the House of Usher」)

譯文:我如此沉湎於自己的想像,以至於我實實在在地認為那宅院及其周圍懸浮著一種它們所特有的空氣。那種空氣並非生發於天地自然,而是生發於那些枯樹殘枝、灰牆暗壁,生發於那一汪死氣沉沉的湖水。那是一種神祕而致命的霧靄,陰晦,凝滯,朦朧,沉濁如鉛。(曹明倫譯)

解析:這個例句選自美國作家愛倫·坡的小說名篇《厄舍府之倒塌》。整段話其實只有一個完整的句子,共70個字,它不僅通過多個消極、晦澀、陰暗的形容詞,如: decayed, grey, silent, pestilent, mystic, dull, sluggish, leaden-hued 來營造一種淒涼、蕭瑟的自然氛圍和壓抑、沉悶的心理氣氛,而且通過一個典型「形合」的長句來烘托這種乏味、陰晦的自然氛圍和心理氣氛。這個「形合」長句主要採用各種語法手段(如並列句、狀語從句、同位語從句、定語從句)以及詞彙手段(如詞彙 atmosphere 的重複)等來表示其結構關係,並進行有機的銜接。在翻譯過程中,原語中「顯性的語法和詞彙手段」不能完全照搬到目標語中,也就是說,不能用帶有各種成分的長句來處理這個句子,否則整個漢語句子就會顯得拖沓、冗長。因此在正確理解原文內容、弄清原文內在結構的基礎上,用三個分句來處理這個長句。分句之間雖然也運用了一定的詞彙和語法手段,如重複「空氣」一詞和運用並列結構「生發於……,生發於……」,分句之間的銜接主要還是靠意義和邏輯關係的連接,先是講我想像的內容,然後講想像內容——「空氣」和周圍環境的關係,最後講這種空氣的實質。三個分句環環相扣,層層展開,如果缺少了分句中意義和邏輯關係的銜接,整個句子就無法成為一個有機而連貫的漢語句子。

例2: She had a very thin face like the dial of a small clock seen faintly in a dark room in the middle of a night when you waken to see the time and see the clock telling you the hour and the minute and the second, with a white silence and a glowing, all certainty and knowing what it has to tell of the night passing swiftly on toward further darkness but moving also toward a new sun. (Ray Douglas Bradbury: *Fahrenheit 451*)

譯文：（她的）容貌那麼清秀，就像半夜裡醒來時在黑暗中隱約可見的小小的鐘面，報告時刻的鐘面。它皎潔而安靜，深知時間在飛馳，深信黑暗雖然越來越深沉，卻也越來越接近新生的太陽。（苗懷新譯）

解析：這個例句選自美國作家布拉德伯利的著名的反烏托邦小說《華氏451度》。整段話共80個字，是一個完整而典型的「形合」句，主要是採用各種語法手段（如被動句、定語從句、賓語從句、並列句）以及運用修辭手法來進行有機的銜接，使原文一氣呵成。在翻譯過程中，正確理解原文內容、理清原文內在結構，原語中「顯性的語法和詞彙手段」，除了兩組重複的詞（「鐘面」「深知」和「深信」）以及前後指代（「鐘面」和「它」）外，大部分都被隱去，取而代之的是漢語中意義和邏輯上的銜接和連貫。譯文充分利用漢語的短句形式，按照原文的邏輯順序，把整個句子切分成兩個單句、七個部分。每個部分間層層相連，環環相扣，讀起來如同有讀原文那種一氣呵成的感覺。如果脫離了漢語句子間意義和邏輯的銜接，整個句子將支離破碎，讀起來拗口、別扭。

Translation Practice

1. I've been spared a lot, one of the blessed of the earth, at least one of its lucky, that privileged handful of the dramatically prospering, the sort whose secrets are asked, like the hundred-year-old man.

2. And so Franklin Roosevelt found that he had, in effect, to recruit an entirely new and temporary government to be piled on top of the old one, the new government to get the tanks and airplanes built, the uniforms made, the men and women assembled and trained and shipped abroad, and the battles fought and won.

Focused Writing

Abstracts

An academic abstract tells a reader what is in a paper or research report. It is normal for all academic papers that are published to have an abstract and it is usually placed at the beginning of the paper—on the second page after the title page.

The purpose of an academic abstract is to identify the focus of the paper or research and to tell potential readers what will be covered in the full text. A well-prepared abstract should enable the reader to identify the content of the text quickly and accurately, and to determine its relevance to their interests.

An abstract should be understandable by itself. It is a brief statement of purpose and scope, thesis, relevant theory and the methodology used in the research. It does not provide detailed results, conclusions, or recommendations. An abstract is usually no more than 250 words.

Note: Some people refer to a summary as an informative abstract. As can be seen in Unit 3, a summary gives the reader an overview of the main points in a text. An informative abstract is rarely longer than one page and should never exceed more than 10% of the length of the original paper; otherwise it defeats its own purpose.

An academic abstract, on the other hand, usually includes many but not necessarily all the following points:

(1) Motivation

Why do we care about the problem and the results? What is the motivation for the research or report? If the report is about one aspect of a larger piece of work this needs to be made clear. This section may also include the importance of your work, any difficulty encountered, and/or the impact it might have if successful.

(2) Problem statement

What problem are you trying to solve? What is the scope of your work (a generalized approach, or for a specific situation)? What is your thesis, what you are proving? Be careful not to use inappropriate jargon unless it will be understood by intended readers.

Note: In some cases it is appropriate to put the problem statement before the motivation, but usually this only works if readers would already understand why the problem is important.

(3) Approach/Methodology/Theoretical Basis

How did you go about solving or making progress on the problem? Did you use simulation, analytical models, prototypes, surveys or quantitative or qualitative analysis of field data? What was the extent of your work? What important variables did you control, ignore, or measure? What, if any, established theoretical works underpinned your research?

(4) Results

What's the answer? Indicate briefly what your results are and what they no room for details, these are in the full report or in appendices.

(5) Conclusion

What are the implications of your results? Is it going to change the world (unlikely), be a significant 「win」, be a nice 「hack」, or simply serve as a road sign indicating that this path is a waste of time. Are your results general, potentially general, or specific to a particular case?

How can you write an effective abstract?

If you're writing an abstract about another person's article, paper, or report, the introduction and the summary are good places to begin. These sections should emphasize what the paper is about.

First, read the article, paper, or report with the goal of abstraction in mind. Look specifically for the main parts of the article, paper, or report: the purpose, methodology, scope, results, conclusions, and recommendations.

Don't merely copy key sentences from the article, paper, or report: you'll put in too much information.

An academic abstract should be no longer than 250 words. If you can convey the essential details of the paper in 150 words, do not use 200.

Keep phrase such as 「this paper...」「this report...」「is described...」「is reported...」to a minimum. It is better to write about the research than about the paper!

There is no need to explain the sections or parts of the paper. 「In the introduction the writer says...」is unnecessary and wasteful of words.

If possible, avoid trade names, acronyms, abbreviations, or symbols. You would need to explain them, and that takes too much room.

Only refer in the abstract to information that is in the document and do not include your own or anyone else's opinion.

An abstract should be written in the third person: use passive verbs to downplay the author and emphasise the information.

The following are sample abstracts in different disciplines. As you read, pay attention to the structure of the abstract.

Sample 1 (Literature)

> Djuna Barnes' experimental modernist novel, *Nightwood*, depicts characters who are variously drunken, bestial, and obscene. In the world of *Nightwood*, depravity is valued over the civilized as a means of accessing the past. This essay identifies three separate 「pasts」: the historical, the developmental, and the evolutionary, all in operation within the characters. The historical past refers to events taking place before the individuals' births but after the evolutionary shift from early animals to present-day humans, such as Felix's past as a Jew in Roman times. The developmental past concerns the early stages in individual life, primarily childhood. The evolutionary past refers to the pre-cultural period, which in *Nightwood* primarily concerns early humans as animals or beasts. The separate pasts are all repeatedly described as degenerate, violent and primitive. The characters that embrace depravity, such as Doctor O'Connor and Robin, are embracing the nature of their historical, evolutionary, and developmental past. Once they recognize where they have come from, they attain a sense of their current position, as well as an ability to simultaneously exist in previous times.

Sample 2 (Social Science)

> This study opens up a discussion of the feminist ethics of Asian Pacific Islander (API) women who are involved in the battered women's movement, based on their occupation within domestic violence agencies. Additionally, there is an examination of the manner in which these ethics are reflected in each respective organizational structure. Central to the research is the understanding that feminist organizational qualities are not simply limited to [collectivism versus bureaucracy]. In not limiting the scope of analysis, the recognition that feminism as an identity is a malleable and varied construct is integrated. The research is based upon in-depth interviews with four women from three domestic violence shelters in the Los Angeles County. As can be concluded from the sample, the API battered women's movement is characterized by fluid factors such as personalities, time commitment, and a general desire to address the problem of domestic violence rather than an unequivocal commitment to any well-defined political philosophy. Also, within the shelters there evidently has not been a transformation from a principally collectivist grassroots structure toward a bureaucratic practice. Rather, a complement of collectivist and bureaucratic approaches effectively responds to changing internal and external dynamics.

Writing Assignment

Write an abstract for a research paper you are writing or have written or of someone else's paper.

Unit 5　Health

Warming-ups

Task 1　Questions for Thought

Think about the following questions, then discuss with your partner.
1. What do you think of the relation between health and living habits?
2. What will you usually do, if you don't feel very well?
3. Do you know how to promote your health?

Task 2　Vocabulary Preview

Complete the following table by writing the English or Chinese equivalents of the words given. Then, check your answers with your partner.

针灸		injection	
手术		aerobics	
中草药		jogging	
急症		yoga	
失眠		symptom	
胃口		stress	

In-class Activities

Task 1　Individual Work

Read the following sentences. Which might you think are good living habits? Tick the items you choose.

Living Habits	Yes	No
Go to sleep early and get up early. Have dinners on time.		
Never get up before 11 am and never have breakfast.		

表(續)

Living Habits	Yes	No
Do some physical exercises regularly.		
Spend most of the time in front of computer or TV.		
Have enough fresh fruits and vegetables every day.		
Drink ten cans of Coca Cola and smoke a pack of cigarettes each day.		
Keep a delightful mood and have positive attitude towards everyday life.		
Always complain about the low wages but never try to make a change.		
Go to doctors if he/she doesn't feel good.		
Have some pills by themselves and never goes to hospitals.		

Task 2　Pair/Group Work

Discuss the following questions.

1. What's the relation between sports and health?

2. How to keep a healthy body?

3. What are the differences between the Chinese medicine treatment and Western medicine treatment?

4. Which one do you prefer? why?

Task 3　Role-play

Read the following dialogue first, and then act it out with your partner.

Each of you should assume a role, and then switch the role.

(Situation: Susan doesn't feel very well recently, so she goes to a clinic for a check.)

Dr. Lee: Come in, please. I'm Dr. Lee.

Susan: I'm Susan. Nice to meet you, Dr. Lee.

Dr. Lee: Nice to meet you, too. Have a seat, please. What seems to be the problem?

Susan: I can't fall asleep and I don't seem to have as much energy.

Dr. Lee: How's your appetite?

Susan: I can't say it's good. Sometimes, my favorite food loses its appeal to me.

Dr. Lee: I see. (after checking the patient) Everything seems to be OK. Any other symptoms?

Susan: No, nothing I can think of. Oh, yeah, sometimes, I feel very tired.

Dr. Lee: OK. And how long have you been like this?

Susan: Well over three months.

Dr. Lee: And how's your work?

Susan: My work? Well, I just changed my job, and this new job keeps me busy all the time.

Dr. Lee: Does this new job give you much pressure as well?

Susan: Yes, you see it's totally new to me, and I have to learn it from ABC.

Dr. Lee: OK. I think you need to relax a bit. Your health's more important that your job.

Susan: I think so. Thank you, Doctor.

Task 4 Debate/Discussion

Everyone knows that smoking is harmful, but there are still lots of people smoking out there. What is your viewpoint? Why?

A: Work in groups and make discussion with your peers.

Argument 1: Smoking should be prohibited. The World Health Organization points out that diseases linked to smoking kill at least three million people each year, one every six seconds.

Your opinion:

Argument 2: Smoking should not be prohibited, for cigarettes give many people a good deal of pleasure much of the time.

Your opinion:

B: After discussing, summarize all the opinions and make an oral speech on:

Smoking and Health

The following might be useful and helpful in the speech:

Words and Expressions:

risk; lung cancer; heart attacks; sore throats; headaches; chronic bronchitis (慢性支氣管炎); pulmonary emphysema (肺氣腫); set up bad examples; non-smokers; indoor and outdoor environment; pleasure; relaxation; inspiration; backbone of economy; increase the revenue

Reference Modal:

In my opinion, smoking should be prohibited. Because scientific research has shown that the risk of developing lung cancer increases with smoking and it's the cause of many other diseases like... Smoking is an expensive habit, for a smoker who consumes a package a day will spend much money every month. And... So I think smoking should be prohibited.

Reading Passages

Passage A

Dieting Your Way to Health

Almost everyone considers going on a diet sometime in his or her life. All, regardless of sex and age, have something in common—losing weight and losing it fast.

Though their common aim may seem basically good, they probably do not realize that misguided dieting can do more harm than good to their health. Going on too strict a diet can destroy the balance of chemicals in the human body. This happens because when the body is suddenly given much less food than usual, it feels as though it is being attacked and tries hard to protect itself by saving energy. It does this by slowing down metabolism, the process by which the food we eat is converted into energy. As energy is supplied to the body at a slower and slower rate, dieters gradually become so weak that they can do nothing. They soon lose interest in everything going on about them, and their resistance to illness becomes so low that they are easily attacked by one illness after another.

Most of those who diet know that foods like rice, bread, potatoes, cakes, sweets, fruits and some vegetables contain carbohydrates, and so can make one fat. What they do not realize, however, is that carbohydrates are our bodies' main source of energy, and that these foods also contain components essential for the composition of substances that are needed to keep the body healthy. As a result, they try to avoid eating these foods and consequently, they become weaker and less healthy. They begin to have difficulty sleeping properly and start to suffer from radical mood changes. In more serious cases, they even begin to show signs of mental illness.

It is strange enough that most strict diets recommend artificial sweeteners to take the place of sugar and other natural sweeteners. In fact, such artificial sweeteners actually increase one's appetite and lead to one's eating even more than usual.

Of course, the fact that misguided forms of dieting result in so many problems does not mean that no dieting is safe or all dieting is harmful to the health. Proper dieting can not only help a person lose ugly excess fat, but can also help him or her to keep it off and to lead a more active, happier and healthier life.

A proper healthy diet is one that includes enough but not too many of the kinds of foods that provide the body with the nutrients that it needs to function properly. The most important of these nutrients are proteins, carbohydrates and fats. The body needs fairly large amounts of proteins and carbohydrates for building material and energy. Meat, fish, eggs, milk, cream, and nuts all contain proteins and foods like rice, bread, potatoes, etc. contain carbohydrates. The body needs fat to keep it from the cold and to provide a protective layer for the organs, but only in small quantities.

Vitamins and minerals such as iron, calcium, are another group of essential nutrients. Water-soluble vitamins like vitamin C and the B-group vitamins do not stay in the body long and so foods containing these vitamins need to be taken rather often. On the other hand, the fat-soluble vitamins, vitamins A, D, E and K stay in the body for long periods of time and so there is no need to take foods containing them so often.

One way of getting enough nutrients while keeping one's weight down is to take substitutes for foods which contain too much fat. For example, instead of regular milk, one can take skimmed milk. In the same way, vegetable oil can be used for cooking instead of animal oil.

Words and Expressions

1. appetite *n.* 食欲, 胃口; 慾望
2. artificial *adj.* 人工的, 人造的
3. balance *n.* 平衡, 均衡認使平衡, 權衡
4. calcium *n.* 鈣 (化學符號 Ca)
5. carbohydrate *n.* (化) 碳水化合物, 糖類
6. chemical *n.* 化學物質
7. component *n.* 組成部分
8. diet *n.* 飲食; (出於健康考慮) 飲食限制, 規定飲食 *v.* 節食
9. dieter *n.* 節食者
10. essential *adj.* 基本的
11. excess *adj.* (only before noun) 過量的, 過分的
12. gradually *adv.* 逐漸地, 逐步地
13. harmful *adj.* 有害的
14. layer *n.* 層, 層次
15. metabolism *n.* (生理) 新陳代謝 (作用)
16. mineral *n.* 礦物, 礦石以力, 礦物 (質) 的
17. misguided *adj.* (想法或行為) 錯誤的
18. mood *n.* 心情, 情緒
19. nutrient *n.* 營養物, 營養品
20. organ *n.* 器官
21. protective *adj.* (usually before noun) 給予保護的, 防護的

22. radical *adj.* 根本的，基本的；急遽的，大幅度的

23. recommend *v.* 推薦，介紹；勸告，建議

24. resistance *n.* 抵抗，抵制；抵抗力

25. skim *v.* 撇去（液體面上的浮物）；瀏覽，略讀

26. soluble *adj.* 可溶解的

27. source *n.* 來源，出處

28. strict *adj.* 嚴格的，嚴厲的；嚴謹的，精確的

29. sweetener *n.* 甜味劑，甜料

30. vitamin *n.* 維生素

31. as a result 作為結果，因此

32. be harmful to 對……有害

33. convert... into 使……轉換成……，使……轉變成……

34. go on a diet 節食

35. have... in common（with sb./sth.）與……有共同點

36. lose weight 減輕體重

37. regardless of 不顧，不管

38. result in 結果是，導致，結果造成

39. slow down （使）慢下來，（使）緩行

40. take the place of 取代……

Content Awareness

Circle the best answer according to the passage.

(1) What is the passage mainly about?

A. How to keep healthy while keeping one's weight down.

B. How to slow down metabolism.

C. How to resist illness.

D. How to get enough vitamins and minerals.

(2) How many types of vitamins are there?

A. One.   B. Two.

C. Three.   D. Four.

(3) Proper dieting has all the advantages EXCEPT _____.

A. helping a person lose ugly excess fat

B. helping a person to keep fat off

C. helping a person to lead a more active, happier and healthier life

D. helping a person gain weight

(4) The most important nutrients the body needs to function properly are _____.

A. proteins, carbohydrates and minerals

B. proteins, fats and vitamins

C. proteins, carbohydrates and fats

D. carbohydrates, fats and vitamins

(5) Which of the following is the body's main source of energy?

A. Vitamins. B. Carbohydrates.

C. Minerals. D. Fats.

Language Focus

1. Fill in the blanks with words or phrases from the passage. Don't refer back to it until you have finished.

A proper healthy (1) d _____ is one that includes enough but not too many of the kinds of foods that (2) p _____ the body with the nutrients that it needs to (3) f _____ properly. The most important of these (4) n _____ are proteins, carbohydrates and fats. The body needs fairly large amounts of (5) p _____ and carbohydrates for building material and (6) e _____. Meat, fish, eggs, milk, cream, and nuts all (7) c _____ proteins and foods like rice, bread, potatoes, etc. contain carbohydrates. The body needs (8) f _____ to keep it from the (9) c _____ and to provide a protective layer (10) f _____ the organs, but only in small quantities.

2. Translate the following into English.

(1) 與……有共同之處_____

(2) 進行太嚴格的節食_____

(3) 減緩新陳代謝_____

(4) 對身體有害_____

(5) 過著更幸福健康的生活_____

(6) 飲用脫脂奶_____

(7) 為……提供保護層_____

(8) 為身體提供營養_____

(9) 減輕體重_____

(10) 對……失去興趣_____

3. Fill in the blanks with the words given below. Change the form where necessary.

diet   harmful   skim   mood   recommend

strict   artificial   appetite   essential   gradually

(1) Poor _____ can affect the unborn baby.

(2) Light is _____ for the healthy development of plants.

(3) The fungus（真菌） is not _____ to humans.

(4) She _____ built up a reputation as a successful lawyer.

(5) The beautiful sunny morning put him in a happy _____.

(6) They are very _____ with their children.

(7) I _____ that you buy a more powerful computer.

(8) _____ the fat off the soup.

(9) The symptoms（症狀） include fever and loss of _____.

(10) She laughed a bright _____ laugh.

4. Complete the following sentences with appropriate expressions given below. Change the form where necessary.

(1) We will continue the race, _____ the weather.

(2) This area obviously _____ a lot _____ with other inner-city areas（內城區）.

(3) _____! You are driving too fast.

(4) They _____ the old school _____ luxury flats（豪華公寓）.

(5) She _____ depression（抑鬱症） for most of her adult life.

(6) DVD systems are rapidly _____ videos（錄像機）.

(7) Tom will be playing _____ me on Saturday.

(8) There is no doubt that stress can _____ physical illness.

(9) It rained heavily this morning. _____, I was late for school.

(10) These worries _____ her _____ sleeping properly.

5. Translate the following sentences into English.

(1) 這次事故導致14名乘客死亡。(result in)

_____

(2) 我們有那麼多共同點。(have... in common)

_____

(3) 我們可以現在就處理這個事情，而不是等到明天。(instead of)

_____

(4) 我越來越胖了，我得節食了。(go on a diet)

_____

(5) 他很快就對周圍發生的一切不感興趣了。(lose interest in)

_____

Passage B

What Is Safe to Eat?

Butter is bad for you—but so is margarine. Coffee raises blood pressure, but may protect against cancer. Alcohol is okay, but only if it's wine.

The confusing studies on what it is safe to eat and drink are enough to make it impossible for anyone to understand what is 「good food」.

Take the margarine – butter debate for example. Studies that linked fat—found mostly in animal products such as meat and butter—with cancer and heart disease sent millions rushing to buy margarine. But then another study found that people who ate a lot of margarine also had high levels of heart disease. For those who have a firm faith in science, this seems to be the end of the world.

But many doctors point out that their advice has never been conflicting. For many years, and in various countries, they have recommended eating less fat.

People in Western countries such as Britain and the United States get about 40 percent of their calories from fat. Doctors say this should be around 30 or even 25 percent.

「We must try to reduce total fat,」said Dr. Robert Richardson of the University of Edinburgh, who has been studying the effects of fat on human health for years.

「We need to go to more such food as bread, in particular brown bread, and more fruit and vegetables.」

Fresh produce may not be so safe, either. Last month the British Government advised consumers to peel their pears before eating, while many Americans briefly avoided apples because of fears over an insect killing chemical.

But Dr. Arnold, a British scientist, said any risk of such poisoning would be outweighed by the costs of nor eating plant foods.

「On balance, if you were to put both risks against each other, the advice has to be eating as much fruit and vegetable daily as possible.」she said.

In general, doctors conclude, variety truly is the best policy.「The general advice is pretty much the same advice that doctors have been talking about for a long time—a varied diet, a mixture of foods and not much of any one.」Arnold said.

Words and Expressions

1. butter *n.* 黃油，奶油
2. margarine *n.* 人造黃油
3. protect *v.* 保護，防護

4. confusing *adj.* 令人困惑的

5. debate *n.* 辯論，爭論，討論

6. link *v.* 聯繫

7. disease *n.* 疾病

8. faith *n.* 信心

9. conflicting *adj.* 衝突的，抵觸的

10. various *adj.* 不同的，各種各樣的

11. calorie *n.* （熱量單位）卡（路里）

12. reduce *v.* 減少，降低

13. produce *n.* （水果、蔬菜等）農產品

14. peel *v.* 削（或剝）去……的皮

15. pear *n.* 梨

16. fear *n.* 害怕，恐懼

17. insect *n.* 昆蟲，蟲

18. chemical *n.* 化學藥品

19. outweigh *v.* 在重要性方面超過

20. conclude *v.* 推斷出，推論出

21. mixture *n.* 混合

22. on balance　總的來說

23. in general　一般來說，大體上

Content Awareness

1. Choose the answer that best completes each sentence or answers each question.

（1）What do the confusing studies tell us?

A. Both butter and margarine may lead to cancer and heart disease.

B. Coffee is better than other drinks.

C. Only wine does good to your health.

D. Foods may have different effects.

（2）The British Government advised consumers to peel their pears before eating because ＿＿＿＿＿.

A. it found that there were insects on the pears

B. it wanted consumers to avoid insect killing chemicals

C. the skin of pears was found to be bad for people's health

D. it was a bad habit not to peel them

（3）The word「outweigh」in Paragraph Nine means「＿＿＿＿＿」.

A. to be heavier than is usual or allowed

B. to be more dangerous than

C. to be greater in value or importance than

D. to be considered less important than

(4) What can we infer from the passage?

A. The studies are somewhat conflicting.

B. Science provides answers to all our questions.

C. We should peel our pears before eating.

D. We should eat plant foods despite the risk of poisoning.

(5) What should we do in order to keep a balance diet?

A. We should have a variety of foods.

B. We should eat less butter.

C. We should eat as much fruit and vegetable daily as possible.

D. We should eat such food as bread, in particular brown bread.

2. Fill in the blanks with appropriate words according to the above reading passage.

To some people, the results of scientific studies may seem _____. For example, we were told by doctors that fat is _____ with cancer and heart disease. This sent _____ of people rushing to buy margarine. But some other studies showed that margarine could also _____ to heart disease. Actually, doctors _____ out that their advice has never been conflicting. For many years and in many countries they have _____ eating less fat. At the same time, people are advised to have as much bread, _____ and vegetable as _____. The most important _____ is to have a varied diet, that is, to eat a _____ of foods but not too much of any of them.

3. Complete the following table and fill in each blank with no more than 3 words.

	Food and Our Diet
Butter	Reason to have it: We get _____ from it. Reason not to have it: It may lead to cancer and _____.
Coffee	Reason to have it: It may _____ cancer. Reason not to have it: It may raise _____.
Fresh Food	Reason to have it: We need it. Reason not to have it: We have to avoid _____.
Advice	(1) We should _____ total fat. (2) We'd better eat as much _____ and _____ daily as _____. (3) We should have a _____, that is, a _____ of foods and not too much of any of them.

Unit 5 Health

Language Focus

1. Fill in the blanks with appropriate words or expressions, with at least one from passage B.

(1) A person's appearance: thin, slight, _____, _____, etc.
(2) Profession: professor, scientist, _____, _____, etc.
(3) Fruit: banana, peach, _____, _____, _____, etc.
(4) Food: meat, rice, _____, _____, _____, etc.
(5) Disease or illness: headache, SARS, _____, _____, etc.

2. Match each word with its definition in column B.

A   B

a. margarine   _____ a strong belief
b. chemical   _____ a substance used in chemistry
c. faith   _____ difficult to understand because of unclear order or pattern
d. fear   _____ considered in terms of a whole situation, group, etc.
e. confusing   _____ keep someone or something sage from harm or damage
f. various   _____ remove the skin from fruit or vegetables
g. safe   _____ an unpleasant feeling of being frightened or worried
h. general   _____ a yellow substance that is similar to butter
i. peel   _____ several; different
j. conclude   _____ not likely to cause any physical injury or harm
k. outweigh   _____ decide after considering all the information
l. protect   _____ be more important or valuable than something else

3. Complete the sentences with appropriate words in their correct form.

debate   debate   debatable

(1) The chairman's point is highly _____.
(2) So far there has been a _____ on the punishment for criminals.
(3) We _____ for several hours before taking a vote.

conclude   conclusion   conclusive

(1) The investigation failed to give any _____ evidence.
(2) The enquiry _____ that the accident had been caused by poor management.
(3) He came to a _____ that he should take no responsibility for the accident.

press   press   pressure   pressure

(1) At the _____ conference held after the game, the football coach apologized to the fans for his team's poor performance.

(2) The _____ of the water caused the wall to break.

(3) The little girl _____ her nose against the window.

(4) She was _____ into agreeing with her parents.

confuse   confused   confusing   confusion

(1) My mother's unexpected arrival threw us into complete _____.

(2) The instructions on the machine are very _____.

(3) Your change of the plan has made us totally _____.

(4) The interviewer _____ me by asking so many questions.

recommend   recommendable   recommendation

(1) The professor wrote a letter of _____ for his student.

(2) Quanjude is s highly _____ restaurant in Beijing. The roast duck there is delicious.

(3) Can you _____ me a good novel?

Skills Development and Practice

Reading Skills

Making Use of Contents and Index

Practice 1: These are the contents of two books Modern Britain: An Introduction and Life in Modern Britain. Read them very quickly. Answer the questions which follow.

Modern Britain: An Introduction

	Contents	
Preface		5
1	Introduction to Britain	9
2	The System of Government in Britain	14
3	Local Government	56
4	The Legal System	61
5	The Welfare State	76
6	Education	89
7	The Industrial State	114
8	Life in Britain Today	128
9	The Mass Media	145
10	Religious Life	154
Glossary		161
Bibliography		167
Index		171

Life in Modern Britain

Contents

Chapter 1	The Country and the People	1
Chapter 2	Government and Politics	15
1	The Queen and the Constitution	15
2	The Government	18
3	The Civil Service	21
4	Elections	24
5	The Conservative and Labour Parties	30
6	The Working of the House of Commons	32
7	The Parliamentary Day	38
8	How Laws are Passed	43
9	Control of Government Expenditure, Taxation and Administration	47
10	The Future of British Politics	49
Chapter 3	The House of Lords	53
1	Will the House of Lords Survive?	53
2	Titles and Honours	57
Chapter 4	Local Government	61
1	The Permanent Principles	61
2	The Reforms in London, 1965—1984	63
3	Local Government outside London	64
4	Ordinary Counties	66
5	The Working of Local Government	67
Chapter 5	Law, the Courts and the Police	73
1	The Courts and Their Judicial Officers	74
2	Crime and Punishment	78
3	The Legal Profession	80
4	The Police	82
Chapter 6	Work and Money	87
1	The Structure of Trade and Industry	87
2	Taxes, Incomes and the Standard of Living	90

Contents

3	Trade Unions	93
4	The Changing Structureof Work	96
Chapter 7	Leisure and Private Life	101
1	Holidays	101
2	Sport	102
3	Theatre and Cinema	107
4	Other Recreations	109
5	Marriage, Home and Family	113
Chapter 8	Houses, Cars and Public Transport	119
1	Housing	119
2	Cars and Roads	124
3	Public Transport	125
Chapter 9	The Welfare State	131
1	Social Security	131
2	The Health Service	134
3	The Social Services	139
Chapter 10	Schools and Universities	143
1	The Educational System	143
2	State Education	146
3	Independent Schools	151
4	Some Educational Problems	155
5	The Universities	157
Chapter 11	Religion	169
Chapter 12	The Press, Radio and Television	179
1	Daily and Sunday Papers	179
2	Local and Regional Papers	186
3	The Weekly and Periodical Press	187
4	Radio and Television	188
Chapter 13	Wales, Scotland and Ireland	195

表(續)

Contents	
1　The United Kingdom	195
2　Wales	196
3　Scotland	199
4　Ireland	204
Chapter 14　Britain and the World	211
1　The Commonwealth	211
2　Europe	214

QUESTIONS:

1. In which sections will you get something about the educational system in Britain?

_____

_____

2. Which sections are most likely to tell us something about newspapers in Britain?

_____

_____

Practice 2: This is a page from the index of the book Modern Britain: An Introduction. Use this to answer the questions that follow.

Index

Administrative Tribunals 69

Art Galleries 139

Arts Council 139

Assizes 63-64

Bank of England 114, 117, 121

Banks 120, 122

Barristers 70-71, 72

Beveridge Report 79

Bill (parliamentary) 22, 40-48, 51, 52, 161

Bingo 140

Birth Rate 129

Bishops 50, 155

Borough 56-59

Boundary Commission 29

British Broadcasting Corporation (BBC) 150-152

British Rail 118
Building Societies 85–86, 162
Comprehensive Schools 94, 99–100
Conciliation and Arbitration Service 127
Confederation of British Industry (CBI) 127, 142
Conservative (Party) 18, 24–27, 31–5, 36, 50, 52, 54, 57, 94–95, 99, 116, 117, 119, 126, 133, 143
Constituency 29–31, 34, 52, 162
Coroners Courts 69
Council Houses 87, 162
Councillors 59
Counties 56–58
County Courts 67
Courts Act (1971) 61
Criminal Courts 61–67
Crown 14–21, 23, 39, 46, 151, 157
Crown Courts 63–64, 67
Crown Estates 19–20, 157
Common Market, see EEC
Commonwealth Immigrants 132–133
Communist Party 27, 149
Cabinet 35–37, 40
Cabinet Ministers 21, 54
Canterbury, Archbishop of 156
Canvassing 31, 162
Central Council on University Admissions 113
Certificate of Secondary Education (CSE) 98
Channel Islands 11, 22
Chief Whips 43
Church of England 30, 49, 50, 90, 96, 154–158, 161
Church of Scotland 158–159
Cinemas 139–140
City (of London) 114, 115, 121–124, 162
Civil Courts 67–69
Civil List 19–20, 162
Colleges of Education 103, 111

Colleges of Further Education 113

Death Rate 129

Department of Education and Science
(DES) 95, 112

Director of Public Prosecutions 65

District Councils 58

Divorce 129-130

Doctors 81-83

Economic Development Committees
(EDCs) 121

Education Act (1870) 90; (1902) 91, 94
(1918) 91, 94; (1944) 91, 93, 95

Elections 23-24, 28-35, 44

Eleven Plus 92-93

England 1-1, 56, 61, 91

Entertainment 134-40

Equal Pay Act (1970) 132, 142

European Economic Community
(EEC) 13, 23, 37, 53, 116

Fabian Society 26, 163

Family Allowances 79, 80

Family Life 129-131

1. Where in the book (on which pages) would you expected to find the account of the following topics?

  a. British Doctors   b. Building Societies
  c. British Family Life   d. England

2. Which of the following topics does the author deal with at length (詳細地), and which seem to be covered briefly?

  a. Education Act   b. Birth Rate
  c. British Rail   d. Conservative Party

Translation Practice

Translation Skills

轉譯詞類：英語副詞可轉譯成漢語的名詞、動詞或形容詞。

Practice 3: Translate the sentences into Chinese, paying attention to the italicized words.

1. Specialization also enables one country to produce some goods more *cheaply* than another country.

_____

2. I love having Fridays *off*.

_____

3. How long will she be *away*?

_____

4. This is *where* you are wrong.

_____

5. I suppose boys think *differently* from girls.

_____

6. Sometimes we have had to pay *dearly* for mistakes.

_____

Practice 4: Translate the sentences into Chinese.

1. If we see a blind person getting off a bus, we watch to make sure that he is in no danger of falling. Members of a family help one another, with particular care for the very young and the elderly.

_____

_____

2. Organizations exist which try to make sure that someone sees when help is needed and does something about it.

_____

_____

3. There are library and shop trolleys to be taken round the wards and at Christmas time decorations to be put up and parties and concerts to be organized.

_____

_____

4. Some cities could not spread out because there was no room to do so. These cities, of which New York is the best example, became more and more crowded.

_____

_____

5. They are looking for unpolluted open spaces and for an independent way of life. They are ready to move from the suburbs to the country.

_____

_____

Practice 5: Translate the sentences into English with the words or expressions given.
1. 我要打電話問清楚會議是否晚上 7 點鐘開始。(make sure)

_____

2. 請幫我搬一下這只重箱子。(lend a hand)

_____

3. 很抱歉，我不能幫你的忙。(in a position to)

_____

4. 我們正在為解決空氣污染問題而努力。(solve)

_____

5. 由於城市太擁擠，許多人準備搬到鄉下去了。(be crowded)

_____

6. 我的秘書去休假時，格林小姐代替她工作了一星期。(take one's place)

_____

Practical Translation

語境與語篇的翻譯

　　語境（context）是指語言交際所涉及的不同環境，離開語境孤立地看語言，是無法準確地理解其真正含義的。語境大致可分為言內語境（linguistic context）和言外語境（non-linguistic context）兩大類。

　　所謂言內語境，就是指文章的上下文以及和語言本身相聯繫的各種因素。例如，volume 這個詞在「The volume of traffic on the roads has increased dramatically in recent years」中，是指「總量」，而在「The volume of the container measures 10,000 cubic meters」中，表示「體積，容積」。

　　言外語境是指語言本身之外的各種主、客觀環境，可分為情景語境和社會文化語境。情景語境指語言交際活動發生時的具體情景。例如，When did you call me last time? 這個句子根據說話人的身分或使用的場景不同，而有不同的解釋，可以表示簡單的詢問或者是抱怨太長時間沒有打電話了。而社會文化語境指交際者各自不同的經驗、經歷、知識、文化背景等。在翻譯中，應該考慮到社會文化差異，並做適當的調整。

　　例 1：The meeting was not hold due to the airline strike. It was held to discuss the impact an aging society would have on our environment.

　　譯文：不是因為航空公司罷工才舉行會議的。召開這個會議是為了討論老齡化社會對環境造成的影響。

　　解析：原文中，如果孤立地看第一句話，就會存在歧義。它可以理解成：①不是因為航空公司罷工才舉行會議的。②因為航空公司罷工，會議被取消了。

聯繫下文，根據言內語境，不難看出第一種理解才是正確的。

例2：There was nothing to do in Lohman the evening except to go to the saloon, an old board building with swinging doors and a wooden side walk awning. Neither prohibition nor repeal had changed its business, its clientele, or the quality of its whisky. In the course of an evening every male inhabitant of London over fifteen years old came at least once to the Buffalo Bar, had a drink, talked a while and went home.

There would be a game of the mildest kind of poker going on. Timothy Ratz, the husband of my landlady, would be playing solitaire, cheating pretty badly because he took a drink only when he got it out. I've seen him get out five minutes in a row. When he won he piled the cards neatly, stood up and walked with great dignity to the bar. Fat Carl, the owner and bartender, with a glass half filled before he arrived, asked, 「What'll it be?」

「Whisky,」said Timothy gravely.

譯文：在洛曼小鎮，晚飯後除了去鎮上唯一的那家酒館便無事可做。酒館是一座老式的木制建築，有一扇轉門，門前人行道上方有一塊木制雨篷。無論是政府的禁酒令還是後來廢除禁酒令的法令都未曾改變過它生意的興隆、顧客的數量，也未曾改變過它威士忌的質量。每天晚飯後，鎮上十五歲以上的男子至少要光顧布法羅酒館一次，喝杯酒，聊聊天，然後回家。

酒館裡常有人玩撲克牌，不過其輸贏聊勝於無。我那位房東太太的丈夫蒂莫西·羅茲就經常在那裡玩單人紙牌遊戲。他玩牌老愛作弊，因為他只在贏牌時才買上一杯酒喝。我曾見過他一口氣連贏五盤。贏牌後他便把紙牌整整齊齊地疊好，然後直起身，神氣十足地走向吧臺。酒館老板兼伙計胖子卡爾不等他走近吧臺便會端起已斟了半杯酒的酒杯問：「來杯什麼酒？」

「威士忌。」蒂莫西總是莊重地回答。（《中國翻譯》，2002年第2期）

解析：原文選自於1938年發表的美國著名作家約翰·斯坦貝克的小說《約翰尼·伯爾》。原文第一段的第二句中，prohibition雖然沒有首字母大寫，但是從作品反應的年代以及小說的上下文來看，prohibition應該指1920—1933年的美國禁酒。而repeal指repeal of the prohibition，即廢除禁酒令的法令。

第二段的最後一句話what'll it be，根據情景的不同，可以有很多不同的理解。不過，原文中該句出現的情景是：在酒館中，酒館老板兼伙計向贏錢後打算買一杯酒喝的客人詢問；並且下文中客人的回答是「威士忌」。據此，這句話的翻譯應該是：來杯什麼酒。

Translation Practice

Translate the following paragraph into Chinese.

I am a journalist, not a historian, and while this book is an effort to describe a moment in the past, it is less a work of history than of personal reminiscence and reflection. Essentially, it is an account of my own observations and experiences in wartime Washington, supplemented by material drawn from interviews and other sources. I have tried to create out of it all a portrait of the pain and struggle of a city and a government suddenly called upon to fight, and to lead other nations in fighting, the greatest war in history, but pathetically and sometimes hilariously unprepared to do so.

This is bound to be somewhere close to the last reporting from that period based on firsthand sources. One after another, with unsettling rapidity, those in positions of power and responsibility during World War II are passing from the scene. Several who agreed to recall and describe their experiences in the war years died before I could get to them.

I have not dealt here in any detail with the grand strategy of the war in Europe and the Pacific. Instead, I have tried to report mainly on what I saw and heard and learned in Washington during years now fading into a misty past, the wartime experience of a country two-thirds of whose people are now too young to remember any of it. The result is a sort of Our Town at war, the story of a city astonished and often confused to find itself at the center of a worldwide conflict without ever hearing a shot fired. A strange city, set up in the first place to be the center of government and, like government itself at that time, a city moving slowly and doing little.

Focused Writing

Resumes and CVs

What is a resume or CV?

A resume or a curriculum vitae (CV) is a document that honestly outlines and summarizes your qualifications, training, work experience, and interests. Prospective employers or admissions committee members will need to know your educational attainments, any work experience you already have and your skills, achievements and interests.

How is resume or CV organized?

A resume (U.S.) or a CV (U.K.) should be limited to one page if possible so that a potential employer can see at a glance who you are and what he or she can expect you to be able to do. Therefore, take time to lay out the page so that it looks tidy and is easy to read. You should tailor your resume or CV to fit the needs and expectations of each company and job position by ensuring the information you include is relevant. There is no point in making a lot of your ability to teach children how to play the flute if you are applying for a position as an accountant—though you should of course mention any abilities that you do have.

What is included in a resume or CV?

Generally speaking, a resume or CV should include any of the following information that is relevant.

Personal details at the top, such as name in bold type, address, contact numbers and, if the subject has one, an e-mail address.

Career objective (This is optional and is not always included in a CV.)

Education: Listing of academic degrees beginning with the degree in progress or most recently earned. Include: name of institution, city and state, degree type (B. A., B. S., M. A., etc.) and area of concentration, month and year degree was (will be) received. If you are an undergraduate and your GPA is 3.5 or higher, it is appropriate to include it.

Work Experience: Listing of jobs (part-time, full-time, volunteer, temporary or permanent). Include: company name, department, agency, or organization; city and state; job/position title; dates; a brief description of your duties and responsibilities, using strong action verbs. List these in reverse chronological order, i.e. latest first.

Honors and Awards (if appropriate): List any competitive scholarships, fellowships or scholastic honors, teaching or research awards, if relevant. Do not include minor awards but these could be referred to in your cover letter, e.g. 「I also received awards for swimming while at university.」

Qualifications or skills: A summary of particular or relevant strengths or skills which you want to highlight.

Publications (if appropriate): Give bibliographic citations fusing the format appropriate to your particular academic discipline) for articles, pamphlets, chapters in books, research reports, or any other publications that you have authored or co-authored. (This section may be omitted but can be referred to in your cover letter, or if comprehensive, listed separately.)

Hobbies and Interests (Optional but you can provide a short list.)

References: (Optional) end a resume or CV with the statement 「Available upon Request.」

Five Cs in writing a resume or CV

Clear—well-organized and logical

Concise—relevant and to the point

Complete—including everything relevant

Consistent—don't mix styles or fonts

Current—up-to-date

A Sample CV

Wang Xiaoming

PERSONAL INFORMATION

Address:	**Tel**: (86-21) 5163-0222
School of Economics and Finance	**Mobile**: (86) 136-8888-2222
Fudan University, Shanghai,	**E-mail**: wxm123@163.com
China, 200043	

EDUCATION

Sep. 2005-July 2009 Fudan University, Shanghai, China

—Bachelor of Economics, Majored in Finance (GPA: 3.98/4, ranked Top 1st in 160 students)

WORK EXPERIENCE

July 2008-Aug. 2008

—Research Assistant at Hengdian Capital, Hangzhou, China. Collected and processed data, developed PowerPoint slides, translated subprime crisis articles in magazines such as Economists and Business Week and wrote an industry analysis report

Summers 2008 and 2007

—Research Assistant at State Street Technology Instit., Shanghai. Produced a review of the evolution of the New Basel Accord, gathered data and helped analysis of sub-prime crisis

PROJECTS AND RESEARCH EXPERIENCE

Sep. 2007-Present「Student Research Training Program」

—Focused on the growing environment and macro-policy influence for small and medium sized enterprises (SMEs) in Shanghai: collated literature, designed questionnaires, and currently conducting field work in Shanghai

June-Aug. 2008「Mid-Term Evaluation of the 11th Five-Year Plan of Shanghai Municipality」Project, Shanghai

—Took charge of the social insurance and social service section, collected local information, and wrote the social insurance and social service part of the report

May 2008「The Present Situation of Shanghai Real Estate Market and Potential Financial Risk」Project, Local Commercial Bank

—Collected and processed data on the real estate market of Shanghai, gathered local real estate market information, and wrote the report

Dec. 2007-Jan. 2008「Developmental Finance Supporting Shanghai」Project, National Development Bank

—Collected data, wrote part of the report, and developed PowerPoint slides

RESEARCH INTERESTS

Econometrics, Financial Economics, and Chinese Economic Reform

LANGUAGE SKILLS

    Native Language: Chinese

    English Language: TOEFL 113/120 GRE V 620/800 Q 800/800 AW 4/6

COMPUTER SKILLS

    Computer Experience: Microsoft Office, Visual Basic, C, Matlab

    Statistical Packages: SPSS, Eviews, Excel

ACTIVITIES AND INTERESTS

    Activities: Volunteer for the 2008 International Workshop on Chinese Productivity Member of IAESTE

    Interests: Swimming, Calligraphy, and Chinese Cooking

REFERENCES

Available upon request.

A Sample Resume

JIM SMITH

jsmith@dd.email.him

Present Address	Permanent Address
123 Riverwood Dr.	222 Hometown Dr.
Collegetown, USA 12345	Parentville, USA 45678
(xxx) 555-7756	(xxx) 444-1111 (after May 15th, 2009)

CAREER OBJECTIVE

    To obtain a position working with environmental issues where I can utilize my analytical skills to assist a company with research goals.

EDUCATION

    University of Nebraska, Lincoln, Nebraska

    Bachelor of Science, May 2009

    Major: Geology Minor: History

    GRA: 3.75/4.00

    Significant Coursework: Research Methods, Peer Leadership, Global Environmental Issues, Technical Writing.

    Computer skills: Lotus, 1-2-3, COBOL, SPSS

表（續）

PROFESSIONAL EXPERIENCE

   Intern, Carson Geological Consultants

   Denver, Colorado, May 2009-August 2009

     * Assisted Senior Geologist with collection of field samples
     * Performed laboratory chemical composition tests
     * Input data for statistical software packages
     * Met with clients to discuss project status

   Student Assistant, University of Nebraska Department of Geology

   Lincoln, Nebraska, September 2008-May 2009

     * Compiled and indexed statistical information from soil sample tests
     * Inspected and cataloged incoming soil sample tests
     * Streamlined procedures for testing and grading core samples
     * Wrote reports summarizing results of soil sample tests

   President, Lambda Lambda Lambda Fraternity

   University of Nebraska, Lincoln, NE, September 2006-August 2008

     * Organized meetings for a group of 25 house members
     * Coordinated activities and intramural participation during Greek Week
     * Proposed new and successful fund raising activities for the house

ACTIVITIES AND HONORS

   Kappa Delta Psi, Geology Honorary, 2006-2008
   Tutwiler Scholarship Award, 2007
   Dean's list, last six semesters
   History Club, 2006-2008

REFERENCES

Available upon request.

Writing Assignment

    Suppose you are applying for an internship at all international manufacturing company. Write your resume for the company so that the Human Resources Department gains a fundamental understanding about you. Remember that special attention should be paid to the layout or format of a resume.

Unit 6 Lifestyle

Warming-ups

Task 1 Questions for Thought

Think about the following questions, then discuss with your partner.

1. What kind of lifestyle do you prefer, the slow, stable old-fashioned life or the fast-paced, mobile modern life?

2. How do you spend your leisure time?

3. In your eyes, what kind of lifestyle is healthy?

Task 2 Vocabulary Preview

Complete the following table by writing the English or Chinese equivalents of the words given. Then, check your answers with your partner.

健康		relationships	
健身		parenting	
美容		cooking	
時尚		gardening	
旅遊		entertainment	

In-class Activities

Task 1 Individual/Group Work

A: Look at these common chores. Check (√) the ones that you do.

_____ pay bills

_____ recycle things at home

_____ wash the dishes

_____ take out the garbage

_____ shop for groceries

_____ feed a pet

_____ clean

_____ return books or videos

B: Look at the chores above again, and discuss these questions.

· Which chore do you dislike doing the most? Why?

· Are there any chores you enjoy doing? Which ones?

· What other chores do you do?

Task 2   Pair Work

If a lifetime could be compressed into a week, this is how much time a person would spend doing these things. Look at the chart. Then discuss the questions below.

A person would spend...				
120 hours	at home		60 hours	in bed
24 hours	at work			
14 hours	watching TV		16 hours	in the bathroom
12 hours	waiting in line		14 hours	eating
10 hours	cleaning house		12 hours	shopping
6 hours	in school and college		7 hours	in meetings
3 hours	traveling		5 hours	on hobbies an interests
1/2 hours	in movie theaters		1 hours	waiting at red lights

●Which statistics are surprising or unbelievable?

●How do you generally spend your time?

Example: I'm surprised a person spends 12 hours waiting in line. I can't believe that I usually...

Task 3   Role-play

Read the following dialogue first, and then act it out with your partner. Each of you should assume a role, and then switch the role.

(Situation: Mike bought a new apartment a few days ago. He meets Tom. Now he is pouring out his trouble to Tom.)

Tom: I heard that you bought an apartment, is that true?

Mike: Yes, my girlfriend threatened not to marry me without an apartment.

Tom: Come on guy. Please not be so sad, now you are a man who has a house.

Mike: The problem is that I need to pay the bank 6,000 yuan per month till I am 55 yesrs old.

Tom: Eh, house really costs too much today.

Mike: Everything costs more than before. Every day I wake up and I start to calculate how much I should earn today to pay all the bills, I think it's better to die.

Tom: Please don't say so. The average price for grave is 50,000 yuan per square meter while apartment is only 20,000 yuan.

Mike: My god! Live or die, both are affliction for such a poor man like me.

Task 4 Discussion

Some people prefer to live in s small town. Others prefer to live in a big city.

A: Would you prefer to live in a big city or small town? Why? Work in groups and make discussion with your peers.

Option 1: Live in big city.

Your Reason:

Option 2: Live in a small town.

Your Reason:

B: After discussing, summarize all the opinions and make a debate about

Live in Big City vs. Live in Small Town

The following might be useful and helpful in the debate:

Words and Expressions:

health; pollution; high living expenses; boring; free more opportunity; pressure leisure; competition; friendly

Reference Modal:

If I were asked to choose whether to live either in a small town or in a big city, I would not hesitate to choose the small town. First of all, there is much more pollution in a city than in a small town. Secondly, ...

Task 5 Questions for Discussion

Prepare for the class discussion based on the following questions.

1. What is the meaning of life? Is your life all that you expected?

2. Are there any episodes in your life that make you feel happy and excited, or disappointed and depressed?

3. Is there any person or event changing your attitude towards life? Explain.

4. What do you dream of becoming? What do you want most in life?

5. Comment on the following statement: In pursuing a dream, one must keep a balance between one's strong wish for the dream to come true and the realities of one's abilities and circumstances.

Reading Passages

Passage A

Our Changing Lifestyle: Trends and Fads

These days lifestyles seem to change very fast. It is more than just clothing and hairstyles that are in style one year and out of date the next; it's a whole way of living. One year people wear sunglasses on top of their heads and wear jeans and boots; they drink white wine and eat sushi at Japanese restaurants; for exercise they jog several miles a day. However, the next year they notice that everything has changed. Women wear long skirts; people drink expensive water from France and eat pasta at Italian restaurants; everyone seems to be exercising at health clubs.

Almost nothing in modern life escapes the influence of fashion: food, music, exercise, books, slang words, movies, furniture, places to visit, even names go in and out of fashion. It's almost impossible to write about specific fads because these interests that people follow can change very quickly.

In the United States, even people can be「in」or「out」. Like people in any country, Americans enjoy following the lives of celebrities: movie stars, sports heroes, famous artists, politicians, and the like. But Americans also pay a lot of attention to people who have no special ability and have done nothing very special. In 1981, for example, an unknown elderly woman appeared in a TV commercial in which she looked at a very small hamburger and complained loudly.「Where's the beef?」These three words made her famous. Suddenly she appeared in magazines and newspapers and on TV shows. She was immediately popular. In 1987 an exterminator in Dallas, Texas decided that he would be very happy if he could find more customers for his small business; he needed more people to pay him to kill the insects and rats in their houses. He put an unusual advertisement in a Dallas newspaper. He offered to pay $ 1,000 to the person who could find the biggest cockroach. This strange offer made him suddenly famous. However, this kind of fame does not last long. Such people are famous for a very short time. They are fads.

What causes such fads to come and go? And why do so many people follow them? Although clothing designers and manufacturers influence fads in fashion because they want to make a profit, this desire for money doesn't explain fads in other areas, such as language. For example, why have teenagers in the past twenty-five years used—at different times—the slang words「groovy」or「awesome」in conversation, instead of simply saying wonderful? According to Jack Santino, an expert in popular culture, people who follow fads are not irrational; they simply want to be part of something new and creative, and they feel good when they are part of an 「in—group」. Fads are not unique to the United States. Dr. Santino believes that fads are common in any country that has a strong consumer economy, e.g., Britain, Japan, and Germany. However, in the United States there is an additional reason for fads: most Americans seem to feel that something is wrong if there isn't frequent change in their lives.

Dr. Santino points out that it's sometimes difficult to see the difference between a fad and a trend. A fad, he says, lasts a very short time and is not very important. A social trend lasts a long time and becomes a true part of modern culture. A trend might be the use of personal computers; a fad might be certain types of computer games. A recent trend is the nationwide interest in good health, but many fads come from this trend: aerobic dancing, special diets, imported water, and the like.

An exciting trend began in Europe in the mid-1990s: the cultural borders between countries began to break down. Travelers from other parts of the world noticed that 「Eurokids,」 from Lisbon to Stockholm, from London to Athens, seemed to be very similar to each other. All followed the same fads in fashion, music and food. These Eurokids had the same lifestyle and values. For example, they were worried about the environment, concerned more about rain forests than clothes. Some of the Eurokids' fads will certainly disappear and others will come along, but it will be interesting to see if the environmental trend continues and becomes a true part of European culture.

Words and Expressions
1. lifestyle *n.* 生活方式
2. trend *n.* 趨向，趨勢；傾向
3. fad *n.* （一時的）風尚
4. hairstyle *n.* 髮式，髮型
5. style *n.* 時髦，時尚
6. sunglasses *n.* ［復數］太陽眼鏡，墨鏡
7. jeans *n.* ［復數］牛仔褲；牛仔服
8. sushi *n.* 壽司
9. jog *vi.* 慢跑
10. pasta *n.* 義大利麵製品
11. escape *vt.* 避免；逃避
12. fashion *n.* （服飾等的）流行式樣；（言語、行為等的）風尚
13. slang *n.* 俚語

14. specific *adj.* 特定的，特有的；具體的，明確的
15. celebrity *n.* 名人，名流
16. politician *n.* 政治家；政客
17. elderly *adj.* 上了年紀的；中年以上的
18. commercial *n.* 商業廣告 *adj.* 商業的，商務的
19. hamburger *n.* 漢堡包
20. beef *n.* 牛肉
21. exterminator *n.* 滅害
22. customer *n.* 顧客，主顧
23. insect *n.* 昆蟲
24. advertisement *n.* 廣告
25. cockroach *n.* 蟑螂
26. manufacturer *n.* 製造商，製造廠
27. profit *n.* 利潤
28. groovy *adj.* ［俚語］頂呱呱的，絕妙的
29. awesome *adj.* 精彩的，絕妙的
30. irrational *adj.* 無理性的，失去理性的
31. rational *adj.* 理性的，理智的；合理的，出於理性的
32. creative *adj.* 創造性的，創造的
33. in-group *n.* 內集團，小團體
34. consumer *n.* 消費者，用戶
35. additional *adj.* 另外的，附加的
36. frequent *adj.* 時常發生的，頻繁的
37. personal *adj.* 個人的，私人的
38. nationwide *adj.* 全國性的，全國範圍的
39. aerobic *adj.* 需氧的，增氧健身法，有氧的
40. diet *n.* 日常飲食，日常食物；特種飲食，規定飲食
41. similar *adj.* 相似的，類似的
42. in/out of style 流行/不流行
43. out of date 過時的
44. on (the) top of 在……之上
45. go/be in fashion 開始/在流行
46. go/be out of fashion 過時，不流行
47. and the like 之類，等等
48. break down 崩潰，坍塌
49. point out 指出

Proper Names

1. Dallas　達拉斯（美國德克薩斯州東北部城市）
2. Texas　德克薩斯州（美國州名）
3. Jack Santino　杰克・桑蒂諾（人名）
4. Lisbon　里斯本（葡萄牙首都）
5. Stockholm　斯德哥爾摩（瑞典首都）
6. Athens　雅典（希臘首都）

Content Awareness

Write down the topic and topic sentence for each paragraph according to the example given below for paragraph 1.

Example:

(para. 1)

Topic: changing lifestyles

Topic sentence: These days lifestyles seem to change very fast.

(para. 2)

Topic: _____

Topic sentence: _____

(para. 3)

Topic: _____

Topic sentence: _____

(para. 4)

Topic: _____

Topic sentence: _____

(para. 5)

Topic: _____

Topic sentence: _____

(para. 6)

Topic: _____

Topic sentence: _____

Language Focus

1. Go over the following sentences and try to figure out the meanings of the underline parts by using context clues and/or word building clues.

(1) These days lifestyles seem to change very fast. It is more than just clothing and hairstyles that are in style one year and out of date the next; it's a whole way of liv-

ing.

　　in style: _____

　　out of date: _____

　（2）Women wear long skirts; people drink expensive water from France and eat pasta at Italian restaurants.

　　pasta: _____

　（3）In 1987 an exterminator decided that he would be happy if he could find more customers for his small business; he needed more people to pay him to kill the insects and rats in their houses.

　　exterminator: _____

　（4）Although clothing designers and manufacturers influence fads in fashion because they want to make a profit, this desire for money doesn't explain fads in other areas, such as language.

　　make a profit: _____

　（5）Why have teenagers in the past twenty-five years used—at different times—the slang words groovy or awesome in conversation, instead of simply saying wonderful?

　　groovy: _____

　　awesome: _____

　（6）People who follow fads are not irrational; they simply want to be part of something new and creative, and they feel good when they are part of an 「in-group」.

　　irrational: _____

　（7）Fads are not unique to the United States. Dr. Santino believes that fads are common in any country that has a strong consumer economy.

　　unique: _____

　（8）It's sometimes difficult to see the difference between a fad and a trend. A fad lasts a very short time and is not very important. A social trend lasts a long time and becomes a true part of modern culture.

　　trend: _____

　（9）The cultural borders between countries began to break down. 「Eurokids」from Lisbon to Stockholm, from London to Athens, seemed to be very similar to each other.

　　「Eurokids」: _____

2. Select the best answer to each of the following questions.

　（1）Which of the following statements best serves as the main idea of the whole text?

　　A. Fashion and fads influence all aspects of modern life.

　　B. Fads are common because clothing manufacturers and store owners make a lot of money if styles change every year.

C. People tend to follow many different kinds of fads because they like to be part of something new and creative.

D. A social trend, when it lasts long enough, becomes a true part of modern culture.

(2) The author supports his ideas mainly by providing _____.

A. facts and examples			B. statistics
C. different people's experiences	D. reasons and explanations

(3) Which of the following best describes the author's attitude towards his writing?

A. Subjective.			B. Critical.
C. Matter-of-fact.		D. Optimistic.

(4) What is the author's purpose in writing this article?

A. To inform.			B. To entertain.
C. To criticize.		D. To persuade.

3. Fill in the following blanks with the words given below. Change the forms where necessary.

advertisement consumer creative customer diet escape
frequent manufacturer profit similar specific trend

(1) She is very careful and nothing important _____ her notice.

(2) They seem to have no _____ plans for dealing with the problem.

(3) According to a recent report, the most _____ cause of death in the U.S. is heart attack.

(4) Paul is so _____ to his brother in appearance that it's very difficult to tell them apart.

(5) You will make a big _____ by selling your house now; if you wait, the price may fall.

(6) I can't keep up with all the latest music _____—they come and go so rapidly.

(7) This is an example of a _____ application of the theory.

(8) 「The _____ is always right」 means that someone who is serving in a shop should try very hard not to disagree with the _____.

(9) The newspaper article claims that tobacco companies failed to warn _____ of the dangers of smoking.

(10) I've lost about twenty pounds since I started this special _____ two months ago.

(11) If your TV set has any basic defect, you should complain to the _____.

(12) If you really want to sell all your books and magazines, why not put an _____ in the local paper?

4. Fill in the following blanks with the phrases given below. Change the forms where necessary.

according to   and the like   break down   come along

go out of fashion   on top of   out of date   point out

(1) It can be very dangerous to go mountain climbing at this time of year, as Tony has just _____.

(2) Loud music with a strong beat _____, and sweeter, softer music is becoming popular again.

(3) _____ today's papers, fifteen people were killed yesterday in a car accident in Liaoning.

(4) Many teenagers in China like McDonald's, Wendy's, Pizza Hut, Kentucky'Fried Chicken, _____.

(5) The book was published five years ago and much of its information is now _____.

(6) His health _____ under the pressure of work.

(7) When the right opportunity _____, be sure to seize it.

(8) Put the letter _____ that pile of books, where it can be seen easily.

Passage B

The Web Lifestyle

If you ask people today why they use telephone to communicate with their friends or why they turn to television for entertainment, they will look at you as if you were crazy. We don't think about a telephone or a television or a car as being oddities. These things have become such an integral part of life that they are no longer noticed, let alone remarked upon.

In the same way, within a decade no one will notice the Web. It will just be there, an integral part of life. It will be only too natural to turn to the Web for shopping, education, entertainment and communication, just as it is natural today to pick up the telephone to talk to someone.

There is incredible interest in the Web. Yet it is still in its early stage of development. The technology and the speed of response are about to leap forward. This will move more and more people to the Web as part of their everyday lives. Eventually, everyone's business card will have an electronic mail address. Every lawyer, every doctor and every business—from large to small—will be connected.

Today in the United States, there are over 22 million adults using the Web, about half of whom access the Internet at least once a day. Meanwhile, the variety of activities on the Web is broadening at an amazing rate. There is almost no topic on which you cannot find fairly interesting material on the Web. Many of these sites are getting excellent traffic flow. Want to buy a dog? Or sell a share? Or order a car? Turn to the Internet. Where are we going to get the time to live with the Web? In some instances, people will actually save time because the Web will make doing things more efficient than in the past. Being able to get information about a major purchase, for example. Or finding our how much your used car is worth. Or what is your cheapest way of getting to Florida. That is very easy to find on the Web, even today. In other instances, people will trade the time they now spend reading the paper, or watching television, for information or entertainment they will find on the computer screen. Americans, particularly young ones, will spend less time in front of a television screen, more on the Web.

Words and Expressions

1. crazy *adj.* 發瘋的，荒唐的
2. oddity *n.* 奇怪的人或東西
3. odd *adj.* 奇特的，古怪的
4. integral *adj.* 不可缺少的
5. remark *v.* 談論，議論
6. incredible *adj.* 難以置信的，不可相信的
7. stage *n.* 階段，時期
8. access *v.* 使用
9. meanwhile *adv.* 與此同時
10. rate *n.* 速率
11. topic *n.* 題目，話題，主題
12. site *n.* 站點，網站
13. traffic *n.* 信息流量
14. instance *n.* 情況
15. purchase *n.* 買，購買
16. the Web 網絡
17. let alone 更別提
18. leap forward 大增長
19. turn to （傾向、注意力等）轉移到

Content Awareness

1. Choose the best answer to each of the following.

(1) How do people look at telephone and television today?

A. They are as important as the Internet.

B. Without them people would become crazy.

C. They are part of people's everyday lives.

D. Few people are aware that they have a telephone or television at home.

(2) According to the author, people turn to the Web for all the following except _____.

A. watching films and TV programs

B. shopping, education and communication

C. getting information

D. doing housework

(3) Many people's business cards will have an e-mail address. What does this imply?

A. Business people can afford to have e-mail service.

B. More and more people will rely on the Internet for communication.

C. Communication by e-mail can save business people a lot of money.

D. Communication by telephone will be out of date for business people.

(4) Which of the following is NOT a reason why people rely on the Web in their everyday lives?

A. People have a great interest in the Web.

B. People can find many interesting materials on the Web.

C. People want to do physical exercise on the Web.

D. People want to get information necessary to their lives.

(5) It can be inferred from the passage that _____.

A. with the quick development of computer technology, people no longer turn to television for entertainment

B. the Web has become the most important source of people's entertainment

C. the Web has greatly changed people's lifestyle

D. people who turn to the Web will have more free time than those who don't

2. Fill in the blanks with appropriate words according to the above reading passage.

Nowadays people still depend on telephone and television for communication and entertainment. But soon it will be _____ for people to turn to the Internet _____ shopping, education, entertainment and communication. The _____ of technological development is so fast _____ more and more people will make the

Web _____ of their everyday lives. Even today, people can find on the Web interesting _____ on almost all _____. That is why Americans, _____ young ones, will spend less time in _____ of a television screen, _____ on the Web.

3. Complete the following chart and fill in each blank with no more than three words.

The Web Lifestyle

Within a decade, the Web will be an integral part of life. People will turn to it for _____ and communication.

Possible reasons for people to turn to the Web:

(1) The technology and the speed of response are about to _____.

(2) The variety of activities on the Web is broadening at _____.

Ways to get time to live with the Web:

(1) The Web will save time because it will make doing things _____ than in the past.

(2) People will _____ the time they how spend reading the paper, or watching television, _____ information or entertainment they will find on the _____.

Although the Web is still in its _____ of development, it will attract _____ people in the near future.

Language Focus

1. Fill in the blanks with appropriate words or expressions, with at least one from passage B.

(1) Ways in which people can communicate with each other: telephone, letter, _____, _____, etc.

(2) Things supporting the main idea of a paragraph: illustration, detail, _____, _____, etc.

(3) Make wider: widen, _____, etc.

(4) Daily activities that can be done on the Web: shopping, communication, _____, _____, etc.

(5) Adjectives describing surprise: unbelievable, amazing, _____, etc.

2. Match the words with the right definition.

A	B
a. leap	_____ send (something) by post
b. broaden	_____ get information from or put information into

  c. entertainment _____ (a computer file)

  c. entertainment _____ jump hard or jump over

  d. traffic _____ make wider; extend in scope, range or area

  e. access _____ a person who is trained and qualified in legal matters

  f. mail _____ a piece of land on which something is located

  g. lawyer _____ vehicles moving along a road or street

  h. site _____ amusement

  i. electronic _____ strange; unusual

  j. integral _____ necessary for completeness; whole

  k. odd _____ very foolish and not sensible

  l. crazy _____ of or concerned with electrons

3. Complete the sentences with appropriate words in their correct form.

efficiency efficient efficiently

  (1) The man worked with great _____ and finished the job quickly.

  (2) The general manager needs a more _____ secretary.

  (3) In the past two years the young man has made great progress and now he can work as _____ as a skilled worker.

technology technological technologist

  (1) Most guests invited to the party are _____.

  (2) Computers are regarded as a great _____ improvement which saves people much time and energy.

  (3) Modem people are enjoying a high level of _____.

information inform

  (1) We were _____ that a big fire had broken out in the center of the city.

  (2) I _____ his mother of his safe arrival.

  (3) These books, which you can get at any bookshop, will give you all the _____ you need.

active act activity action

  (1) There have been a lot of _____ in the town today.

  (2) _____ speak louder than words.

  (3) He is an _____ member of the school's English club.

  (4) Think well before you _____.

communicate communication communicative

  (1) After graduation, we'll _____ with each other by e-mail or telephone.

  (2) He is very _____. If he is given a chance, he will talk on without stopping.

(3) All _____ with the north was stopped by the snow storm.

Skills Development and Practice

Reading Skills

Recognizing Punctuation (標點符號)

Practice 1: A good knowledge of PUNCTUATION, like other reading skills, helps us understand the written materials better. Different punctuation marks may make the sentences different in meaning. Look at the examples to see how the meaning change with the punctuation marks.

EXAMPLES:

1. a. He agrees with you.

b. He agrees with you?

c. He agrees with you!

2. a. Do you know her mother?

b. Do you know her, mother?

3. a. His boss says Mr. Wang works very hard.

b. His boss, says Mr. Wang, works very hard.

4. a. I didn't go, because I am afraid.

b. I didn't go because I am afraid.

QUESTION: The sentences in each group seem to be the same at the first sight, but they are different in meaning. What are the possible differences?

Practice 2: Tell the difference of the each pair of sentences.

1. a. The boy thinks his father will come back.

b. The boy, thinks his father, will come back.

2. a. When I looked into the room, I saw Mary seated at the desk; Jim was at work on the computer and did not hear me call.

b. When I looked into the room, I saw Mary; seated at the desk, Jim was at work on the computer and did not hear me call.

3. a. He didn't understand the question clearly.

b. He didn't understand the question, clearly.

4. a. He is too proud to do it.

b. He is, too, proud to do it.

5. a. The policeman wants to know the following: exactly where the man fell, what happened to the broken car, who was using it, when the accident took place.

b. The policeman wants to know the following: exactly where the man fell, what happened to the broken car, who was using it when the accident took place.

6. a. The street was narrow, and the houses were on either side; like guards, dark grey, watchful (警惕的) dogs stood waiting.

b. The street was narrow, and the houses were on either side like guards: dark, grey, watchful; dogs stood waiting.

Translation Practice

Translation Skills

轉譯詞類：英語動詞可轉譯成漢語名詞。

Practice 3: Translate the sentences into Chinese, paying attention to the italicized words.

1. The man I saw at the party *looked* and *talked* like an American.

2. She *designs* for a famous shop.

3. I *weigh* less than I used to.

4. He *aims* to enter the university next year.

5. The electronic computer is chiefly *characterized* by its accurate and rapid computation.

6. What's that? It is *shaped* like a ball.

Practice 4: Translate the sentences into Chinese.

1. Apparently, many people believe that the more time a person spends at work, the more she or he accomplishes. However, the connection between time and productivity is not always positive.

2. Although many working people can do their job effectively during a regular 40-hour work week, they feel they have to spend more time on the job after normal working hours so that the people who can promote them see them.

3. In such fields as advertising, show business, and journalism, the glamour and publicity are worth more than any monetary benefit.

4. People frequently have garage sales before they move and on weekends when the weather is nice. Sometimes several families gather their unwanted household goods and sell them together.

5. Cleaning, organizing, pricing, and moving merchandise is hard work, out the opportunity of flea markets and garage sales proves that many Americans work for fun!

Practice 5: Translate the sentences into English with the words or expressions given.

1. 似乎沒有人知道發生過什麼。(It seems that…)

2. 別花那麼多時間來打扮自己。(dress oneself)

3. 為了不遲到,我想現在就走。(so that)

4. 除了幾張桌子和椅子外,整個房間空蕩蕩的。(except)

5. 整整一下午,他都在因特網(the Internet)上尋找一些有趣的網址。(search)

6. 他常常去跳蚤市場買一些家庭用品,然後再出售,賺一點額外的小錢。(flea markets, household items)

Practical Translation

修辭的翻譯

修辭是藝術,也是科學。修辭手段使用得當,能使文字激發聯想,喚起美感,增強表現力、說服力和感染力,做到語言形式與表現內容完美和諧的統一。

根據修辭格的特徵，修辭可分為詞語修辭、結構修辭和音韻修辭三個方面。

詞語修辭側重營造詞語的形象感，常用的修辭格有明喻（simile）、隱喻（metaphor）、擬人（personification）、誇張（hyperbole）、對照（contrast）、借代（metonymy）及提喻（synecdoche）等。

結構修辭著重呈現句式結構的均衡美，常用的修辭格有反覆（repetition）、排比（parallelism）、對偶（antithesis）、設問（rhetoric question）和突降（anticlimax）等。

音韻修辭意在表現語言的音韻美，常用的修辭格有頭韻（alliteration）、尾韻（rhyme）和擬聲（onomatopoeia）。

從翻譯的角度來看，有些修辭格是可譯的、有些是很難譯的、有些其實是不能譯的，對不同類別的修辭格主要有三種翻譯方法，即直譯法、意譯法和彌補法。

1. 直譯法

直譯，即保留原文句子結構和修辭，努力再現其形式、內容和風格。平時使用頻繁、英漢語言中有對應修辭格的辭格（如明喻、暗喻、擬人、誇張、轉喻、反語、設問、反問、排比等），一般可以通過直譯法處理。

（1）One plunges into the surf and rescues a swimmer from drowning; another dashes into a burning house and carries a stranger to safety; others snatch a child from the wheels of death; many give their blood that others may live.

譯文：有人躍入水中拯救溺水的泳者；有人衝進火場將陌生人帶出險境；有人從死亡的車輪下救出孩子；許多人獻出鮮血使他人生命得以延續。

解析：這個句子的修辭格是排比，四個同等結構的單句表達的內容圍繞同一個主題，反覆強調了同一個觀點，即上文提到的 Man's inherent goodness, moreover, is revealed by his countless acts of heroism, unselfishness and sacrifice. 讀起來音韻悠揚，給人留下深刻印象。漢語譯文運用了相應的排比句式，通過直譯法既保留了原文結構的美感，也再現了原文表達的力度和感染力。

（2）The spirit is perfect, but when it inhabits human structures, it participates in the imperfections of the latter.

譯文：精神是完美的，但它棲居到人類肉體結構中後，便參與其中，表現出後者的不完美。

解析：動詞 inhabits 和 participates in 將 the spirit 和 human structures 的關係擬人化為人和住所之間的關係。譯文直譯了原文擬人的修辭格。inhabits 和 participates in 分別譯為「棲居」和「參與」，完整地體現了原文形象和生動的表達。

2. 意譯法

由於英漢語法、語音、語言形式或文化背景的差異，有時直譯法會使譯文生硬晦澀，影響翻譯效果。為了傳達原文的確切意義，只能捨棄原文辭格的形式，從而使譯文自然貼切，具有較強的可讀性，即使找到相似的修辭方式，也要認真地加工，以增強譯文的表達效果，這就是意譯法。對偶、擬聲、腳韻、雙關、反覆等修辭，常採用意譯的處理方法。

（1）I have never seen such a wreck of humanity.

譯文：我從來沒有看到過如此衰敗的人。

解析：Wreck 原指飛機船只失事後的殘骸，這裡喻指身心遭受毀滅性重創的人。漢語中沒有能直接表達相應或相似意思的詞彙，直譯成漢語「我從沒有見過這樣的人的失事殘骸」語義不通。所以譯出句意、拋棄原文的喻體形象是較明智的選擇。

（2）The youngsters have been devoted cheerleaders of the new video game.

譯文：年輕人一直都是這種新型視頻游戲的忠實粉絲。

解析：原句的 cheerleaders 屬於比擬用法，並不真的存在著這樣的啦啦隊，即便存在，年輕人也並不都是隊長。所以這裡採取了意譯的方法。

3. 彌補法

對無法翻譯的辭格（如頭韻、聯邊、回文、鑲字、仿詞等），可根據不同的語境採用不同的策略：內容重要非譯不可的可通過換格、加重語氣、加上腳註等辦法補救；與原作思想力度和情節發展無重大關係的修辭格，乾脆不譯。

（1）But the spirit, the inner man, remains untouched and undefiled by evil.

譯文：但是精神——內在的人——卻仍然免遭邪惡的染指和玷污。

解析：這裡的修辭格是押韻，untouched and undefiled 包含了頭韻和尾韻兩種押韻方式，通過重複相同的前綴 un- 和後綴 -ed，使結構整齊漂亮，音律鏗鏘有力，增加了和諧與美感。押韻給人以聽覺衝擊或視覺美感，卻是翻譯中較難處理的修辭格，特別是押頭韻的手法歷來被認為是很難譯的。要在譯文中再現原文鮮明的修辭特點，獲得形和聲兩方面的美，絕非易事。本句中 untouched and undefiled 的頭韻和尾韻無法完整地再現到譯文中，但處理成「染指和玷污」，其中「染」和「玷」韻母相同，也算是一種較好的補救辦法。

（2）Countless unnamed and unrecorded men have given their lives for their fellowmen, not only on the battlefront but on the home-front as well.

譯文：數不勝數的不知姓名、不被記載的人們，不僅在戰場上，而且還在戰爭的大後方為了他們的同胞獻出了生命。

解析：這又是一個押頭韻和尾韻的例子，unnamed and unrecorded 重複了相同的前綴 un- 和後綴 -ed，雖然做不到將頭韻和尾韻全部保留到譯文中，但作為彌補手段，選擇了兩個都以「不」開始的短語，「不知姓名和不被記載」，在一

定程度上體現了原句的表達效果。

Translation Practice

Translate the following paragraphs into Chinese.

Paragraph One

The constancy of human nature is proverbial, as no one believes that a man can fundamentally change his nature. This is why it is so difficult for one who has acquired an unsavory reputation to re-establish himself in public confidence. People know from experience that an individual who in one year displays knavish characteristics seldom in the next becomes any different. Nor does a thief become a trustworthy employee, or a miser a philanthropist. Nor does a man change and become a liar, coward or traitor at fifty or sixty; if he is one then, he has been one ever since his character was formed. Big criminals are first little criminals, just as giant oaks are first little acorns.

Paragraph Two

I recalled his high spirits, his vitality, his confidence in the future, and his disinterestedness. It was impossible that it was the same man, and yet I was sure of it. I stood up, paid for my drink, and went out into the plaza to find him. My thoughts were in a turmoil. I was aghast. I could never have imagined that he was reduced to this frightful misery. I asked myself what had happened. What hopes deferred had broken his spirit, what disappointments shattered him, and what lost illusions ground him to the dust? I asked myself if nothing could be done. I walked round the plaza.

Focused Writing

Letters of Recommendation

What is a letter of recommendation?

A good letter of recommendation can be an asset to any application. For example, during admissions to post graduate courses, most universities expect to see at least one, preferably two or three, letters of recommendation for each applicant.

A letter of recommendation is a written document from your referee to an employer or graduate school that discusses your skills, abilities and worthiness for the position or program into which you are seeking enhance.

What is included in a letter of recommendation?

All letters of recommendation differ; however, most good letters of recommendation need at least three paragraphs containing the following types of information. The letter should spill over onto a second page, if possible.

· Identify yourself and the student. Explain your affiliation, the capacity in which you have come to know the student, and for how long you have known him or her. Include course names. State what grades the student earned in your course and mention how you would rank the student in relation to other students that you have known.

· Make detailed references to specific projects or activities in which the student participated, or work that was produced. You should be detailed and fulsome (豐富的;大量的) where appropriate and highlight any relevant aspects from the following:

—Intellectual ability (overall intelligence, analytical skills, creativity, academic record, retention of information)

—Knowledge of area of specialty

—Communication skills (writing skills, oral articulateness)

—Personal qualities (industry, self-discipline, motivation, maturity, initiative, flexibility, leadership, team work spirits, perseverance, energy, competitiveness)

· Referees should be willing to receive follow-up calls from employers or schools, so you should include your business or home phone number and email in the letter.

What should be noted?

Bear in mind the following particular 「do's」 when producing a letter of recommendation.

1. Do be specific. Give examples of the student's work, completed projects, participation in extra-curricular activities and any relevant information that shows the student's abilities and character.

2. Do be objective. Although you are giving a personal recommendation, you must be fair and reasonable. Report specific examples to back up your comments. If you want to attest to a student's interpersonal skills, mention how you observed the student's interactions with others, rather than merely stating what a 「nice person」 she or he is.

3. Do be both honest and positive. If your experience with the student is negative in any way, ask the student to find another letter writer. Obviously, making negative comments about a student's performance will have serious consequences on the student's chances at the job, scholarship, or acceptance being sought. Remember that your experience with the student may not be typical, so the student should find someone who can make positive comments. In addition, writing negative comments can potentially affect you as well, if there is ever any doubt about the reliability of your judgment with respect to the student.

Sample 1

School of Sciences
Zhejiang University
Hangzhou, China,
310058

December 22nd, 2009

To Whom It May Concern:

    It is my great pleasure to recommend Ms. Ma for the Masters Finance and Economics program at the London School of Economics. As her former calculus professor, I have known Ma Xiaoming since autumn 2005 and have met with her regularly over the past four years. I knew that she had made up her mind to pursue a degree in finance at LSE some years ago and I am delighted she has asked me to write a letter of recommendation for her.

    Ms. Ma is a gifted, diligent and intensely rigorous student with strong academic performance. At the very beginning of my calculus course at the Chu Kochen Honors College, affiliated to Zhejiang University, she appeared to be no more than a diligent student who always sat at the right corner of the front row. Yet soon, she stood out as one of the few very outstanding and talented students who come along from time to time. She easily understood my lectures and often raised thought-provoking questions. Through questions and discussions, I found her intensely meticulous and persistent, for she would never stop scrutinizing (詳審) a problem until all uncertainty was unraveled. As you know, these qualities are most useful in research and I strongly believe that she will go on to make an excellent PhD candidate one day. Her scores at Zhejiang were exceptional, achieving 99%, the highest grade, in both Calculus I and Calculus II final papers. I understand from her other professors that she has performed equally well in all her other mathematics courses such as Linear Algebra, Probability Theory, Mathematical Statistics, and Ordinary Differentiation. I believe Ms. Ma's undergraduate training in mathematics and exceptional learning ability will undoubtedly prove useful to her graduate study in finance and economics.

    Another point that I would like to mention is her enrollment in the Mathematical Modeling Competition. During the competition, she combined her knowledge of mathematics and finance so well that her team won Second Prize. In addition, as the leader of her team, she skillfully managed the available resources and drew out the potential of each team member. Such experience and the leadership she showed indicated a level of maturity somewhat beyond her years.

    Ms. Ma is warm-hearted and straightforward. My recollection is of her frequent and patient explanations to confused classmates before and after my calculus classes. During my 4-year contact with her and her classmates, she was always willing to offer her help and was a great comfort to a classmate who lost her Father in tragic circumstances. She shows excellent time management skills, her assignments were always handed in on time and she has been able to combine a healthy social life in the Debating Society and on the tennis courts with her studies.

    I know she is very keen to study for a degree in your program, and your positive consideration will be greatly appreciated. Please do not hesitate to contact me at 086-571-88206033 if I can be of any further assistance in her application.

Yours faithfully,
YY
Dean of Department of Mathematics, Zhejiang University

The salutation can also be 「Dear Admissions Committee Members」.

Opening: stating how you knew the applicant and your pleasure to recommend her.

Main body: supporting evidence ① of the applicant's academic abilities.

Supporting evidence ② of the applicant's extracurricular achievements.

Supporting evidence ③ of the applicant's good character and personality.

Closing: indicating willingness to be contacted and offer of further help.

Sample 2

> 55 Baima Lu
> Changsha
> Hunan
>
> November 19th, 2009
>
> To Whom It May Concern:
>   I have great pleasure in writing to recommend Yang Hailin. I have known him in my capacity as a friend of the family and Neighborhood Watch Officer since he was a child and watched him grow into an intelligent and hard working young man. His school years were marred by difficulty as his Father died when he was only six and his Mother struggled to support the family. Despite this Hailin has completed his high school diploma showing especial aptitude in art and Chinese literature. He would seem to be ideally suited for a job in advertising where his artistic ability would provide interesting and unusual images.
>   At school he was a diligent student who worked hard at his studies and entered into the school life with a quiet commitment. His attendance was excellent and he was well liked by all the teachers. He helped to organize optional artistic outings for students so that they could expand the types of subjects they could draw and showed such enthusiasm for making the event fun yet productive that they became very well attended. He made a number of good friend.
>   Hailin was a quiet yet thoughtful child and has grown into a caring and considerate adult. He has shown great kindness to an elderly neighbor who he has spent many hours reading to and showing her how to paint. Hailin was also a willing and conscientious member of the team that cleaned and replanted out local pond and has helped each year to plant trees in our neighborhood. He is honest, careful and sensible in all he does and will be a loyal asset to any company that employs him. I have no hesitation in recommending this excellent young man.
>
> Yours faithfully,
> Yang Fanmei
> Deputy Neighborhood Watch Officer

Writing Assignment

1. Suppose you are a professor at Peking University. Write a letter of recommendation for Li Ming, one of your students, who aims to pursue a course of study at Harvard University.

2. Suppose you are a high school teacher. Write a letter of recommendation to a potential employer about one of your students.

Unit 7   Man and Technology

Warming-ups

Task 1   Questions for Thought

Think about the following questions, then discuss with your partner.

1. Can you list some electronic inventions influencing your life?
2. How would your life be different without these inventions?
3. In your opinion, what is the most important invention in the 21st century? Why?

Task 2   Vocabulary Preview

Complete the following table by writing the English or Chinese equivalents of the words given. Then, check your answers with your partner.

機器人		digital TV	
網上衝浪		cellphone	
克隆		hacker	
新能源		high-tech	
宇航員		netizen	
短信		manned spaceship	

In-class Activities

Task 1   Individual Work

Do you know the following words and expressions related to a computer?

CD-ROM		chip		disk	
disk drive		hard disk		hardware	
keyboard		memory		modem	
monitor		mouse		multimedia	
software		system			

Task 2　Pair Work

1. Suppose you work in the Service Department of an air-conditioner company. You receive a phone call from a man, whose air-conditioner does not work. Try to answer the call. An example is given to you.

A: Hello. Is this the Service Department?

B: Yes. What can I do for you?

A: My air-conditioner does not work. Could you tell me what I can do?

B: Do you know which part of your air-conditioner is broken?

A: No. I have no idea.

B: Well. I'll go to your place and have a look.

A: That would be nice.

B: May I have your name?

A: My name is John Smith.

B: Your address?

A: No. 5 Washington Street.

B: How about two o'clock this afternoon?

A: Two o'clock would be fine.

B: See you then.

A: See you.

2. Suppose you haven't seen your best friend after graduation from high school. Talk about your college life and how to use the computer with him/her on the Internet after class. An example is given to you.

A: Hello, Linda! I just logged on.

B: Hey, Jan! Long time no see.

A: How's it going?

B: Not bad. I think I have adapted to my college life. Now I keep practicing how to use computer proficiently. I couldn't be behind the times!

A: Sounds good! What do you usually do on the Internet?

B: That's really interesting. I send E-mails to my friends instead of writing letters. Sometimes I watch movies and TV, and download my favorite songs. How about you?

A: Me too. Shopping online is really convenient and not expensive.

B: That's awesome! Can you teach me how to use it next time?

A: Sure. A piece of cake!

B: You are really kind.

Task 3　Role-play

Read the following dialogue first, and then act it out with your partner. Each of you should assume a role, and then switch the role.

(Situation: Davis is a college student. His parents live in another city. He was writing to his parents in the dorm when Barbara came in.)

Barbara: Hey, Davis. What are you doing?

Davis: Hey, Barbara. I'm writing to Papa and Mama. I miss them very much.

Barbara: Me, too. But I often make phone calls.

Davis: I'd like to call my parents, but long distance is quite expensive.

Barbara: Then, why not send emails? They're cheap.

Davis: Really?

Barbara: Yeah, and they are fast, too.

Davis: Sounds great. But...

Barbara: You can even chat with your parents on the Net.

Davis: But I know very little about the computer.

Barbara: I can help you if you like.

Davis: That's really very nice of you.

Barbara: I will be free this afternoon.

Davis: Shall we say two o'clock?

Barbara: OK. See you then.

Davis: Bye.

Task 4　Debate

Intelligent machines such as robots are increasingly being used. They can do many things that used to be done by human. Most people believe they can help us create a new world. But some people are afraid that in the near future the human being will be under robots' control because of their high intelligence.

What's your attitude toward robot? Work in groups and carry out a debate on:

Can Robots Defeat Human Being?

The following might be useful and helpful in the debate: shorten work time, more efficient/convenient, do some dangerous work, make life relaxing, high intelligence, provide service, undercut job opportunities, overdependence on machines, unwilling to think/create

Reference Modal:

Positive Side:

Robots can not defeat human being. But it can helps us make life easier and more convenient.

Negative Side:

In the near future high intelligent robots will make human being lose their job opportunities. People would be unwilling to think.

Reading Passages

Passage A

The Dangers of Television
Harriet B. Fidler

When television was first introduced into American society thirty years ago, writers and social scientists thought that this new invention would better American life. ⌈Television is going to bring American families closer together,⌋ predicted psychologist Joel Gold in 1949. Pictures which advertised television in the 1950s invariably showed a happy family gathered together in the living room, sharing the TV viewing experience. Who could have guessed that a quarter of a century later mother would be in the kitchen watching a daytime drama, dad would be in the living room watching a ball game, and the children would be watching cartoons in their bedroom?

Television has certainly changed American life, but not the way the first critics predicted. The first televisions were enormously expensive, so most families owned only one. By 1975, however, 60% of American families owned two televisions or more; some middle-class families had as many as five television sets under one roof. Such multi-set families may keep family members in the same house, but that hardly brings them ⌈together⌋. In fact, family outings—hiking, going to the movies, going out to dinner—are often limited by TV because one or more family members don't want to go: ⌈I'll miss my program⌋ is the common complaint.

Perhaps more important than the lack of family outings is the destruction of family time together at home. Social scientists in the 1950s could not have realized how much television Americans would watch in the 1980s; the average American watches 6 hours of TV a day. That leaves little time for the special family characteristics and traditions that used to be formed during long evenings together. The time devoted to games, songs, and hobbies—all shared activities—in the years before TV is now dominated by ⌈the tube⌋. And especially damaging to family relationships is the elimination of the opportunities for talking: chatting, arguing, discussing. Without such communication, family lite disintegrates.

Dominationis the key word. Families in America today schedule their lives around the television. Children rush home from school to watch their programs while they do their homework. Mother shops between her special programs. The ski slopes are nearly empty on Super Bowl Sunday; football on TV takes precedence. The family may even eat meals in front of the television. Moreover, television is used as a baby-sitter; small children nationwide spend countless hours in front of the TV, passively investing whatever flashes before their eyes. Addiction of some sort inevitable follows; TV becomes a necessary part of life, and receiving a TV for his own room becomes the wish of most children. Moreover, parents use the television as a source of reward and punishment:「If you mow the lawn, you can watch TV an extra hour tonight,」or「No TV for you. You didn't do your homework.」Ultimately, life-style s revolve around a regular schedule of eating, sleeping, and watching television.

Isn't there a better family life than this dismal, mechanized arrangement? According to social scientist. Mary Helen Thuente,「The quality of life is diminished as family ties grow weaker, as children's lives grow more and more separate from their parents, as the opportunities for living and sharing within a family are eliminated.」Indeed, if the family does not accumulate shared experiences, it is not likely to survive. Consequently, if parents and children alike do not change their priorities, television will continue to exert its influence on American family hie as baby-sitter, pacifier, teacher, role model, and supplier of mores and morals, thus supplanting the place of the family in society.

Words and Expressions

1. disintegrate *v.* 瓦解，解體，分裂，崩潰
2. ingest *v.* 食入，攝入，咽下
3. diminish *v.* 減少，削弱，減小，貶低
4. pacifier *n.* 平定者，撫慰者
5. take precedence 優先，居優先地位

Content Awareness

Decide whether the following statements are true (T) or false (F).

(1) _____ When first introduced into American families, television was supposed to change people's lives for worse.

(2) _____ In the 1950s, most families owned only one TV because family members were closer to each other.

(3) _____ Lack of family outings is worse than anything else in weakening family ties.

(4) _____ Active participation in various activities gives way to passive activity when family members are watching TV programs.

(5) _____ Using television as a baby-sitter is a common poor practice nationwide.

(6) _____ Watching too much television makes children drug addicts.

(7) _____ The author does not believe the current situation can be improved.

(8) _____ The author thinks it is the family, not television, that should take the responsibility for teaching and setting role models for the young.

Language Focus

1. Fill in the blanks with the appropriate form of the given words (and phrases).

disintegrate   dominant   ultimately   consequently   supplant
eliminate   dismal   predictable   enormous   invariably
devote   take precedence   exert... influence on

(1) The war against terror will end in _____ victory for us.

(2) He was a _____ figure at the opening of this year's World Summit on Sustainable Development.

(3) The report describes the catastrophic _____ of the aircraft after the explosion.

(4) Our low spirits were made worse by the _____ weather.

(5) The farmers suffered a severe drought and there was a _____ shortage of food in the markets.

(6) _____ of poverty is mankind's long-cherished dream.

(7) The rent and cost of maintenance of such an apartment are _____; we can't afford it.

(8) His _____ of time and money to the project was not well compensated for.

(9) Price control _____ over every other consideration.

(10) Peter's _____ courtesy won him many votes from his fellow students, especially the girls.

(11) The press _____ great _____ public opinion.

(12) The stock markets seem to be teeming with _____ risks, and veteran analysts always disagree about the overall trend.

(13) Machinery has largely _____ hand-labor in making shoes.

2. Structure:

A rhetorical question differs from an ordinary question in that it does not need an answer. A positive rhetorical question resembles a strong negative statement, whereas a negative rhetorical question is like a strong positive statement. Therefore, the idea expressed in the form of a rhetorical question has a special force, and gains greater emphasis.

Examples

Who could have guessed that a quarter of a century later mother would bein the kitchen watching a daytime drama, dad would be in the living room watching a ball game, and the children would be watching cartoons in their bedroom? (Nobody could have guessed that...)

Isn't there a better family life than this dismal, mechanized arrangement?

(There is surely a better family life...)

Use rhetorical questions to give the following sentences greater emphasis and force.

(1) They are really wonderful dresses.

_____

(2) You don't call that poem.

_____

(3) If winter comes, spring is surely not far behind.

_____

(4) We can surely learn from the tragic experiences of others.

_____

(5) There are surely other alternatives to the chemical control of insects.

_____

(6) You surely know that this is a highly classified document.

_____

3. Functional Training

(1) Build a network of an associative field for *television*.

(2) Underline the transitional sentences in the text and discuss how they bind the paragraphs together.

(3) Discuss the common function of the following underlined words in the context.

The first televisions were enormously expensive, <u>so</u> most families owned only one.

<u>Ultimately</u>, life-styles revolve around a regular schedule of eating, sleeping, and watching television.

<u>Consequently</u>, if parents and children alike do not change their priorities, television will continue to exert its influence on American family life as baby-sitter,

pacifier, teacher, role model, and supplier of mores and morals, thus supplanting the place of the family in society.

Passage B

It's Not 「All in the Genes」

It is no surprise that virtually every list of the most influential people of the 20th century included James Watson and Francis Crick, alongside Churchill, Gandhi and Einstein. In making out the double-helical nature of DNA, Watson and Crick paved the way for understanding the molecular biology of the gene, the dominant scientific accomplishment of the postwar era. Sequencing the human genome will indicate that the revolution produced by the two talented scientists has come to a sort of end.

At the same time, it's also not surprising that many people get nervous at the prospects of that scientific milestone. It will no doubt be a revolution, but there are some fundamental questions about how we will think about ourselves. Will it mean that our behaviors, thoughts and emotions are merely the sum of our genes, and scientists can use a genetic roadmap to calculate just what that sum is? Who are we then, and what will happen to our cherished senses of individuality and free will? Will knowing our genetic code mean we will know our irrevocable fates?

I don't share that fear, and let me explain why. At the crux of the anxiety is the notion of the Primacy of Genes. This is the idea that if you want to explain some big, complex problem in biology (like why some particular bird migrates south for the winter, or why a particular person becomes schizophrenic), the answer lies in understanding the building blocks that make up those phenomena—and that those building blocks are ultimately genes. In this deterministic view, the proteins unleashed by genes 「cause」 or 「control」 behavior. Have the wrong version of a gene and, barn, you're guaranteed something awful, like being pathologically aggressive, or having schizophrenia. Everything is preordained from conception.

Yet hardly any genes actually work this way. Instead, genes and environment interact; nurture reinforces or retards nature. For example, research indicates that 「having the gene for schizophrenia」 means there is a 50 percent risk you'll develop the disease. It occurs only when you have a combination of schizophrenia-prone genes and schizophrenia-inducing experiences. A particular gene can have a different effect, depending on the environment. There is genetic vulnerability, but not inevitability.

The Primacy of Genes also assumes that genes act on their own. How do they know when to turn on and off the synthesis of particular proteins? If you view genes as autonomous, the answer is that they just know. No one tells gene what to do; instead, the buck starts and stops there.

However, that view is far from accurate too. Within the staggeringly long sequences of DNA, it turns out that only a tiny percentage of letters actually form the words that constitute genes and serve as code for proteins. More than 95 percent of DNA, instead, is 「non-coding」. Much of DNA simply constitutes on and off switches of regulating the activity of genes. It's like you have a 100-page book, and 95 of the pages are instructions and advice for reading the other five pages. Thus, genes don't independently determine when proteins are synthesized. They follow instructions originating somewhere else.

What regulates those switches? In some instances, chemical messengers from other parts of the cell. In other cases, messengers from other cells in the body (this is the way many hormones work). And, critically, in still other cases, genes are turned on or off by environmental factors. As a crude example, some carcinogens work by getting into cells, binding to one of those DNA switches and turning on genes that cause the uncontrolled growth that constitutes cancer. Or a mother rat licking and grooming her infant will initiate a series of events that eventually turns on genes related to growth in that child. Or the smell of a female in heat will activate genes in certain male primates related to reproduction. Or a miserably stressful day of final exams will activate genes in a typical college student that will suppress the immune system, often leading to a cold or worse.

You can't dissociate genes from the environment that turns genes on and off. And you can't dissociate the effects of genes from the environment in which proteins exert their effects. The more science learns about genes, the more we will learn about the importance of the environment. That goes for real life, too: genes are essential but not the whole story.

New Words

1. irrevocable *adj.* 無法改變的，不可更改的

2. deterministic *adj.* 確定性；決定性的

3. preordain *v.* 事先規定

4. autonomous *adj.* 自治的，有自治權的，自主的，有自主權的

5. initiate *v.* 開創，開始，提出，制定

6. activate *v.* 激活，使活動，使活化

7. dissociate *v.* 否認同……有關係，表明無關

Content Awareness

1. Read Passage B once quickly and answer the following questions.

(1) How many points of view are posed in the text towards sequencing the human genome?

(2) What is author's purpose in writing this article?

2. Underline the essential parts in the following complex sentences from passage B.

(1) It is no surprise that virtually every list that appeared of the most influential people of the 20th century included James Watson and Francis Crick, right up there alongside Churchill, Gandhi and Einstein.

(2) It will no doubt be a revolution, but there are some fundamental questions about how we will think about ourselves.

(3) For example, research indicates that 「having the gene for schizophrenia」 means there is a 50 percent risk you'll develop the disease occurs only when you have a combination of schizophrenia-prone genes and schizophrenia-inducing experiences.

(4) Or a mother rat licking and grooming her infant will initiate a series of events that eventually turns on genes related to growth in that child.

3. Reading Comprehension

(1) James Watson and Francis Crick are regarded as the most influential people of the 20th century because _____.

A. they succeeded in sequencing the human genome

B. their discovery was the most Important scientific accomplishment after the Second World War

C. they understood the molecular biology of the gene

D. their discovery was fundamental in understanding molecular genetics

(2) In paragraph 2 「that scientific milestone」 refers to the _____.

A. molecular biology of the gene

B. sequencing of the human genome

C. discovery of the double-helical nature of DNA

D. Theory of Relativity

(3) According to the Primacy of Genes theory, _____.

A. if you carry the wrong gene, you are doomed to die an early death

B. genetics provides answers to all problems

C. if you have the gene for schizophrenia, your chance of suffering the disease is 50% higher than those who do not

D. a gene is the fundamental element of any biological phenomenon

(4) The example of 「a 100-page book」 is meant to _____.

A. illustrate that genes are not autonomous

B. demonstrate the complicated nature of genetics

C. illustrate the relationship between DNA and proteins

D. show the vulnerability of genes

(5) The example of a college student catching a cold as a result of a stressful day best illustrates that _____.

A. chemical messengers from other parts of the cell activate the gene in question

B. the gene in question is turned on by environmental factors

C. the gene in question is turned on by messengers from other cells in the body

D. the gene in question is activated by carcinogens

(6) Which of the following statement is NOT true according to the article?

A. DNA has extremely long sequences.

B. Genes work through the synthesis of proteins.

C. Our fates are fixed from conception.

D. Environmental factors can counteract genetic influences on a person.

(7) The article probably first appeared _____.

A. in the popular science column of a newspaper

B. as a preface to a book on biology

C. in an academic journal of biology

D. as a presentation in a seminar

(8) The article is mainly concerned with _____.

A. predicting the impact on people's lives of knowing human genetic codes

B. analyzing the historical importance of sequencing the human genome

C. disputing the notion of the Primacy of Genes and illustrating that the environment is equally important as the genes

D. dispelling people's doubts about themselves

Language Focus

1. Micro-writing Skills Practice

In passage B, there are many words with affixes, such as「dis-」「-ate」「-ous」「-ic」「-ity」「pre-」「ir-」「over-」. Choose proper affixes for the following words and complete the sentences.

engage   poet   public   valid   envy   rational   work   caution

(1) We are exhausted from _____.

(2) Coal mines should and must take all _____ against accident.

(3) The writer's vision of the rainbow was _____.

(4) The concert was a good one, but because of bad _____, very few people came.

(5) He did not look ashamed about his _____ behavior.

(6) Linda was always _____ of her sister's beauty.

(7) He accepted the invitation, but was later forced to _____ himself.

(8) The experiment was designed to _____ Professor Clare's hypothesis.

2. List all the scientific terms in the text. Discuss how to classify the words according to word formation and how your knowledge of word formation helps you understand the scientific vocabulary.

3. Underline the colloquial expressions in the text. Discuss how they balance the scientific terms and make this popular science article more easily readable to a general reader.

4. Below are the specific ideas regarding the Primacy of Genes. Find the author's point of view as opposed to these ideas and identify the way he starts his points.

This is the idea if you want to explain some big, complex problem in biology (like why some particular bird migrates south for the winter, or why a particular person becomes schizophrenic), the answer lies in understanding the building blocks that make up those phenomena—and that those building blocks are ultimately genes.

· the author's opposing point:

The Primacy of Genes also assumes that genes act on their own.

· the author's opposing point:

Skills Development and Practice

Reading Skills

Understanding Reference (指代關係)

指代是英語中常見的現象。明確替代詞的具體指代內容，可以幫助我們在閱讀中正確、清楚地理解句子的意思。

Practice 1: Study the samples carefully and decide what those words refer to according to the passage.

EXAMPLE:

Part of the problem is understandable. When **employers** evaluate employees, *they* often consider the amount of time on the job in addition to job performance. **Employees** know this. Consequently, *they* work longer hours and take less vacation time than *they* did nine years ago. Although many working people can do *their* job effectively during a regular 40-hour work week, *they* feel *they* have to spend more time on the job after normal working hours so that the people who can promote *them* see *them*.

QUESTION: In the paragraph above, the reference of the first two 「theys」 has been made clear by arrows, hasn't it? Now please do the same with the rest of the paragraph.

Practice 2: Tell what the italicized part refers to in each of the sentences or paragraph. Write your answers in the blanks next to each one.

1. Tom was not angry at first, but became *so* after a little while. ＿＿＿＿

2. Mary arrived on Tuesday and John arrived *then*, too. ＿＿＿＿

3. The man was deaf, but *he* did not think that many people noticed it. ＿＿＿＿

4. 「The old man fell on his way to the hospital.」
「Yes, and I'm afraid he *did the same* the other day.」＿＿＿＿

5. When I was seventeen. I left my native village. *That* was more than fifteen years ago. ＿＿＿＿

6. 「Did Mr Li take a plane to the United States today?」
「No. but his wife *did* to Canada.」＿＿＿＿

7. Because he had a cold. Mr White decided to stay in bed the whole day. ＿＿＿＿

8. Men have been interested in the stars ever since ①*they* first looked up into the sky. Some of these stars may have ②*their* own planets. If ③*that* is true we can suppose that intelligent (有理解力的) life may exist on one of ④*them*. The problem is that the nearest star is four light years away. In other words, light from ⑤*it* has been travelling for four years when ⑥*it* finally reaches us. Probably nobody from earth will ever visit ⑦*that* star because it would take a rocket a hundred years to reach ⑧*it*.

①＿＿＿＿ ②＿＿＿＿ ③＿＿＿＿ ④＿＿＿＿ ⑤＿＿＿＿
⑥＿＿＿＿ ⑦＿＿＿＿ ⑧＿＿＿＿

Translation Practice

Translation Skills

轉譯詞類：英語介詞可轉換成漢語動詞。

Practice 3: Translate the sentences into Chinese, paying attention to the italicized words.

1. Are you *for* or *against* the plan?

＿＿＿＿＿＿＿＿＿＿＿＿＿＿＿＿＿＿＿＿＿＿＿＿＿＿＿＿＿＿＿＿

2. I paid fifty yuan *for* an old bicycle.

＿＿＿＿＿＿＿＿＿＿＿＿＿＿＿＿＿＿＿＿＿＿＿＿＿＿＿＿＿＿＿＿

3. What's *on* the television tonight?

4. He went out *with* his hat on.

5. He is leaving *for* Beijing at 10 this morning.

6. It gives me a great pleasure to be here *with* you today.

Practice 4: Translate the sentences into Chinese.

1. Now he holds the record for the most gold medals won at a single Olympics: a total of eight, in the 2008 Beijing Olympics.

2. After winning his seventh gold medal in the Beijing Olympics, Phelps said that tying Mark Spitz's record had been his goal.

3. Believing in yourself and your ability to achieve your dream is a must if you're to really get there, and no dream is too big.

4. I'm 23 years old and despite the successes I've had in the pool, I acted in a youthful and inappropriate way, not in a manner people have come to expect from me.

5. Whether it's flawless technique, or simply a gift from the heavens, Chusovitina has turned into an inspiration to gymnasts all over the world.

6. 「She's quick,」said German national coach Ursula Koch,「You cannot teach that. She's a phenomenon.」

Practice 5: Translate the sentences into English with the words or expressions given.
1. 為了使大家都能聽見，他只得使用話筒。(resort to, microphone, so that)

2. 他生在北京，由他奶奶撫養長大。（bring up）

_____

3. 聽到他打破了一項世界游泳紀錄的消息，我們都感到非常高興。（noun+that-clause）

_____

4. 不管你是游泳運動員還是體操運動員，任何領域的成功歸根到底在於你的態度。（whether... or，come down to）

_____

5. 菲爾普斯向自己的支持者道歉，說自己做出了令人遺憾的行為。（engage in）

_____

6. 他的醫療帳單堆積如山，而在目前情況下他沒錢支付。（circumstances）

_____

Practical Translation

語篇的翻譯方法——摘譯

在英漢翻譯中，主要有兩種翻譯方法：全譯和變譯。全譯是將原文幾乎沒有遺漏地翻譯成另一種文字，主要用於文學作品和社科哲學類作品，其目的在於把原文全面地展現給譯文讀者。變譯是對原文採用擴充、取捨、濃縮、補充等方法傳達信息的中心內容或部分內容的一類宏觀方法，包括摘譯、編譯、改譯等。

摘譯是摘錄和翻譯的結合，即摘取原文的精華加以翻譯，主要用於新聞或科技文體的翻譯。摘譯必須遵循以下原則：①整體性原則，即保持原文宏觀結構上的完整性；②針對性原則，即選擇原文中重要的或讀者感興趣的內容進行翻譯；③簡要性原則，即譯文傳達的信息必須簡潔明瞭；④客觀性原則，即譯文中不可加入譯者的個人觀點。

摘譯應該先摘後譯，在通讀並充分理解原文的基礎上，摘取該文獻的主要內容或譯文讀者感興趣的內容進行翻譯。摘取的單位可以是詞語、句子、段落或者章節。一旦選取了擬翻譯的信息，就要遵循全譯原則，將其完整地翻譯出來。

例 1：Apple expects to have a fix this month for a vulnerability in the iPhone that could allow an attacker to gain control of the device remotely via SMS, according to CNET NEWS. com.

An attacker could exploit a weakness in the way iPhones handle SMS messages to do things like use GPS to track the phone's location, turn on the microphone for eavesdropping, or take control of the device and add it to a botnet, Charlie Miller, co-author of The Mac Hacker's Handbook and principal security analyst at Independent Security Evaluators, said in a presentation at the SyScan conference in Singapore. The presentation was covered by IDG News Service.

Miller said that under an agreement with Apple, he was barred from providing too much detail on the vulnerability. He plans to give a more detailed presentation on the hole at the Black Hat conference in Las Vegas at the end of the month.

Despite the SMS hole, the iPhone is more secure than OS X on computers, Miller said. That is because the iPhone doesn't support Adobe Flash and Java, only runs software digitally signed by Apple, includes hardware protection for data stored in memory, and runs applications in a sandbox, he said.

Apple representatives did not immediately respond to an email request for comment.

譯文：據美國 CNET 科技資訊網報導，蘋果公司預計將於本月修復 iPhone 中存在的一個安全漏洞，這一漏洞使黑客能夠通過發送短信遙控手機。獨立安全評估公司的首席安全分析師查理・米勒聲稱，黑客能夠利用 iPhone 處理短信服務中存在的漏洞，採用全球定位系統來跟蹤 iPhone 的位置，打開手機麥克風竊聽用戶通話，或者控制手機，把手機變成「僵屍網絡」中的一員。米勒指出，儘管存在這一短信服務漏洞，不過相對於電腦上的 OS X 系統，iPhone 還是比較安全的。

解析：譯文中保留了原文的主要信息，即 iPhone 的短信服務功能存在安全漏洞，這一漏洞的潛在危害，以及蘋果公司預計何時修復該漏洞。第四段的第一句雖然和全文關係不是非常緊密，但很可能是讀者非常關心的信息，所以也包含在譯文中。

例 2：A 36-year-old Swiss amateur parachutist made a successful 650-metre drop using a replica of a parachute designed more than 500 years ago by Leonardo da Vinci. 「I came down... smack in the middle of the tarmac at Payerne military airport,」 said Olivier Vietti-Teppa, 「A perfect jump.」 Vietti-Teppa is the first person to have made it safely to the ground with the Leonardo model. In 2000, Britain's Adrian Nicholas tried it but had to pull the ripcord on a modem backup parachute to complete his descent safely.

Vietti-Teppa jumped from a hovering helicopter and the Leonardo parachute opened at 600 meters, he reported. The parachute he used was made using modem fabric along lines designed by the Renaissance genius. The specifications were found in a text dating from 1485. The parachute consists of four equilateral triangles, seven meters on each side, made of parachute fabric, Vietti-Teppa explained. The base of the pyramid is a square of mosquito net, which enables the parachute to open. A wooden frame originally conceived by da Vinci was not used on the model in action on Saturday. One drawback: it is impossible to maneuver or steer the Leonardo parachute. 「You come down at the whim of the wind,」 said Vietti-Teppa, who carried out advance tests using a scale dummy model launched from a remote, controlled model helicopter.

譯文：瑞士一名 36 歲的跳傘愛好者成功地從 650 米的高空降落，而他用的降落傘可是 500 多年前萊昂納多·達·芬奇設計的降落傘的複製品。維耶提—特帕是第一個用達·芬奇設計的這款降落傘安全降落到地面的人。他解釋說，降落傘是由 4 個邊長為 7 米的等邊三角形構成，由降落傘綢製作而成。

解析：摘譯中包含了原文的主要信息，即該跳傘者用達·芬奇設計的降落傘的複製品成功地完成了高空跳傘，成為完成這一嘗試的史上第一人；該降落傘的構造。其他未翻譯的句子中，有些是對主要信息的重複，比如第二段的前兩句；有些則是與主旨關係不緊密，故刪去不譯。

Translation Practice

Translate the following passage into Chinese using the translation method you've learned above.

Prime Minister Gordon Brown of Britain disclosed Saturday that an eye examination showed two tears in his right retina—a revelation that could embolden critics who want him to step down before a national election.

Downing Street moved quickly to quash speculation over Brown's health, issuing the statement only one day after a regular examination at a London eye hospital. Brown's office said his eyesight remained unchanged and that no operations were planned to address the situation.

「Were there to be any change? he would of course make a further statement,」Brown's office said in a statement.

Brown, who lost the use of his left eye in a sporting accident when he was a teenager and had surgery to save the sight in the other one, has been dogged by questions about his eyesight in recent months.

During a visit to the United States for the Group of 20 summit, he was forced to deny that he was slowly going blind.

NBC Nightly News anchor Brian Williams had questioned Brown over reports that he was using larger and larger text sizes as his remaining vision declined.

「I had all sorts of operations」, Brown said during the September interview.「I then had one operation on the other eye and that was very successful, so my sight is not at all deteriorating,」he said.

The same month he told the BBC that「it would be a terrible, terrible indictment of our political system if you thought that because someone had this medical issue they couldn't do their job.」

The September comments came as former Home Secretary Charles Clarke told the-

London Evening Standard newspaper that he hoped rumors Brown would quit—perhaps on health grounds—would come true.

Brown must call a general election by June 2010. Recent polls overwhelmingly suggest that the opposition Conservative Party will win after 13 years out of power.

British prime ministers rarely disclose details about their health unless they need to take time off work—as in 2004, when Brown's predecessor Tony Blair had a surgical procedure to correct an irregular heartbeat.

Som Prasad, a consultant ophthalmologist at Arrowe Park Hospital in northwest England, said retinal tears affect 3% of people over 40 in Britain, and only occasionally cause serious problems.

Unit 8 Job Interview

Warming-ups

Task 1 Questions for Thought

Think about the following questions, then discuss with your partner.

1. Do you know how to make an English resume? What kind of personal information your resume is supposed to cover?

2. What kinds of channels can you turn to when hunting a job?

3. Do you know how to make preparation for a job interview?

Task 2 Vocabulary Preview

Complete the following table by writing the English or Chinese equivalents of the words given. Then, check your answers with your partner.

簡歷		interviewee	
面試		international company	
申請者		personality	
職業的		qualification	
自信		energetic	
壓力		diligent	

In-class Activities

Task 1 Individual Work

When hunting for a job, how important are these things to you? Put them in order (most important first).

Items	Your Order
1. good salary	

表(續)

Items	Your Order
2. pleasant working environment	
3. working in a team	
4. having a challenge	
5. good career prospects	
6. high job status	
7. flexible working hours	
8. being able to work from home	

Task 2 Pair Work

A: What qualities do companies look for in people that would be their employees? Look at the following lists and check √ for the five most important qualities for each job. Then compare your answer with your partner.

Qualification	Secretary	Import/Export Manager	Attorney	Delivery Driver
experience				
good communication skills				
honesty and integrity				
lots of confidence				
problem-solving skills				
qualifications				
professional appearance				
strong leadership				

B: If you want to apply for a job, normally you need to send a resume. Which of the following items should be included in the resume? Discuss with your partner.

Items	In China	In USA
address		
telephone number		
email address		

表(續)

Items	In China	In USA
place of birth		
date of birth		
nationality		
primary school education		
secondary school education		
college/university education		
other qualifications		
marital status		
hobbies		
languages		
references		
photograph		

Task 3　Pair Work

1. Suppose you are going to a company for an interview. Your partner is a receptionist. Start a conversation; ask him/her the way to the manager's office. An example is given to you.

A: Good morning, sir. Can I help you?

B: Yes, thank you. I'm here for an interview. Could you tell me where the Personnel Department is, please?

A: It's on the third floor. The lift is just over there. When you come out of the lift, just go along the corridor, turn left at the corner, and it's the fourth door on your right.

B: Third floor... along the corridor... turn left... the fourth door.

A: That's right. You can't miss it.

B: Thank you.

2. Suppose you are an applicant and your partner is an interviewer. Try to start a conversation with him/her. An example is given to you.

A: Come in, please.

B: Good afternoon. I've come here for an interview.

A: Oh, please come in. I'm John Smith, the office director. Take a seat please.

B: Thank you. I'm glad to meet you, Mr. Smith.

A: So, What can you tell me about yourself?

B: I'm a good student – good grades. And I've served as class monitor for three years.

A: What kind of person do you think you are?

B: Well, I am always energetic and enthusiastic. That is my strongest personality.

A: What are your strengths and weaknesses?

B: Em, as I have said, I am diligent and industrious. On the other hand, sometimes I'm too hard-working and I put myself under too much pressure to make things perfect.

A: What qualities would you expect of persons working as a team?

B: To work in a team, in my opinion, two characteristics are necessary for a person. That is, the person must be cooperative and aggressive.

A: How do you spend your leisure time?

B: I like playing games and having sports. They are my favorite hobbies.

A: So, what kinds of sport do you like most?

B: Oh, it's hard to narrow it down to just one. I mean, I like all kinds of sports, basketball, swimming, bike riding and so on. Maybe it is just the reason why I am so energetic and vigorous.

A: What do you think you are worth to us?

B: I feel I can make some positive contributions to your company in the future.

Task 4　Role-play

Read the following dialogue, and then practice with your partner. Each of you should assume a role, and then switch the role.

(Situation: Fay needs advice from Jerry on how to succeed in a job interview)

Fay: Hi Jerry. I'm thinking of applying for a job with a multinational company, but I'm worried about having an interview in English. Can you give me any good tips?

Jerry: Hmm. That's a tough one. I guess the first thing is to try to make say,「You never get a second chance to a good impression. We often make a first impression」. You really need to get off to a good start.

Fay: That sounds like good advice. But how do I make a good first impression?

Jerry: To begin with, you should firmly shake the interviewer's hand while greeting him or her with a smile. Be sure to keep eye contact, especially when listening to the interviewer.

Fay: Ah,「body language」is really important, isn't it?

Jerry: Yes, it is. The second thing is to have confidence. You get confidence from being prepared. You should learn a little bit about the company before the interview.

Find out what they do, how long they've been in business, what their business motto is that kind of thing. You should also anticipate possible questions, and think about how you will answer.

Fay: Should I memorize my answers beforehand?

Jerry: No! Definitely not! That sounds very mechanical. You should be natural when you speak. Just think about how you want to answer, and choose the right words at the time of the interview. That way, you can use the interviewer's own words in your answer, which shows you've been listening. Then you're sure to make a good impression.

Fay: I never thought about that before. You're really smart, Jerry! But what should I do if I can't remember an English word when I'm answering a question?

Jerry: In that case, you have to paraphrase. In other words, you have to explain what you want to「manufacturing」, you can say「making a product」instead. Or instead of「statistics」you could say「using many big numbers to describe something」.

Fay: That's very helpful, Jerry. Thanks so much. Ah, one more thing. Should I ask about the salary during the interview?

Jerry: No, either let them bring up the topic of money, or else wait for a second interview. If you prepare well, make a good first impression, have confidence, and use English naturally, you're almost certain to be interviewed again. Good luck!

Task 5 Discussion/Presentation

Most newly-graduated college students choose to enter an enterprise unit or public institution (企事業單位) after graduation, while a small portion choose to start business of their own (self-employment).

A: What is your viewpoint? Work in groups and make discussion with your peers.

Option 1: Entering a private enterprise/company (working for others)

Your opinion:

Option 2: Entering public institution (working as public official/civil servant).

Your opinion:

Option 3: Starting business oneself (self-employment).

Your opinion:

B: After discussing, summarize all the opinions and make an oral speech entitled
Is Self-employment a Wise Choice?

The following might be useful and helpful in the speech:

Words and Expressions:

employment pressure; less pressure and stable earnings; public official/civil servant; regular/fixed/guaranteed/wage/salary; welfare/fringe benefit (福利); innovation ability; risk; entrepreneurship（創業精神）; promising

Reference Modal:

After graduation from university or college, some people choose to work in an enterprise (company or factory). A small potion of lucky ones passed the national examination for the admissions to the civil service（公務員考試）and works in pubic unit or an institution, which is really a good choice in most people's eyes, because of the guaranteed salary and welfare/fringe benefits. While there are some newly-graduated students who give up working for others and start their own business. Then, which options is better, work for others or work for oneself? In my opinion...

Reading Passages

Passage A

Choosing an Occupation or Career
by *Gerald Corey*

What do you expect from work? What factors do you give the most attention to in selecting a career or an occupation? In my work at a university counseling center I've discovered that many students haven't really thought seriously about why they are choosing a given vocation. For some, parental pressure or encouragement is the major reason for their choice. Others have idealized views of what it will be like to be a lawyer, engineer, or doctor. Many people I've counseled regarding career decisions haven't looked at what they value the most and whether these values can be attained in their chosen vocation. In choosing your vocation or evaluating the choices you've made previously, you may want to consider which factors really mean the most to you.

Making vocational choices is a process that spans a considerable period of time, rather than an isolated event. Researchers in career development have found that most people go through a series of stages in choosing the occupation or, more typically, occupations that they will follow. The following factors have been shown to be important in determining a person's occupational decision-making process: self-concept, interests, abilities, values, occupational attitudes, socio-economic level, parental influence, ethnic identity, gender, and physical, mental, emotional, and social handicaps. Let's consider some of these factors related to career decision making, keeping in mind that vocational choice is a process, not an event. We'll look at the role of self-concept, occupational attitudes, abilities, interests, and values in choosing a career.

Self-Concept

Some writers in career development believe that a vocational choice is an attempt to fulfill one's self-concept. People with a poor self-concept, for example, are not likely to picture themselves in a meaningful or important job. They are likely to keep their ambitions low, and thus their achievements will probably be low also. They may select and remain in a job that they do not enjoy or derive satisfaction from, based on their conviction that such a job is all they are worthy of. In this regard, choosing a vocation can be thought of as a public declaration of the kind of person we see ourselves as being.

Occupational Attitudes

Research indicates that, among the factors that influence our attitudes toward occupational status, education is important. The higher the educational requirements for an occupation, the higher its status.

We develop our attitudes toward the status of occupations by learning from the people in our environment. Typical first-graders are not aware of the different status of occupations. Yet in a few years these children begin to rank occupations in a manner similar to that of adults. Other research has shown that positive attitudes toward most occupations are common among first-graders but that these preferences narrow steadily with each year of school. As students advance to higher grades, they reject more and more occupations as unacceptable. Unfortunately, they rule out some of the very jobs from which they may have to choose if they are to find employment as adults. It is difficult for people to feel positively about themselves or their occupation if they have to accept an occupation they perceive as low in status.

Abilities

Ability, or aptitude, has received as much attention as any of the factors considered significant in the career decision-making process, and it is probably used more often than any other factor. There are both general and specific abilities. Scholastic aptitude, often called general intelligence or IQ, is a general ability typically considered to consist of both verbal and numerical aptitudes. Included among the specific abilities are mechanical, clerical, and spatial aptitudes, abstract reasoning ability, and eye/hand/foot coordination. Scholastic aptitude is particularly significant because it largely determines who will be able to obtain the levels of education required for entrance into the higher-status occupations.

Interestingly, most studies show little direct relationship between measured aptitudes and occupational performance and satisfaction. This does not mean that ability is unimportant, but it does indicate that we must consider other factors in career planning.

Interests

Interest measurement has become popular and is used extensively in career planning. Interests, unlike abilities, have been found to be moderately effective as predictors of vocational success, satisfaction, and persistence. Therefore, primary consideration should be given to interests in vocational planning. It is important to first determine your areas of vocational interest, then to identify occupations for which these interests are appropriate, and then to determine those occupations for which you have the abilities required for satisfactory job performance. Research evidence indicates only a slight relationship between interests and abilities.

Values

It is extremely important for you to identify, clarify, and assess your values so that you will be able to match them with your career.

Incounseling college students on vocational decision making, I typically recommend that they follow their interests and values as reliable guides for a general occupational area. If your central values are economic, for example, your career decisions are likely to be based on a desire for some type of financial or psychological security. The security a job affords is a legitimate consideration for most people, but you may find that security alone is not enough to lead to vocational satisfaction. Your central values may be social, including working with people and helping people. There are many careers that would be appropriate for those with a social orientation.

Of course, the factors I've mentioned are only a few of the many considerations involved in selecting a vocation. Since so much time and energy are devoted to work, it's extremely important to decide for ourselves what weight each factor will have in our thinking.

In short, you stand a greater chance of being satisfied with your work if you put time and thought into your choice and if you actively take steps toward finding a career or an occupation that will bring more enrichment to your life than it will disruption. Ultimately, you are the person who can best decide what you want in your work.

New words

1. occupation *n.* 職業，工作
2. counseling *n.* (對個人、社會以及心理等問題的) 諮詢服務
3. idealize *vt.* 使理想化；使合於理想
4. evaluate *vt.* 評價；求……的值 (或數)；對……評價
5. previously *adv.* 以前；事先；倉促地
6. vocational *adj.* 職業的

7. derive *vt.* 得到；源於，來自
8. conviction *n.* 定罪；信念；確信；說服
9. declaration *n.* 宣言，布告，公告，聲明
10. aptitude *n.* 傾向；才能，資質，天資
11. scholastic *adj.* 學校的，教育上的
12. verbal *adj.* 言辭的
13. numerical *adj.* 數字的
14. spatial *adj.* 空間的
15. coordination *n.* 協調，和諧
16. moderately *adv.* 適度地；普通地；溫和地；不過度地
17. appropriate *adj.* 適當的；合適的；恰當的
18. orientation *n.* 取向
19. enrichment *n.* 豐富
20. disruption *n.* 擾亂
21. ultimately *adv.* 根本；最後，最終；基本上

Proper Names
Gerald Corey 杰拉爾德·科里（人名）

Notes
1. This text is taken and adapted from *I Never Knew I Had a Choice: Explorations in Personal Growth* (Seventh Edition) by Gerald Corey and Marianne Schneider Corey. Wadsworth Publishing Co., 2005.

2. Gerald Corey: a professor emeritus（榮譽退休的）of Human Services and Counseling at California State University at Fullerton and a licensed psychologist. With his colleagues he has conducted workshops in various countries with a special focus on training in group counseling.

3. IQ: IQ (intelligence quotient) is a number that shows a person's level of intelligence, measured by a special test called an IQ test. An IQ of 100 is the average. The test consists of problems related to letters, numbers, and shapes. Some people criticize this test because it only measures one specific type of intelligence, and it may not be fair to people from certain races or social backgrounds.

4. Others have idealized views of what it will be like to be a lawyer, engineer, or doctor. → Other students have unrealistically high hopes of what it means to be a lawyer, engineer or doctor.

5. If your central values are economic, for example, your career decisions are likely

to be based on a desire for some type of financial or psychological security. →If what you want most out of life is money, for example, you will probably choose a job that is likely to be a good and steady source of income.

6. you stand a greater chance of being satisfied with your work if you put time and thought into your choice and if you actively take steps toward finding a career or an occupation that will bring more enrichment to your life than it will disruption. →if you take the matter of career decision seriously and if you can find out what kind of occupation may enrich your life and bring about a sense of true fulfillment, then you are more likely to end up with a career that is going to make you happy.

Content Awareness

1. Find the right definition in Column B for each italicised word in Column A. Put the corresponding letter in the space provided in Column A. The number of the paragraph in which the target word appears is given in brackets. The first one has been done for you.

Column A
(1) ___e___ *idealized* views (Para. 1):
(2) _____ the choices you've made *previously* (Para. 1):
(3) _____ *ethnic* identity (Para. 2):
(4) _____ *Scholastic* aptitude (Para. 6):
(5) _____ *mechanical*, clerical, and spatial aptitudes (Para. 6):
(6) _____ *predictors* of vocational success (Para. 8):

Column B
a. before now of before a particular time
b. of a racial, national, or tribal group
c. of schools and/or teaching
d. those who can describe a future happening in advance
e. imagined or represented as perfect or as better than reality
f. of machinery

2. Fill in each blank in the following sentences with a phrase from Text B. Both the meaning and the number of the paragraph in which the target phrase appears are given in brackets.

Example: That area's future weather pattern might <u>consist of</u> long, dry periods. (be made up of: Para. 6)

(1) It often helps to talk to someone when you're _____ a crisis. (suffering of experiencing; enduring: Para. 2)

(2) The union is the largest in the country and _____ is best placed to serve its members. (in this respect: Para. 3)

(3) The police haven't yet _____ murder after days of investigation into the case. (stopped considering the possibility of: Para. 5)

(4) You'll _____ of getting a better job if you hold a Master's degree. (have the possibility of succeeding or achieving sth.: Para. 12)

3. Paraphrase the following sentences, paying special attention to the italicised parts.

(1) Many people I've counseled regarding career decisions haven't looked at *what they value the most and whether these values can be attained in their chosen vocation.* (Para. 1)

_____

_____

(2) In this regard, choosing a vocation can be thought of *as a public declaration of the kind of person we see ourselves as being*. (Para. 3)

_____

_____

(3) *It is difficult for people to feel positively about themselves or their occupation* they have to accept an occupation they perceive as low in status. (Para. 5)

_____

_____

(4) Interestingly, most studies show *little direct relationship between measures optitudes and occupational performance and satisfaction.* (Para. 7)

_____

_____

(5) Interests, unlike abilities, have been found to be *moderately effective as predictors of vocational success, satisfaction, and persistence.* (Para. 8)

_____

_____

Language Focus

1. Complete the following sentences with an appropriate word form the box.

job	career	post	position
profession	trade	vocation	work

(1) Teaching children ought to be regarded as a _____ , not just as a

means of earning a living.

(2) The company advertised some _____ for university graduates in yesterday's newspapers.

(3) Some professional people used to look down upon people who are engaged in _____ .

(4) The factory closed down last month and she lost her _____ again.

(5) It is difficult to find _____ in the present economic climate.

(6) Dr. Green showed great ability in pleading for the accused. After all, he is a lawyer by _____ .

(7) As a diplomat, he spent most of his _____ in the United States of America.

(8) She retired from her _____ as marketing director due to health reasons.

2. Turn the following complex sentences into simple sentences.

Example: We couldn't agree as to whom we should select.

We couldn't agree as to whom to select.

(1) I don't remember I have ever borrowed anything from you.

_____

(2) She'll stay here for a couple of weeks before she goes on to New York.

_____

(3) The prospect that Professor Smith was to come to visit us cheered us all.

_____

(4) Jim, who was a man of strong character, naturally didn't give in.

_____

(5) When he arrived at the school gate, he found his classmates had already assembled.

_____

3. Complete the following passage with words chosen from this unit. The initial letter of each is given.

Most people have work to do. With work, they can e_____ their lives. However, people who did p_____ labor were looked down upon in the past. Many people were c_____ to take manual labor because it was an absolute n_____ for them to earn a living and to s_____ their families. By contrast, people who did m_____ work were highly respected. Under the influence of this idea, even today some people still i_____ their future when making choices for their career. What they care most about is whether the job can give them enough social s_____ rather than whether they can realize their v_____ in it. In their eyes, those who do manual labor should still be c_____ as inferior in social status.

In fact, there is no e_____ difference between those who work with their hands and those who work with their m_____. Whether a job is labor of work does not depend on the job itself but on people's a_____ towards it. As long as you like your job, you will think you are f_____ enough to take it and you will do it enthusiastically.

4. Translate the following sentences into English, using the words or expressions given in brackets.

（1）隨著她個人生活的細節越來越多地被媒體披露出來，她不得不辭去公司總經理的職務。(compel)

（2）她對自己的新工作很滿意，因為這份工作正好與她的興趣相符。(coincide with)

（3）我買了這件襯衣，因為它的價格從300元降到了80元。(reduce)

（4）為了把孩子們撫養成人，這位母親真是歷經了各種磨難。(go through)

（5）警方在老太太的死亡案中已經排除了謀殺的可能性。(rule out)

（6）市政府承諾將盡快採取有效措施，解決空氣污染的問題。(take steps)

（7）因為腿部受傷，我沒有參加上個月學校舉行的網球錦標賽。(go in for)

（8）要是能得到大多數女生支持的話，你贏得選舉成為學生會主席的機會是很大的。(stand a chance)

（9）他寫的書並非都像這一本這麼成功，所以我建議你從圖書館把它借來讀一下。（recommend）

_____

_____

（10）在 2004 年雅典奧運會上劉翔打破男子 110 米欄（110-meter hurdles）世界紀錄，獲得冠軍，這個記錄以前是由一個美國運動員保持的。（previously）

_____

_____

Passage B

Changing Attitudes to Lifelong Employment

This fall, as usual, companies and corporations are busily hiring new graduates. Major cities are crowded with young men and women who have just graduated from high school or college and who are hunting for a job.

One high school graduate says that the employment season represents judgment day for many students. 「Our whole lives are decided during this period when we're looking for a company to work for,」 she says, 「I know that when I finally find a job, I'll probably be with that company for the rest of my life, and that makes the job search very important.」

For some employers, the policy of lifetime employment is particularly important because it means that they can put money and effort into training their staff. The personnel manager of one large firm reports that the policy here is different from most other countries, where companies employ people who are already trained and whose skills can be used immediately. 「What we do here, however, is to select young people who have potential and who can be trained,」 he said, 「We then give them the kinds of skills that will make them suitable employee for us.」

One recently employed graduate says that she is receiving a great deal of valuable training from the company. 「This means that I will be a loyal employee,」 she says, 「And it also means that the company will keep me. I am an important investment for them. So the policy is a good one because it is of great benefit to both the employer and the employee.」

Recently, however, attitudes toward lifelong employment are beginning to change. Employees are slowly beginning to accept the idea that lifelong employment is not always in their best interest and that changing firms can have career advantages. Companies are also developing more flexible employment policies. 「I thought I had a job for life,」 says one young woman who lasted just six months in her first job,「However, when the company lost a big international order, I was laid off. I'm now looking for another job.」

Words and Expressions

1. attitude *n.* 態度
2. lifelong *adj.* 終身的，一生的
3. employment *n.* 職業
4. corporation *n.* 公司
5. hire *v.* 雇用
6. represent *v.* 代表，象徵
7. employer *n.* 雇主
8. policy *n.* 政策，方針
9. particularly *adv.* 特別，尤其
10. staff *n.* 全體人員
11. personal *n.* 人事（部門）
12. firm *n.* 商行，公司
13. suitable *adj.* 合適的
14. employee *n.* 受雇者，雇員
15. investment *n.* 投資
16. advantage *n.* 好處，優勢
17. flexible *adj.* 可變通的，靈活的
18. be in somebody's (best) interest 最有利於某人
19. lay off 解雇

Content Awareness

1. Fill in the blanks with appropriate words or expressions according to the above reading passage.

Many high school and college graduates have the idea that once they are employed, they will be _____ that company for the _____ of their lives. At the same time, some _____ have adopted a lifetime employment _____. Once they hire people, they can put money and _____ into training them, and make them _____ employees for the companies. _____ some extent, this policy is good because it is of great benefit to both employers and _____. Recently, however, some employees are beginning to change their _____ toward the lifelong employment and they think changing firms can bring them career _____.

2. Choose the best answer to each of the following.

(1) Why is the employment season so important for many graduates?

A. It is difficult to find a company they would like to work for.

B. The graduates have to make fight judgments in that season.

C. Companies have the policy of lifelong employment.

D. The graduates believe they will stick to the job they find all their lives.

(2) Employers who like lifelong employment are willing to _____.

A. look for people with skills that can be used in their lifetime

B. employ people who have already received necessary training

C. spend money and effort on their employees to make them work better

D. select young people who are educated for the jobs in their companies

(3) Which of the following is NOT mentioned as an employment policy?

A. Be prepared for employees' quitting jobs frequently.

B. Spend money on training the employees.

C. Employ people with the required skills and knowledge.

D. Be flexible in choosing your employees.

(4) When a company spends a lot of money on the training of its employees, _____.

A. it will get the money back

B. it will not lay them off easily

C. it will change the attitude to lifelong employment

D. it will mean that the company is loyal to the employees

(5) The sentence 「I thought I had a job for life」 means that _____.

A. she had found a job to make a living

B. she would work as long as she was living

C. she had never thought about changing her job

D. she thought the job was good for her life

3. Complete the following chart according to the passage.

Aspects of Lifelong Employment

(1) Benefits of lifelong employment for employees:

a. They can _____.

b. They can _____.

(2) Benefits of lifelong employment for employers:

The company can have _____.

(3) Reasons why some employees begin to change their attitudes to lifelong employment.

a. Lifelong employment is _____.

b. Changing firms can _____.

4. Write down at least three more comprehension questions of your own. Work in pairs and ask each other these questions. If you can't answer any of these questions, ask your classmates or the teacher for help.

(1) _____

(2) _____

(3) _____

Language Focus

1. Fill in the blanks with appropriate words or expressions, with at least one from passage B.

(1) Organizations that do business or make products: factory, _____, _____, _____, etc.

(2) A place that provides education to students: university, _____, _____, etc.

(3) To attempt to find something: look for, _____, _____, etc.

(4) Employment: job, work, _____, _____, etc.

(5) To pay somebody to work for you: hire, _____, etc.

2. Match the words in Column A with the right definition from Column B.

A	B
a. select	_____ symbolize or to be a representative for
b. lay off	_____ pick out, or choose from a number of alternatives
c. lifelong	_____ search
d. suitable	_____ send workers home, usually for economic reasons
e. attitude	_____ a plan or course of action, as of a government, etc.
f. policy	_____ a mental state involving beliefs and opinions
g. represent	_____ a beneficial factor or profit
h. hunt	_____ the act of laying out money or capital in an enterprise, etc.
i. investment	_____ involving two or more nations
j. advantage	_____ responsive to change; adaptable
k. flexible	_____ appropriate for a condition or purpose
l. international	_____ continuing through life

3. Complete the sentences with appropriate words in their correct form.

value   valuable   evaluate

(1) Nothing is more _____ than time, but nothing is less valued.

（2）Some of us _____ health very highly. Others _____ money.

（3）The business has only been open for six months, so it's too early to _____ its success.

train　training　trainer　trainee

（1）The boxer has been _____ hard for the big fight.

（2）The tiger attacked the animal _____ and killed him.

（3）The company's salary scale range from 5,000 for a _____ to 50,000 for the managing director.

（4）You mustn't drink beer; you're in strict _____ for your next race.

important　unimportant　importance

（1）It is _____ for people to keep themselves strong and healthy.

（2）This problem is of great _____ to all people.

（3）It is _____ for me whether you go abroad or not.

represent　representation　representative　representational

（1）These few books are _____ of the ones we use in the school.

（2）The foreign minister will _____ his country at tomorrow's conference.

（3）This painting is a _____ of a storm at sea.

（4）The tiger is a common _____ of the cat family.

develop　development　developed　undeveloped

（1）Such disease is not considered a serious problem in _____ countries.

（2）Scientists are _____ new drugs to treat AIDS.

（3）There are still vast _____ areas in China's West.

（4）We all keep an eye on the latest _____ of the event.

Skills Development and Practice

Reading Skills

Recognizing Logical Connectors（邏輯連接詞）

邏輯連接詞是表示句內或者句子間語義聯繫的結構詞，如：first, second, next, finally, therefore, 以及 in conclusion, on the other hand, as a result 等。確切地瞭解它們所表達的聯繫，對句子、段落乃至全篇文章的理解，關係甚大。

Practice 1：Study the example carefully and pay attention to the logical connectors.

EXAMPLE：

Most of us rely on the telephone for quick and easy communication, but this medium is limited to communication by voice. To communicate by telephone, we have to talk to each other. A lot of information, <u>however</u>, is not in the form of speech, so that if we want to find out, <u>for example</u>, if our library has a certain book or what the president said in a recent speech, we have to read a written text. It is not easy to get such information through the telephone. Pictures are another problem for the telephone. We cannot see what a person, a news picture, a piece of art, or an illustration in an encyclopedia actually looks like. The fax machine does allow us to send written materials and pictures over telephone lines, <u>but</u> it is often slow, expensive, and limited in quality.

QUESTIONS:

1. What functions do the underlined words have?

2. Does the paragraph become easier and clearer for you to understand if you pay attention to those words underlined?

Now read the following paragraph and pay attention to the words or phrases underlined. Tell their relationships and put your answers in the blanks.

There are millions of books in the world, <u>and</u> thousands of new books come out every year. It is no good hoping to read all these books. <u>Even if</u> we try hard, we can read only a few. <u>So</u> we must be careful in deciding what to read, <u>for</u> there are bad books <u>as well as</u> books really worth reading. We may read good novels, <u>but</u> most of our reading should be serious.

and: _____   even if: _____   so: _____
for: _____   as well as: _____   but: _____

Practice 2: Fill in the blanks with the words given.

so   for example   but   as a result   then   however   first

Life in a new country can be confusing. _____, one day I wanted to go to a local bank to open an account. _____ my aunt gave me the address of the bank. _____ when I arrived downtown, I got lost. _____ I went to a big office building. A lady there told me to walk three blocks south. I walked for three blocks north instead, _____. _____ I asked a policeman for help. _____, he drove me right to the door of the bank. From my story, you can see that I had a hard time being on my own in the new place.

Translation Practice

Translation Skills

增詞譯：在譯文中增加原文雖無其詞而有其意的一些詞。

Practice 3: Translate the sentences into Chinese.

1. More recently, Americans have been moving from the cities to the suburbs.

2. Matter can be changed into energy, and energy into matter.

3. We must serve the people heart and soul.

4. The latest type of the TVR system is light, inexpensive and easy to manipulate.

5. You may apply in person of by letter.

6. Let's do it in the way of business.

Practice 4: Translate the sentences into Chinese.

1. I once found myself in an airport bar with a man on the same flights as me. Our flight had been called three times, but he insisted we stay for another round.

2. And when we finally take off, all us wimps know that not only will that late luggage be the first off the plane, but it is probably sitting on top of our luggage, crushing our shirts.

3. I was too embarrassed to say that I arrived at airports early so I wouldn't have to hurry.

4. The man, equally keen to break the embarrassing silence, gave Arthur a detailed explanation of the different grades of German wine.

5. Anyway, it didn't matter, because the evening ended well. Everyone said goodnight, and Arthur went back to his hotel, able to relax at last.

Practice 5: Translate the sentences into English with the words or expressions given.

1. 我正要離家，天就開始下雨了。(be about to)

2. 當時我窘得說不出話來。(too... to)

3. 隨著下午慢慢地過去，他變得越來越放鬆了。(wear on)

4. 老實說，我當時感到很尷尬，真希望地上能裂開一個口子把我吞滅。(to tell the truth)

5. 他覺得總得有人要設法使談話繼續進行下去。(keep... going)

6. 一旦一些平常的話題講完了，交談也就結束了。(once)

Practical Translation

拆譯法

　　相比漢語而言，許多英語文本，尤其是英語議論文和科技文獻，句子一般較長，且包含許多信息。這些信息通過「形合」法連接成句，進而形成語篇。英譯漢時，如果應用語法分析和邏輯判斷的手段，對英語語篇加以分析拆解，就能使譯文更加體現漢語「意合」的特點。我們稱這種化整為零的處理方法為「拆譯法」（division）。拆譯法需要按照意群，將英語句子中某些成分，比如詞、短語、複合句從句子的主幹中拆分出來，或變成短句，或變成獨立句等。這些成分可根據邏輯順序和英漢兩種語言的差異，改變它們在原句中的位置，有利於譯文句子的總體安排，使譯文自然、流暢。

　　一、拆譯單詞
　　例1：He shall be glad of your company on the journey.
　　譯文：如果你能陪他一塊兒去，他會很高興的。
　　例2：She had a sound fleeing that idiom was the backbone of a language and she was all for the racy phrases.
　　譯文：她感到習語是語言的支柱，因此特別主張用生動的短語，她的想法是完全正確的。
　　解析：這兩個句子雖然不長，但都包含多層意思。例1包含兩層意思：「他高興」和「你陪他一塊兒去」，因此原句中的 glad 在譯文中被拆分出來，譯成了一個短句「他會很高興的」。例2包含三層意思：「她的想法完全正確」「習語是語言的支柱」和「她主張用生動的語言」，因此原文中的 sound 在譯文中被拆分出來，譯成了短句「她的想法是完全正確的」。在翻譯這類句子時，我們要先對

句子進行有效的拆分，譯出句子的層層意思，然後按照漢語「先分析，後結論」的句式特點，得出地道、連貫的譯文。

二、拆譯短語

例3：「But we have a lot of small, very disruptive day-in-and-day-out problems on the factory floor,」one industrialist said.

譯文：一位實業家說：「在工廠辦公樓裡，我們面臨許多很小但破壞性卻很大的問題，它們日復一日，無休無止地發生。」

例4：Thunderstorms in spring and summer often come with intensity great enough to cause flash-flooding.

譯文：春夏兩季，雷雨交加，猛烈異常，往往會導致暴雨成災。

解析：這兩個句子都是完整的長句。例3中的problems前面有四個修飾語：a lot of, small, very disruptive, day-in-and-day-out，如果不作任何拆譯，讓所有的修飾語全部作定語修飾problems，那定語部分就會顯得過長，句子會出現「頭重腳輕」的問題。因此有必要對句子進行拆譯，讓直接修飾problems的定語前置，而把說明問題發生頻率的短語day-in-and-day-out置於句尾，譯成一個獨立句，這樣句子的意思和結構就變得清晰明了。例4的原文是一個完整而有氣勢的句子，但如果我們不作任何拆譯，句子的結構就會顯得拖沓，意思表達不清，讀者會不知所雲，因此有必要拆譯句子，並用漢語中常用的「四字格」來處理，句意清晰，氣勢依舊。

三、拆譯複合句

例5：In the course of decay of the vegetable and the animal matter in the soil, various acids and gases are formed which help to decompose the rock particles and other compounds needed for the plan foods.

譯文：動植物在泥土裡腐爛的過程中，形成各種酸和氣體。這些酸和氣體有助於分解岩石粒和其他化合物，以供植物作養料。

例6：Considerable attention has been focused on the dilemma presented by the patient with chest pain who, on angiographic study, has normal coronary arteries and no other objective evidence of heart disease.

譯文：有一種胸痛病人，其冠狀動脈造影檢查正常，又無心臟病的其他客觀特徵，其診斷上的困難引起了人們的極大重視。

解析：這兩個句子都是含有定語從句的複合句，對於這類句子，我們往往可以按照句子的意群，使用拆譯法將從句和主句分開譯。例5的關係代詞which前面是一個完整的句子，我們可先譯出前面的句子，而which所指代的acids和gases又是後面句子的主語，因此我們可以重複這兩個先行詞，再譯後面的句子。而後面句子中的needed其實是另一個定語從句which are needed省略which are而來，因此按照意群，我們可以在這裡進行第二次拆譯，將後半句譯成兩個語義連貫的短句。例6的情況也是一樣，我們可以按照句子的意群，將關係代詞who作

為拆譯的一個標誌詞，在它的前面進行拆分，將句子一分為二。而這個定語從句本身是一個並列句，我們有必要將並列的兩個成分進行拆分。從思維方式來說，原句是典型的「先結論，後分析」的英語句子結構，譯成漢語時，要使句子符合漢語的邏輯思維，就需採用「先分析，後結論」的句子結構，因此對整個句子的結構和順序進行了較大的調整。

四、拆譯整個句子

例7：This development is in part a result of experimental studies indicating that favorable alterations in the determinants of myocardial oxygen consumption may reduce ischemic injury and that reduction after load may be associated with improved cardiac performance.

譯文：從某種程度上講，這方面的進展是實驗研究的結果。實驗結果表明，有效改善心肌耗氧量的決定因素可減輕局部損害，並且負荷的減輕也能改善心肌功能。

例8：Could any spectacle, for instance, be more grimly whimsical than that of gunners using science to shatter men's bodies while, close at hand, surgeons use it to restore them?

譯文：例如，炮兵利用科學毀壞人體，而就在附近，外科醫生用科學搶救被炮兵毀壞的人體，還有什麼情景比這更怪誕可怕的嗎？

解析：這兩句如果按照英文結構直接翻譯成漢語，勢必造成邏輯關係混亂，表意不清，使人難以理解。因此我們要根據漢語多用短句的句法特點，按照英語原文的意群，將較長的英語句子拆譯為兩個或兩個以上的單位，以求在充分「達意」的基礎上，符合漢語的表達習慣。因此例7的譯文將原句拆譯成兩個完整的句子，含五個分句，例8的譯文將原句拆譯成五個分句，這樣處理後，句子層次分明、表意明確、邏輯性強。

但是，拆譯是有一定限度的，拆譯的目的並不是要把句子弄得七零八落，支離破碎。拆譯應該按照英文原句的意群，使拆譯後的漢語主謂結構完整、層次分明、邏輯清晰，否則拆譯的意義也就不復存在了。

Translation Practice

Translate the following sentences into Chinese, using the technique of division.

1. They vainly tried to find out the stranger's name.

2. The infinitesimal amount of nuclear fuel required makes it possible to build power reactors in that mountainous area.

3. It all began in the mid-1850s, when Lowe's experiments with balloons led him to believe in the existence of an upper stream of air that moved in an easterly direction, no matter what direction the lower currents flowed.

4. More puzzling is the remarkable increase in occurrence of this disease which has happened since World War II in a number of western countries where standards of hygiene were continuously improving.

Focused Writing

Personal Statements

When you are applying for scholarships, for graduate schools, or for a number of post-graduate positions, you are usually required to write a personal statement (also called Statement of Purpose or Personal Goals Statement), as an introduction to the selection committee. This document requires you to indicate what type of person you are, and why you would be a suitable candidate for the program. You should outline your strengths as confidently and concisely as possible, a task that requires thought, takes time and can prove quite challenging.

What is a personal statement?

Though the requirements differ from application to application, the purpose of a personal statement is to represent your goals, experiences and qualifications in the best possible light, and to demonstrate your writing ability. Put it simply, a personal statement is a picture of you as a person, a student and a potential scholarship winner and gives an indication of your academic abilities, priorities and judgment.

How is a personal statement organized?

As mentioned above, the requirements for personal statements differ, but in general a personal statement includes the following information.

Introduction

Mention the specific name of the program, the position and/or the title of the degree you are seeking, in the first paragraph.

Detailed Supporting Paragraphs

Subsequent paragraphs should explain clearly:

1. Why you are interested in your subject. Give as specific reasons as you can. 「It seems interesting」 is not sufficient!

2. Why you want to study at that specific institution. You should have done your research and be able to show that you know about the university and what it has to offer in specific terms. For example, what are the professors in the Department where you want to study publishing? Be able to show that you know and have read their recent work and how or where it relates to your field of interest.

3. Information about your academic achievements and levels to date. Flesh out what

is on your CV by including any awards or honors you have received.

4. A paragraph indicating your background, interests and any accomplishments outside of your studies along with mention of any long-term goals to help show what type of person you are. Universities usually like to know that their students are well-rounded and interesting people.

5. Address any specific questions relating to the application that may have arisen. Each paragraph should be focused and should have a topic sentence that informs the reader of the paragraph's emphasis.

Conclusion

Tie together the various issues that you have raised in your personal statement, and reiterate your interest in the specific program or position. You might also mention how the job or degree is a step toward a long-term goal in the closing paragraph.

Sample

As a senior student currently majoring in finance at Zhejiang University, I believe that my solid academic background in mathematics, economics and finance makes me an excellent candidate for the distinguished doctoral program in Economics at Duke University. I am particularly interested in econometrics and financial economics, and I am determined to return to China and to be a professor of economics at a university after graduation.	Introduction: mentioning the name of the program, the title of the degree, and above all, her interest in it.
During my undergraduate years, I had an outstanding academic track record. For the past three and a half years, my GPA has been the highest among the 160 students of my major, which has ensured me the First Prize of Excellent Achievement Scholarship for three consecutive years. Besides courses listed in my transcript, I have also audited Advanced Econometrics for Finance and presently I am taking Advanced Financial Economics as my elective in order to be well prepared for advanced research.	Supporting Paragraph 1: a brief description of her educational assets.
My interest in economics was initially cultivated by my participation in a student-organized economics discussion group in my freshman year. Our informal meetings often started with a student's presentation on a pre-chosen topic, followed by a discussion. Our readings were diversified, ranging from The Nature of the Firm by Ronald Coase to Portfolio Selection by Harry Markowitz. Although our discussion was not in-depth, this informal group did ignite my interest in economics and exposed me to a variety of economic materials.	Supporting Paragraph 2: How her interest in economics was fueled.
The courses I took during my sophomore year on theories of Probability, Mathematical Statistics, and Econometrics triggered my interests in the field of econometrics. I enjoyed the Intermediate Econometrics course and the textbook Econometric Analysis by William Greene, for they offered me both basic techniques in applied econometrics and a general insight into econometric theories. Also at that time, I enrolled in a mathematical modeling team and participated in the Mathematical Modeling Competition, which was indeed a perfect opportunity for me to integrate my mathematics knowledge, financial economics knowledge, and econometric techniques and put them into practice. Quite by accident, the	Supporting Paragraph 3: How her interest in economics was enhanced.

problem to be solved that time was a financial one, mainly focusing on the optimum decision in subscribing new shares in the Chinese stock market. We collected relevant data such as the new share returns ratio and the lot winning rate, developed a mathematical model based on the optimization method, and later applied it to the practical problem. Our team won Second Prize From this experience, I learned the importance of 「digitalizing」economic theories so as to link the economic theory to tangible economic data, as well as empirical analysis which aims to ensure the consistency of economic theories and data. What's more, the combination of analytical rigor and applied focus attracted me so much that I was determined to further my education in this field.	
Currently, I am involved in a Student Research Training Program focusing on the growing environment and macro-policy influence for small and medium sized enterprises (SMEs) in Zhejiang Province. I have collated literature, designed questionnaires, and I am now conducting field work in Zhejiang under the guidance of my professor in order to gain first-hand data before performing a quantitative analysis. During the reading collation period, I was surprised to find that in much Chinese economic literature, econometric methods are misused without consideration of the conditions or assumptions required for them to be valid. For example, some literature even neglected the sample size requirement when conducting time series analysis. These findings, though disappointing, further spurred me to go abroad and pursue a rigorous econometrics training.	Supporting Paragraph 4: Her current participation in a program helped crystallize her reasons for pursuing her doctoral degree in the United States.
I really hope to be able to attend the economics doctoral program at Duke because this program satisfies my needs and Interests perfectly by its dedication to anchor all teaching and research firmly in core disciplines and the diversity of its professors' specialities. The program not only would help consolidate my foundation in econometrics, but also would offer me another opportunity to find out what field truly interests me. Since I have a firm econometrics background and currently major in finance, I would like to find a held which combines the theories and applications of the two. Duke's system just provides me with such an opportunity. I am interested in both theoretical research in time series and its application in financial markets. Also, since my mentor in China has just decided to start a project on the application of extreme value theory in the Chinese stock market and I am in charge of data collection, I would also like to further my research in that area. Besides what I have mentioned above, I am willing to conduct rigorous research in other fields as well.	Supporting Paragraph 5: How she is eligible for further study and her interest in research.
In conclusion, I firmly believe that I have the intellectual aptitude, perseverance, and motivation to succeed in my study in econometrics at Duke and future academic career. I am confident that my solid economics and mathematics foundation and my rich research experience, will make me a valuable member of your program. I Sincerely hope that you will feel the same.	Conclusion: reiterating the reason for choosing the program, and concluding the essay positively.

Sample 2

My interest in science dates back to my early childhood. I have always excelled in physical sciences and have received numerous awards in mathematics in high school. At age 18, I attended Beijing Normal University, majoring in physics. Four years of extensive study on physics and my current work in surface science inspire me to undertake a greater challenge in pursuing a doctorate degree in physics. My aspiration to be a research scientist also makes the graduate study an absolute necessity for me.

As an undergraduate student, I specialized in Physics, mathematics, and computer science. And in my Junior year, I studied computational physics in Applied mathematics III, during which I developed a 2-dimensional model with the finite size effect as a course project. In addition to being elated (歡欣鼓舞的) by my computer simulated phase transition phenomena, I was also pleased with the computed values of the critical exponents which closely agree with theoretical values. During the two-year course on the fundamentals of experimental physics, I diligently studied the techniques of operating experimental equipment, such as the epitaxy systems, lithography, and computer controlled data acquisition interfaces. I enjoyed these hand-on experiences. My current duty, as a research assistant, is to set up diamond film growth kinetics experiments which is designed to verify whether the mechanism of H atoms destroying C-H bonds in diamond film growth is the bottleneck reaction to diamond film formation. The results will give valuable insights and better enhance the research efforts of another group here. In the meantime, I am learning about the scanning probe microscopy, charged particle optics, energy analyzers and instruments used in surface science through the seminars held in my group.

In order to be knowledgeable in the breadth of physics, I have attended workshops and symposiums in different fields. In the symposium on Symmetries in Subatomic Physics held in 1995 in Beijing, I worked as an interpreter and edited the article 「Conceptual Beginnings of Various Symmetries in the Twentieth Century Physics」from Prof. C. N. Frank Yang's speech and translated it into Chinese. Not only did I keep an open mind to get experiences in academics, I also actively participated in extracurricular activities in my university years. In the senior year, I was a part-time teaching assistant grading exams and answering questions in the courses, A Journey to Subatomic World and From Quarks to Black Holes. I also had a part-time position as the bulletin board system administrator for the Physical Society of PRC. I am currently constructing their WWW home page to improve information exchange and science education in China.

Accumulating these valuable experiences, I am preparing myself for a career in scientific research. Being exposed to surface science, I am interested in mesoscopic systems and nanostructure materials. I plan to concentrate on condensed matter physics. Having carefully read the content of the graduate studies and on-going research programs at University of Washington at Seattle, I believe that UW is the best place for me to be. I am confident in that my diverse research experiences together with a firm commitment to physics have merited me to be qualified to undertake graduate study at the University of Washington at Seattle.

Applicant * * * *
mm/dd/yy

Writing Assignment

Suppose you are applying for a place on a doctoral degree program at a foreign university. Choose a university and write your Personal Statement. Base it on your real situation.

國家圖書館出版品預行編目（CIP）資料

大學生必懂的英語學習 / 馬予華 主編. -- 第一版.
-- 臺北市：崧博出版：崧燁文化發行, 2019.07
　　面；　公分
POD版

ISBN 978-957-735-907-0(平裝)

1.英語教學 2.高等教育

805.103　　　　　　　　　　　　　　　108011287

書　　名：大學生必懂的英語學習
作　　者：馬予華 主編
發 行 人：黃振庭
出 版 者：崧博出版事業有限公司
發 行 者：崧燁文化事業有限公司
E - m a i l：sonbookservice@gmail.com
粉 絲 頁：　　　　　　網　址：
地　　址：台北市中正區重慶南路一段六十一號八樓 815 室
8F.-815, No.61, Sec. 1, Chongqing S. Rd., Zhongzheng Dist., Taipei City 100, Taiwan (R.O.C.)
電　　話：(02)2370-3310　傳　真：(02) 2370-3210

總 經 銷：紅螞蟻圖書有限公司
地　　址：台北市內湖區舊宗路二段 121 巷 19 號
電　　話:02-2795-3656 傳真:02-2795-4100　　網　址：
印　　刷：京峯彩色印刷有限公司（京峰數位）

本書版權為西南財經大學出版社所有授權崧博出版事業股份有限公司獨家發行電子書及繁體書繁體字版。若有其他相關權利及授權需求請與本公司聯繫。

定　　價：280 元
發行日期：2019 年 07 月第一版
◎ 本書以 POD 印製發行